KATHRYN
SPRINGER

THE
CHARMING
LIST

Steeple
Hill
Café

Published by Steeple Hill Books™

STEEPLE HILL BOOKS

ISBN-13: 978-0-373-78622-0
ISBN-10:   0-373-78622-0

THE PRINCE CHARMING LIST

www.SteepleHill.com

Printed in U.S.A.

Each one should use whatever
gift he has received to serve others,
faithfully administering God's grace
in its various forms.

—*1 Peter* 4:10

To Kayla,

Who proves that a girl can wear really
cute shoes while walking with God!
Your enthusiasm and encouragement during
the writing of this book were blessings—
and so are you!

THE Prince CHARMING LIST

Chapter One

it feels like everyone is watchng me. Im so paranoid. (Text message from Heather Lowell to Bree Penny)

u r not paranoid. they r watchng u. welcome to prichett. (Text message from Bree Penny to Heather Lowell)

I caught the bridal bouquet.

This happened exactly thirty seconds after I told God that all I wanted to do was fade into the beautiful woodwork of Faith Community Church for the rest of the day.

I'm sure He was laughing when I walked out of the bathroom after a quick lipstick check and was swept into the center of a cluster of women whose eyes reflected deadly intent. Kind of like Mom's koi when they saw the mysterious hand poised above them, ready to drop food pellets into the water.

I looked in the direction of whatever it was everyone was fixated on—just in time to see a floral missile hurtling our way. What happened next was something I'd only experienced in the mosh pit at a Christian rock concert the summer before. But this time everyone was wearing pastels.

Candy Lane, Prichett's mayor, was short but agile, judging from the way she vaulted out of the pack toward the ceiling.

Someone stepped on my toe and I bounced to the left, putting myself between Bree, who could have unwound the ribbon from her hair and lassoed the thing, and Prichett's very own resident artist, Marissa Maribeau, who looked as confused as I did that she'd been caught up in this weird ritual.

As luck would have it, the bouquet rocketed right to Marissa like it was on a programmed course, but she decided to change the rules. As soon as it touched her hands, she popped it back into the air like we were playing hot potato. If she'd been a Green Bay Packer quarterback, she wouldn't have been signed on for the second season.

Gravity did its duty and when the bouquet returned to earth, it ricocheted off Bree and landed with a fragrant thump against my arm, then spiraled toward the floor. The competitive instinct—the one that drove me to set my sights on Boardwalk and Park Place when I played Monopoly—kicked in and I grabbed it. Now I was in the crosshairs. Panicked, I realized my only option was to imitate Marissa's move, but just as I was about to launch it back into space, there was no one there to catch it. My former opponents suddenly muttered their congratulations and shape-shifted from future bride-zillas to supportive, can-you-feel-the-love sisters. And they headed toward the cake table together.

"I think this belongs to you." I snagged Marissa's elbow before she escaped.

"Not a chance." Marissa backed away, staring in horror at the flowers I grandly offered.

Future psychology majors take note. This would be a fascinating study. Why intelligent women who've grown up in the modern world react in unpredictable ways when the bridal bouquet is headed in their direction like a ribbon-trailing asteroid. It's not like anyone really believes that the girl who catches it is going to be the next one to walk down the aisle. I'm twenty-one years old and I've already figured out that in the age group twenty to thirty, there's a ratio of one Christian guy to a bazillion Christian women. Okay, a slight exaggeration. Then again, maybe not.

I buried my nose deep in the lilacs and white roses and when I emerged a few seconds later, at least a dozen disposable cameras were aimed in my direction.

"Say cheese." Bree grinned.

For all I knew, the good old dairy state of Wisconsin had been the birthplace of the expression.

I silently pounded my head against my inner wailing wall.

"I wanted to fade into the woodwork," I muttered.

Bree's blue eyes flashed in amused sympathy. "If you want to fade into the woodwork, go back to the Twin Cities. In Prichett you've got a starring role."

A starring role.

Not quite what I had in mind, God.

Why was He so determined to shake up my life? There's no doubt that what's happened to me since last summer can only be the result of God's intervention. Divine fingerprints. My life is full of them. Okay, confession. Maybe I had a hand in getting the whole thing started. Initially.

Dad insists that I can't leave things alone. Supposedly this endearing characteristic can be traced to a package of Oreos and the VCR when I was four years old. Unfortunately, Mom has the pictures to prove it. Which leads me to ask a question—why are parents wired with a twisted sense of humor that drives them to take photos of their children's most embarrassing moments when they are too young and helpless to prevent it? Those photos have an annoying habit of surfacing years down the road like the risqué, before-they-were-famous poses of models that the tabloids gleefully print. Case in point, the infamous Oreo-VCR photos have come back to haunt me at my sixteenth birthday party, high school graduation open house and my first (and only) date with Chad Benson. Although I don't think there was a direct correlation. Really.

As if the Oreo photos and the accompanying script my mom loves to recite when she displays them aren't enough, she's put them in a special album, which I like to refer to as Heather Lowell's Childhood Bloopers. Also included in my repertoire is the photo where I'm perched in Dad's leather recliner, wearing nothing but a diaper and draped from head to toe in yards of shiny tape—which in a former life had been the movie *E.T.* Mom is convinced I thought he was trapped in there somewhere and it was up to me to save him.

As far as I'm concerned, *all* diaper and birthday-suit bathtub photos should be burned on a kid's tenth birthday. Middle and high school are right around the corner. Think about it.

So maybe I can be forgiven for being a bit camera shy. For years I thought everyone's parents came automatically equipped with a 35-millimeter and telephoto lens. I learned the sad truth at my kindergarten graduation, when my mother, armed with enough film to take a head shot of everyone in the Twin Cities, was besieged by mothers who'd (gasp) *forgotten* their cameras. My mother, being the good Christian woman that she is, cheerfully took pictures of my entire class. And the faculty.

I heard one of the moms whisper that after her fourth child, she was lucky she remembered to check to be sure both her shoes matched before she left the house, let alone remember to bring a camera. Mom had leaned over and whispered back that I was an only child and every precious moment needed to be recorded.

I may have been five years old, but that's when I figured it out. The camera fixation and the bulging photo albums had something to do with my being adopted.

Mom and Dad were never secretive about it. I grew up being told that I was a special gift to them from God. That I was the child of their heart. I was so cocooned in love and attention that I never felt like I was lacking anything. Some of my closest friends were adopted, too, so I didn't think there was anything strange about it at all. In fact—minus the never-ending photo sessions—it was kind of cool.

Until my freshman year of high school. On Career Day. A day that will go down in history as the day I started to wonder—for the first time—about my birth parents. Particularly my mother. I blame the guidance counselor and Rhianne Wilson: the guidance counselor for handing out the questionnaire that was designed to point kids who still watched Saturday morning cartoons in the direction of their future career; Rhianne Wilson for getting caught in a downpour on the way to school, which caused her to slink into the gymnasium through the side door and huddle between the rows of lockers, where I practically tripped over her.

The guidance counselor had decided that Career Day would be more fun if the students came to school *dressed* for their future career. If we had a clue what that was. Which I didn't. I attended a private school called His Light Christian Academy, so even though I could've borrowed my dad's scrubs and pretended I was thinking about following in his respected footsteps, it wouldn't have been completely honest. And honesty is a big thing at a Christian school. Not to mention that everyone knew from an unfortunate incident in third grade that I faint at the sight of blood—whether it's mine, a fellow classmate's, the classroom hamster's…

But that's a different subject.

"I'm supposed to be a model," Rhianne had wailed. "Look at me. Everyone is going to think I want to be a drowned rat when I grow up."

"It's not that bad." I was an optimist, but I still felt the need to ask God to forgive me for stretching the truth.

I skipped algebra to put Rhianne back together. By the time she got to study hall, three boys had asked her out. By lunchtime, half the girls in the school were begging me to give them tips on makeup and hairstyles.

"I guess we know what you'll be doing with your life," Rhianne said, linking her arm through mine and forcing me to match her catwalk sashay—hip roll to hip roll—to history class.

"What?"

She gave me a *well, duh* look. "Hair. Makeup."

"No way."

My parents weren't snobs but I'm sure there was an unspoken agreement between them and God that He wouldn't choose a path for me that involved anything less than four years at a Christian college and included at least two semesters of Bible study.

"You have talent. A gift." Rhianne could be pretty dramatic when she was wearing the right shade of eye shadow. I hadn't known that. "It's in your genetic makeup. Wow. That was one of those…you know…"

"Puns?" Okay. I don't mean to be uncharitable, but sometimes it's a good thing a girl can go far on her looks.

"Right." Rhianne had tossed her long blond hair with one of those graceful head rotations that only girls with long blond hair have perfected.

When we parted company, I sat through an hour of American history in a daze, remembering the Christmas I'd begged for one of those plastic mannequin heads topped with the glossy artificial hair you could style any way you wanted. I got a piano instead. Disjointed memories returned, of the times I coordinated Mom's outfits when she had a women's ministry luncheon, making sure she chose the right pair of shoes or insisting she surgically remove the shoulder pads from a blazer she'd bought on the same day there was a two-for-one special on leg warmers.

It wasn't a talent, I told myself. And it certainly wasn't infused into the strands of my DNA. That was impossible. I just had a…knack…that's all.

But Rhianne had started me wondering. How much of who I was were pieces of two people I'd never met?

Suddenly I was noticing things I'd never paid much attention to before, like my green eyes (Mom and Dad's were brown) and my perfectly straight nose (which I have to admit I was a trifle conceited about). And it wasn't just the differences in my looks, either. Mom and Dad were quiet while I had a hard time not voicing my thoughts out loud. Every one of them. And I had that impulsive thing going.

Even as the questions about my background rushed into my mind, guilt rushed into my heart. Mom and Dad wouldn't understand. I didn't quite understand it, either, so I ignored it. But sometimes over the next few years the wondering would return and take me by surprise. When I laughed, was it the echo of someone else's laughter? As a senior in high school, when the mailbox was crammed with college catalogs, why did I dump them all in the trash one day and take a year to travel around Europe? And when I got home, why did I walk away from a full scholarship at the University of Minnesota and sign up for cosmetology school?

Who was responsible for my quirks? I needed someone to blame!

That's how I ended up in Prichett, Wisconsin.

"Wait! I want a picture, too." Bernice Strum-Scott hurried over. She owns the Cut and Curl Beauty Shop on Main Street and even a photophobe like myself couldn't refuse to pose for her. She was the bride, after all. Obediently, Bree and I put our faces together— cheek to cheek—and I could smell Bree's cinnamon gum. I'm pretty sure she chewed it in her sleep.

"Here, let me. It's nice to be on this end of a camera for a change." Alex Scott took the camera from Bernice and winked at me.

Alex Scott was a real live movie star and he looked every inch of it today in his black tux. There were no helicopters flying over the church, though, because Alex confided to me that he'd spent years cultivating a life apart from Hollywood and it was finally paying off. Just in time. He could get married without ending up on the cover of *People* magazine. I did see Sally Repinski from the café take some discreet snapshots that would probably be on the Prichett Pride and Joy Wall by morning. I'd heard all about the Pride and Joy Wall from Bree's mom, Elise. She'd won the Proverbs 31 pageant and only Annie Carpenter's twins had finally displaced her from the wall—but that had taken almost a year. Bree told me her mom has been trying to keep a low profile since then.

Just as the flash went off, Bree and I stuck out our tongues. Bernice laughed and Alex shook his head.

"That's one for the mantel," he said. "Now let's get one for this year's Christmas card. No tongues, please."

"Killjoy," I mumbled. The flash went off and I reached for the camera. "My turn."

Bernice and Alex leaned against each other. Her veil drifted toward his face and he batted it away. Just as I pressed the button, they both stuck their tongues out at me.

I scowled but I guess I wasn't very convincing, because they started to laugh. And in Bernice's laughter, I heard a deeper, a richer, echo of my own. Because even though I initially came to Prichett to find the source of my quirks, the bride and groom—my birth parents—were the reason I came back.

Chapter Two

Supper 2 nite? 2 celebrate frst day on the job? (Bree)

If no 1 runs me out of town. B there at six. (Me)

Whoever described small towns as sleepy had never been to Prichett. Tiny as it was, Prichett packed the energy of a double shot of espresso. I'd finally fallen asleep about four in the morning and that was only because Snap, Bernice's cat, suddenly decided to live up to her name and hissed at me when I rolled onto her tail. Apparently my restlessness was the only thing keeping her from her beauty sleep. I settled down out of embarrassment and the next thing I knew it was six o'clock and the sound of voices was tapping against my dreams.

Wrapping an afghan around my shoulders, I scuttled over to the window to check out the early birds. The recycling truck was idling on the street right below and one of the guys started to whistle an upbeat version of "Going to the Chapel." I recognized him from the reception. The ceremony had been small, but the guest list for the reception afterward must have included most of the town.

Bernice and Alex had left for their European honeymoon just a few hours after the gift opening the day before, leaving me to take up Bernice's exalted scissors and run the Cut and Curl for the next eight weeks. Being a Minnesota girl myself, I knew that eight weeks was all the summer a person could hope to squeeze out of this part of Wisconsin.

One glance at the clock on the wall and I should have been sprinting toward the shower. Instead, I leaped back into bed and dove under the covers. What had I been thinking? All I had was a certificate from cosmetology school in my suitcase and four—count them—encouraging parents who didn't seem to have a doubt that I could manage the salon. *Manage*.

Bernice had planned to close the salon for the summer until I'd blithely told her that I didn't have any plans yet (translation: no job) and if she wanted to keep the salon open, I could run it for her. It had seemed so doable. Then. Now, I was in a panic. Curse my impulsive tendencies. No wonder Mom and Dad had to put me on one of those wrist tethers when we went to Disney World (yet another unforgettable photo in my Blooper album) when I was two.

I did a quick search above the comforter and my fingers brushed against Snap's silky ear. Aha. Animals were therapeutic. A warm, seven-pound stress reliever.

The next best thing to chocolate chip cookie dough. I wrapped my hand around her belly and pulled her under the covers, into the tunnel of denial. She must have sensed my distress because instead of signing her name on my face with her claws, she burrowed closer and hiccupped. Which jump-started a soothing, uneven purr.

Lord, I am absolutely crazy. Mama B has a ton of loyal customers and please, just please, let them hang in there until she gets back….

Bernice hadn't even given me a list of things to do at the salon. Since she wasn't just the owner of the Cut and Curl but also the only employee, she said it really wasn't that complicated. There were no internal struggles, either, unless a person counted the battle between her and her self-control over the candy drawer in the back room. Which she'd stocked before she left. I'd checked. She'd given me a turbo-lesson in how to do the banking and assured me the "regulars" would fill me in if I had any questions. And I could call her anytime—day or night—if I needed anything.

When I'd looked over her shoulder at the appointment book, I noticed the month of June was already booked solid. That would make it easy. Then Bernice had mentioned she'd deliberately penciled in the *low-maintenance* customers after one o'clock so I'd end the day on a good note. I was pretty sure that low maintenance had nothing to do with their hairstyle.

The memory opened up a hole that my stomach dropped through.

"We can do this, can't we, Snap?"

Her eyes narrowed in kitty amusement.

"Everyone else believes in me." I felt the need to remind her. "And if this isn't going to be a relationship based on mutual encouragement, I'm going to bring Colonel Mustard to live with us for the next two months."

Colonel Mustard was a basset hound everyone thought Alex had taken in out of the goodness of his heart, but he'd told me, when Bernice wasn't around, it had really been a pathetic need to win friends and influence people in Prichett. When I persuaded them to let me move into Bernice's apartment above the Cut and Curl instead of her and Alex's house just outside of town, Bree had told me the Colonel could bunk with Clancy, their golden retriever, for the summer. So far, the dogs were doing fine, but if Snap needed empathy lessons, I was sure I could get him back.

Alex and Bernice had planned to fix up the apartment and rent it out when they got back from their honeymoon. Bernice's snow globe collection had been carefully transported to the new house, but she'd left most of her furniture behind. It was perfect.

There were three reasons I wanted to live in the apartment but only two I was willing to share if anyone asked me why I preferred a cramped apartment with no shower to an adorable remodeled house in the country. The first two were easy—the apartment was convenient and it was so unique I'd fallen in love with it. The plaster ceilings were high, and the walls in the living room were the original brick. The polish on the hardwood floor had been scuffed to the bare wood in places. The wall-to-wall row of windows that overlooked Main Street welcomed the sunlight all day and I'd already decided to fill the space with plants.

The third reason—the one only my journal knew about—was harder to put into words. Even for me. Bernice and I had only met the summer before and had slowly been getting to know each other through long-distance telephone calls and e-mails. I thought that by living in her apartment, I might get to soak in a bit more of who she was. She'd welcomed me with open arms when I'd shown up unexpectedly at the Cut and Curl one day. She was a new believer—God's timing is always amazing—and she told me she was happy to have a chance to know me, but she'd let me set the boundaries of our relationship. Which was easy because I couldn't think of any.

The alarm went off, rudely reminding me that I was a working girl now. Not that I hadn't held a job before, but this couldn't compare to making smoothies at the Fun Fruit Factory.

On my way to the kitchen, I passed the black-and-white movie posters that Bernice had left on the wall. *Giant. Camelot. To Catch A Thief. You've Got Mail.* Even though I loved movies, I'd only seen the last one. Bree didn't know it yet, but I planned to lure her to the apartment with M&M's for a movie marathon some weekend.

I popped a bagel into the toaster. Now it was time to face the *big* question. What to wear on my first day of work? Dressy or casual? If I went too dressy, I could be labeled a snob. Too casual and it would look like I didn't care. Again being labeled a snob.

There was a knock on the door and I squeaked in surprise. It was only seven o'clock in the morning. I had an hour before the Cut and Curl opened. Maybe it was Bree bearing cinnamon rolls. Yum.

"Hey!" I swung the door open. "You're a—"

A strange guy.

I slammed the door and put my shoulder against it, my fingers fumbling against the frame for a row of locks that didn't exist. My mother had taught me well.

There was a few seconds of silence and then another hesitant tap on the door.

"Who is it?" I winced. What a dumb question. He could make up any name he wanted and, being the new kid on the block, I wouldn't recognize it.

Bernice's door was oak and I could barely make out the muffled mutterings of Strange Guy. I opened it a crack, glad that Dad had insisted I take self-defense classes in high school.

I have a brown belt, buddy. And, according to the Psalms, a few angels camped around me.

Strange Guy stood on the top step and, from what I could see of him through the few inches that separated us, he looked pretty harmless. He was tall but more lanky than muscular.

"Heather, right?"

"Yes." I drew the word out, not sure how much info to give him as my brain quickly downloaded the Stranger Danger curriculum I'd learned in second grade.

"I'm Ian Dexter." *And you must be paranoid.*

I could read it in his eyes. Eyes that were centered behind thick black frames.

"Didn't Mr. Scott mention I'd be stopping over?"

The handyman. Heather thy name is Stupid. Alex had mentioned that he'd hired Pastor Charles's nephew, who was staying with them for the summer, to do some general fixer-up type of stuff while I was at the salon during the day. I just didn't think he'd show up at seven in the morning. And I assumed it would be a teenager, not someone close to my age.

"I guess so. He just forgot to mention you'd be here so early." *Or that you'd be here today.*

"I wanted to talk to you before you left for work," Ian said, injecting a tiny pause between each word in the same tone a person might use if they were talking someone down from a ledge. "If I know your schedule, I won't get in your way."

Too late!

I sucked in my bottom lip. "Can you come back in fifteen minutes? I got up late and I'm not exactly…ready for company."

He stared at me, puzzled. Right away I knew what box to put Ian Dexter in. I'd seen that expression before. He lived in an alternate universe. The alternate universe where moving to the next level is the reason for existence. The world of video games.

"I'm not dressed yet." I'd learned with this type of guy you just have to spell things out. They were really good at defeating fire-breathing monsters but not so skilled at holding up their end of a conversation. Unless I was a two-dimensional fairy princess. Then maybe.

"Oh. Right." Ian's face turned the same shade of scarlet as Bree's cowboy boots. "I'll, um, come back then."

"Ten minutes."

Ian's unexpected appearance shaved precious minutes off my dressy versus casual quandary. By the time I remembered my bagel, I found it lodged in the bottom of the toaster, resembling a charred hockey puck. No time for breakfast. No time to linger over the contents of my closet now.

When in doubt, upgrade to suede. In questionable weather, go with leather.

They weren't exactly pearls of wisdom for modern man, but they had the potential to solve a possible wardrobe malfunction. I decided on a cute skirt—suede, of course—a shirt with a geometric print I'd bought when I was in Paris and a comfortable pair of shoes because I'd be on my feet all day.

The butterflies in my stomach, which had settled briefly while I decided what to wear, came to life and began to perform impressive loops and dives. Maybe it was a blessing I hadn't eaten that bagel.

Snap wound herself around my feet as I poured myself a glass of juice. "At least one of us has time for breakfast," I muttered, serving her a dish of fish-shaped kibbles and replenishing her water bowl.

My Bible was on the counter and, while I rummaged in the drawer for a granola bar, I leaned over to skim the page in a search for spiritual sustenance. As devotional times went, this was pretty sad. Especially when I needed God's strength more than ever to get me through my first day at the Cut and Curl. For some reason, my Bible was open to Haggai, which consisted of a whopping two chapters, easily overlooked between the two Z's—Zephaniah and Zechariah.

In the interest of time, I couldn't turn to the Psalms, my devotional favorite. Haggai would have to be it. I skimmed through the verses until one jumped out at me.

Then Haggai, the Lord's messenger, gave this message of the Lord to the people: "I am with you," declares the Lord.

I am with you.

Just the reminder I needed. And humbling. Like going to a potluck dinner empty-handed and leaving with a full tummy. I'd offered God the crumbs of my chaotic morning and He responded with a banquet...

Ian Dexter was at the door again. I studied him without making it obvious I was studying him. Looks-wise, he fell into the same category as my brown leather purse. Not attractive enough to gush over and show off to your friends but not stash-in-the-closet unattractive, either. His short hair was dark brown; his nose was straight and narrow and clearly not up to the task of supporting those heavy glasses. His eyebrows were full but at least there were two of them. He was wearing a pair of paint-spattered blue jeans straight out of a bin from a discount store and a sweatshirt with a faded, peeling logo that I couldn't decipher. School of Zelda perhaps?

"What did Alex hire you to do?" I didn't want him

changing things too much. As far as I was concerned, the apartment was as close to perfect as you could get.

Instead of answering my question, he pulled a piece of paper out of his pocket and handed it to me. Cheat sheets. Why wasn't I surprised?

"Paint bathroom. Replace faucet in tub and sink. Cabinets in kitchen—rip out and replace or paint. Heather's choice." I smiled when I read that. "Varnish floor in living room. Pantry needs shelves. Wow, you're going to be pretty busy, Ian."

"Everyone calls me Dex." He refolded the list carefully and tucked it back into his pocket. "What time are you done with work?"

"Five o'clock on Mondays, Wednesdays and Fridays. Seven o'clock on Tuesdays and Thursdays. Three o'clock on Saturday. Closed on Sunday." I recited Bernice's standard hours. She'd told me I could close at five on Tuesdays and Thursdays, too, but I didn't want to test anyone's loyalty. My goal was to gain a few new clients by the time Bernice got back from Europe, not lose any of her regulars.

"I'll make sure I'm gone by then," Dex said. He wouldn't look at me. Probably because I wasn't spinning like a tornado or wielding a sword.

"The cat's name is Snap." I grabbed my purse and headed toward the door. "Make sure she doesn't sneak out on you, okay?"

"Okay." I could see him process the information. Cat. Outside. No. The tension that had cinched my stomach into a knot when I'd wondered if Alex's handyman was going to disrupt my peaceful abode un-raveled. Unless he was battling for control of the golden key, Dex would simply do the job he was hired to do. No threat. No drama. On the quiet side but seemed like an okay guy.

I sent up a quick prayer that the rest of my day would be as easy as handling Ian Dexter.

Chapter Three

What about womn? (Text message from Tony Gillespie to Ian Dexter)

Been here 48 hrs. (Dex)

So? Has 2 b grls there. (Tony)

Havent seen any. (Dex)

All work and no play... (Tony)

Gets me to S America fastr. (Dex)

I started brewing the coffee as soon as I let myself in. Bernice had mentioned that people stopped by the Cut and Curl at various times during the day just to grab a free cup of coffee so she always kept the pot full.

There was a loud thump above my head and the light fixture on the ceiling quivered. Great. What was Dex doing up there? Painting or replacing drywall?

"Where's Bernice?"

I heard the voice and the bells above the door jingle at the same time. It was hard to believe the petite grand-motherly woman tottering toward me was one of Bernice's high-maintenance clients. The circles of coral powder on her cheeks matched the lipstick that followed a crooked path across her lips. I glanced at the appointment book. "Good morning. You must be Mrs. Kirkwood."

"No. I'm Lorelei Christy. Florence has a mission circle meeting this morning so we traded appointments. Where's Bernice?"

Traded appointments. Was this allowed?

"Bernice is on her honeymoon." I knew Bernice had told all her clients she'd be gone for the summer but if Mrs. Christy had forgotten, I wasn't going to argue the point. "I'm Heather Lowell and I'm helping Bernice out this summer."

I scanned the appointment book. Sure enough, Lorelei Christy was supposed to be my four o'clock. *The last shall be first and the first shall be last.* According to Bernice's system, that meant she was a "low maintenance." Which meant that Mrs. Kirkwood, my last appointment for the day…wasn't.

"All right." Lorelei slipped off her lavender cardigan and draped it across the back of a chair. "I'm sure if Bernice hired you, we'll get along just fine. Right, dear?"

As far as I was concerned, Lorelei Christy was the dear.

"What would you like me to do today, Mrs. Christy?"

"Just a shampoo and set. The yellow rollers work the

best. And I like the shampoo that smells like coconut. It reminds me of the cruise Edward and I took for our fiftieth wedding anniversary."

By the time I was finished, I wanted to adopt Mrs. Christy and add her to my grandparent collection. She'd told me all about her family, recited her recipe for rhubarb pie, quizzed me afterward, and filled me in on her plans for the summer—which involved knitting slippers for the upcoming preschool class.

"Oh, I almost forgot your tip." Mrs. Christy turned back to the counter and reached into her purse. "Here you go." She handed me a neatly folded dishcloth.

If I shook it, would a five-dollar bill fall out?

"I crochet them myself. If you don't like pink I have a green one in here somewhere—"

"No. Pink is fine. I love pink."

"You're a sweet girl. I'll see you next week. Four o'clock."

That wasn't so bad. One down, four to go.

Five minutes after Mrs. Christy left, a harried-looking mom pulled four-year-old twin girls into the salon. I checked the appointment book. Natalie and Nicole. Adorable. They were even dressed alike. This was one of the times I got that wistful I-wish-I-had-a-sister feeling.

They each picked out a chair by the window but their sweet, identical smiles disappeared as soon as their mother announced she needed to run to the grocery store for a gallon of milk. *Because she'd only be gone for a few minutes and the girls would be fine without her.*

"Who's first?" I patted the back of the chair.

The girls linked arms in a show of defiant solidarity. A scene from *Lady and the Tramp*—the one with the Siamese cats—came to mind. No one at cosmetology school had coached me through this scenario.

"One at a time." *Come on, Heather. Don't let them get the best of you.*

Natalie scowled at me. "Where's the elephant chair?"

"I want the elephant chair, too," Nicole whined.

Could four-year-olds smell fear?

"Can I have a sucker now?"

Aha. Leverage. "No suckers until *after* you get your hair cut."

"Bernice lets us."

I knew this was a big fat fib. Bernice would never let kids get sticky until they were about to go home. "I'll get the elephant chair while you two decide who's going to be first." *There you go, Heather. Pleasant but assertive.* Fortunately, I'd paged through a few of Mom's parenting books over the years!

While my back was turned, I heard their low, candy-sweet voices planning their next move.

Think fast, Heather.

"You girls are lucky today—you get the ten-o'clock special," I said, pretending I didn't see Nicole stick her tongue out at me as I turned around.

"What's that?" Natalie tilted her head and Nicole elbowed her in the side.

"A manicure—and you even get to pick out the nail stickers." I stared at the clock. "Oh, oh. Only ten minutes left… I don't know if I'll have time…"

"I'll go first!" Natalie bounded over to the elephant chair while her sister crossed her arms and pouted.

Yes! Divide and conquer.

By the time their mother strolled in forty-five minutes later, holding a cup of coffee from Sally's Café, I was just finishing up Nicole's manicure. There'd been a tense moment when the girls had tried to talk me into letting them each take home an extra set of stickers but after I'd gently pointed out that other little girls might want them, too, they hadn't pushed the issue.

I was going to be a wonderful mother someday, I just knew it….

"Look, Mommy! She painted my fingernails. And I have pony stickers." Nicole spread out her fingers for her mom to admire.

Mom frowned.

"No charge," I said quickly, and winked at the girls. "The ten-o'clock special."

"My stickers are better," Natalie announced. "Mine are kitties."

"*Purple* kitties." Nicole tossed her head. "Kitties aren't really purple, so mine are better."

Wait. What was happening here? My brilliant idea was being hijacked by a pair of three-foot-tall divas.

"You didn't give them the *same* stickers?" Mom turned accusing eyes on me.

"Ah, I let them pick out the ones they wanted." What kind of pre-parenting mistake had I just made? I was an only child. Was this something I was supposed to know?

The look she gave me was both pitying and resigned.

"How long do the stickers usually last?"

"About a week."

She nodded. And sighed.

"You have a pink pony." The war waged on around us. "There aren't *pink ponies,* either!"

"Duh! On the merry-go-round."

"Girls!" In the time it took for Mom to put her cup down, Natalie had launched herself at her sister and they were locked in battle. In the elephant chair. Which began to teeter.

In slow motion, I saw the chair begin its downward descent and I managed to catch Nicole as she pitched out of it. Fortunately Mom must have been working out because she practically vaulted over the counter. It was her oversize purse—which I'd thought looked a bit outdated when I first saw it—that broke Natalie's fall.

The elephant chair wasn't as lucky. His trunk snapped off.

"You killed him!" Nicole shrieked.

Natalie burst into tears.

"Here. You can each have another set of stickers. How's that?" The second the words were out of my mouth, the tears stopped and they politely opened their little palms.

After they left, I slumped in the chair and closed my eyes. I was *so* ready for lunch. Except I had a broken elephant and another little girl coming in for a first haircut.... But wait, I had a handyman right upstairs, didn't I?

I collected elephant parts, locked the door and dashed up the back stairs.

"Dex?" I burst in, expecting to find him wrench-deep in home improvement.

He was asleep on the sofa. With Snap wrapped around his neck like a shawl. Was he hungover? And did I have the authority to *fire* Alex's *un*-handyman?

"Rise and shine, you two."

Dex opened his eyes—he was still wearing his glasses—and stared at me like he'd never seen me before.

"Come on. Wake up. Time to scale the reality wall," I told him. I only had half an hour to eat lunch and get my elephant fixed and his nap was wasting precious seconds.

"I fell asleep." He peeled Snap off his neck and sat up.

"Really?" I rolled my eyes. On the inside. I'd been well trained not to do it on the *outside*. It wasn't polite. And it had been grounds for an hour of detention at His Light Christian Academy. "Do you think you can fix this?"

"What was it?"

"It *is* Bernice's elephant chair. A booster for pre-school kids." I spread the pieces out on the coffee table to give him an idea how they fit together. "And I need it back by one o'clock. If you're not too busy."

I couldn't prevent the tiny bit of sarcasm that oozed into my question. *Sorry, Lord!*

"Did you try it out or something?" He knelt down to examine the damage and I glowered down at him. Only a guy totally unaware of the statistics on eating disorders would make a comment like that!

"It will go down in history as the place where Nicole and Natalie fought a battle over nail stickers a few minutes ago."

"You didn't give both of them a set of stickers?" He picked up the elephant's trunk and studied it. I couldn't help but notice that almost every one of his fingers was wrapped in a colorful Band-Aid, like graffiti on an overpass.

"I did give them each a set of stickers but one of them said her ponies were better than kitties because the kitties were purple and everyone knows kitties aren't *really* purple…."

Dex tilted his head. He had the same expression on his face that the girls' mom had had. "You didn't give them the *same* stickers?"

"One wanted ponies, the other wanted kitties. I thought I was being nice."

"You thought you were being nice. What you really were being was *deluded*. Any bank teller at the drive-up window will tell you that you give a green sucker to every kid in the minivan. It's known as *the same game*." Dex picked up the hammer he must have dropped when he fell asleep and tapped in a loose nail.

I felt the need to defend myself. "How was I supposed to know that?"

His eyebrows disappeared as they dipped behind his glasses. "Brothers and sisters?"

"I'm an only child."

"Didn't you babysit to pad your 401(k)?"

He looked serious. I tried not to smile. "No."

"Can you get me the wood glue in the bucket over there?" Dex rocked back on his heels. "So how did the nail-sticker war end?"

At last I could redeem myself. "I gave them each another set."

"No kidding." Dex pushed a nail between his lips, but it looked like he was trying not to laugh.

"What?"

"That was probably their scheme all along."

"There was no *scheme*." I rolled my eyes again. This time on the outside. "They're four years old! They were upset. Natalie thought she killed the elephant. I wanted them to stop crying. Case closed." It suddenly occurred to me that those tears had stopped awfully fast when I'd handed them another set of stickers. The stickers they'd wanted earlier but I'd told them they couldn't have.

Dex nodded the second I became enlightened. "Uh-huh."

"They set me up." I'd been scammed. Conned. Taken advantage of.

"I need some more nails."

Dex had a courtside seat to view my humiliation and it was clear he was hanging out at the concession stand. This was the upside of conversing with someone who lived in an alternate universe.

While Dex pounded on the chair, I worked my way through half a box of crackers and the three pieces of string cheese I'd found in the fridge.

"You're eating my lunch." Dex flicked a glance at me as I inched closer to check his progress. I had less than five minutes to get back to the salon.

"I'm sorry." I shoved the last hunk of string cheese toward him. "Here."

"It's all yours." He leaned away from me and jumped to his feet.

As good as new. Except for the extra fifty nails that formed an uneven line across the back. But I wasn't going to be picky.

"Thanks." I wrapped my arms around the elephant and hauled it toward the door. "You saved my life."

He shrugged. "It's your first day. Cut yourself some slack."

"Yeah, you, too." I couldn't resist.

He lifted his hands and studied the Band-Aids. "That obvious, huh?"

I mimicked him and shrugged. Then I waited for him to apologize for falling asleep on my couch and beg me to let him keep his job.

"I better get back to work. I didn't get much done this morning." That's all he said.

"You probably should take it easy fighting those kickboxing kangaroos all night," I muttered.

"Video games?" Dex's eyes widened behind his glasses. "I never play them."

Yeah, right.

Chapter Four

not sure I can make dinr. (Me)

whatsup (Bree)

2 wrds. mrs. kirkwood. (Me)

Recovry group at 7. Wear jeans. (Bree)

Mrs. Kirkwood walked in at four o'clock on the dot and there was no way this pleasant-looking woman could be a high-maintenance customer. She had a soft swirl of snow-white hair that reminded me of the meringue on Mom's banana-cream pie and her cheeks were as round and smooth as a baby's. If she hadn't been wearing a pink cotton dress and dainty sandals, she would've looked like a storybook drawing of Mrs. Claus.

She hopped up in the chair and her smile was so sweet it should've been accompanied by a warning from the American Dental Association. Maybe Bernice had been right to schedule Natalie and Nicole in the morning, but Mrs. Kirkwood must have been a mistake….

"Aren't you that girl Bernice gave up for adoption?"

I had turned my back for a second to organize my workspace when her sugarcoated missile struck my starboard side.

"I'm Heather Lowell." My name was the only thing I could come up with when I spun around and found myself caught in the dead center of Mrs. Kirkwood's lasers…oops, those were her eyes.

"I suppose that movie star is your dad? You have the same nose." Mrs. Kirkwood patted my hand. "I'm surprised you have to work after falling into all that money."

Suddenly I knew why Bernice had scheduled Mrs. Kirkwood as my first appointment. She must have known I'd need the entire day to recover. Lorelei Christy—my original four o'clock—was supposed to be the cheerful memory at the end of my first day. To soothe me after Florence Kirkwood—the nightmare at the beginning of it.

"Bernice and Alex *aren't* supporting me…" There were several things I was suddenly tempted to do to Mrs. Kirkwood's hair but I was pretty sure none of them would have been approved by my parents, the faculty at His Light Christian Academy or—and this is the one that saved Mrs. Kirkwood from waking up bald the next morning—God Himself.

"I saw on the news last week that just about anyone can get a degree off the Internet nowadays. But I'm sure you went to school for this. It's never bad to have family connections, is it?" Her tinkling laugh sounded just like the bells over the door. *Internal memo:* Remove bells before post-traumatic stress disorder sets in.

"Shampoo chair," I managed to gasp. Although maybe asking her to put her head into a deep sink wasn't a very good idea at the moment.

In the six steps it took us to walk across the room, she told me it was too bad that young women today weren't concerned with modesty and, just out of curiosity, where *had* I bought my skirt?

It continued downhill from there. By the time the clock on the wall assured me it was closing time, I'd gotten over my initial shock and in one of those weird out-of-body type of experiences, I was a bit awed at the way Florence Kirkwood could simultaneously smile and cut someone off at the knees. It reminded me of a handy little kitchen gadget Mom had affectionately dubbed "the chopper" because it could take a whole onion and reorganize its molecular structure in seconds. When Florence Kirkwood finally left the salon, I knew exactly what that onion felt like.

Fortunately Dex wasn't asleep on the couch again when I slunk up the back stairs to the apartment. I could melt into a puddle without witnesses.

"Snap!" I wailed. "I need pet therapy."

Wherever she was hiding, she wouldn't come out. Right then I renamed her Miss Fickle. All right, if there wasn't purring, then there could be bubbles. Or chocolate. Or both.

Except there was no longer a faucet in the tub. Someone pretending to be a handyman so he could get some extra sleep during the day had lopped it off.

I dialed Pastor Charles's number. Dex answered the phone.

"Where *is* it?" I said.

There was a moment of silence. "I'm…I don't know."

"You don't know?" I counted to ten. Actually, I skipped five, six and seven because I didn't think it would make a difference anyway. "How can you lose something that important?"

"It just disappeared. I think it planned to escape."

"I hate to tell you this, but it's only in *your* world that inanimate objects come to life. Faucets can't *plan* anything."

"Faucets? I thought you were talking about your cat."

I sagged against the wall. "Snap? You let Snap out?"

"No. I think it snuck out when I propped open the door to clear out the…never mind. I left you a note."

"Where? On the refrigerator?"

"The mirror. I figured you wouldn't miss it there."

And did I want to analyze that? I stepped over to the mirror and read the message on the piece of paper stuck to it.

"I can't find your cat."

"Dex, Snap isn't *my* cat." I felt the need to clarify that. "She's Bernice's cat and Bernice is very attached to her. Did you try to call her?" *Because that works so well for me.*

"Cats don't come when you call them."

I closed my eyes and tried not to think about the busy Main Street just outside. So maybe it wasn't like rush hour in the Twin Cities but there *were* a lot of pickup trucks with really big tires and Snap was an inside cat, used to being fed and pampered....

Something brushed against my leg. I shrieked and jumped three feet in the air. When I crash-landed back to earth, Snap was in the bathtub, checking out the gaping hole where my faucet had been.

"Never mind. I found her." Relief poured through me. "She must have been hiding from you."

Snap flicked her tail and meowed, reminding me that only one of my problems was solved. The other one was big enough for a raccoon to crawl through.

"I can't use the tub, Dex."

"I know. I'll have it done tomorrow. Scout's honor."

You better or you won't get your Plumbing badge.
"Dex, are you sure you know, um, how to do this kind of stuff?"

"I'm trying to raise support for the mission field."

Oh, sure. Play the missionary card!

"Fine. I'll see you tomorrow. Please put the faucet first on your list...." I was talking to dead air. He'd hung up on me!

"You'd think he'd be a teensy bit more grateful, wouldn't you, Snap?" I shed the skirt Mrs. Kirkwood had implied was too short and reached for the pair of jeans I'd slung over the hamper that morning.

One day down. Fifty-six more to go.

* * *

"My name is Heather and I'm a hairstylist."

"That bad, huh?" Bree met me on the front steps of the Penny farmhouse and waved a cheeseburger under my nose to revive me. We plopped down on the porch swing and I didn't take a breath until I'd worked my way through half of it.

"Someone could have warned me about Mrs. Kirkwood," I finally mumbled.

"You wouldn't have believed us."

That was true. "She hinted I was after Alex's money, questioned the amount of experience I've had *and* insisted she'd seen my shirt—the one I bought in *Paris*—on sale at Kmart last week."

Bree chuckled. "Try having her for home economics two years in a row."

"She's a *teacher?* How'd you end up so normal?"

"If you call breaking out in cold sweat whenever I see a sewing machine *normal*." She raised an eyebrow at me and we both burst out laughing.

It was amazing how close Bree and I had become. The day I'd met Bernice for the very first time, she'd introduced me to Bree. On our way to the Penny farm for dinner that evening, Bernice had condensed her ten-year history with Bree while I tried to form a picture of the girl who must have received the bulk of my birth mother's attention. She loved horses. She was dating a boy named Riley Cabott. She was an only child.

Did you ever wish you knew me *that well,* I'd wanted to interrupt. But I didn't. The resentment bubbling up at Bernice's obvious love for Breanna Penny had surprised me into silence. The only thing that prevented it from flowing out and staining our conversation was when I remembered my Grandma Lowell's words.

"This woman you're meeting has a life, Heather. And so do you. God has given you both a new starting point…a place where your lives are going to intersect again. It's up to you where you go from there. I would make it an opportunity for grace."

That was one of Grandma's favorite sayings. *Make it an opportunity for grace.* It wasn't the first time I'd applied it, although I can't say it was always easy. When Bree and I came face-to-face, I took a deep breath and searched her eyes—expecting to see them full of anger that I'd dare to show up and turn Bernice Strum's world upside down. But all I could see in them was warmth. And welcome. That's how accepting Bree was. She loved Bernice. She'd love me, too. It was as easy as that.

It's strange how someone can enter your life and instantly become such a part of it you can't imagine there was ever a time they weren't there. Over the past year, Bree and I had kept in touch and she'd been just as excited as I was that we were both coming back to Prichett for the summer.

Bree rose to her feet and stretched like Snap after a long nap. "Are you ready for your recovery group?"

"I thought that was the cheeseburger." There was more?

"That was only phase one."

We tossed our plates in the dishwasher and Bree paused a moment, inspecting me with a critical eye.

How could she find fault with my favorite pair of DKNY jeans and yellow high-top tennies?

She frowned. Apparently she had.

"You'll have to wear my boots." She dug into the hall closet and tossed her red cowboy boots at me. I'd worn them before as a fashion statement but suddenly I was beginning to get suspicious about what Bree Penny considered *relaxing*.

"Come on. I've got a surprise for you."

And it was waiting in the barn.

I'd ridden before. Once. With Bree. Her horse, Buckshot, was an equine skyscraper, but riding him hadn't seemed so scary when I was with someone who knew which end of a horse was which.

"Her name is Rose. Don't ask me why, but the Cabotts like to name their horses after flowers." Bree opened the stall and Rose stepped out quite daintily for something the size of a Neon. "Riley brought her over this afternoon. He said we can keep her here all summer for you to ride."

Rose stretched out her neck and blew on my hand, parting the hair all the way up my arm.

"She likes you." Bree grinned. "Here, take her out in the yard while I saddle up Buck."

"We're going riding *now?*" I think I needed more time to get used to the idea. Like two or three years.

"Sure. You're going to love it. This is the best time of year to ride. Before the flies get too bad." Bree gave Rose a gentle swat on the behind and she accompanied me agreeably to the door. She seemed harmless enough.

Until I was looking at how far away the ground was a few minutes later.

This can't be any more complicated than riding a bike, I reasoned. Pull on the left rein, she goes left. Pull on the right rein, she goes right.

"Loosen your reins a bit. Sit back in the saddle. Drop your heels," Bree instructed as soon as she saw me.

At the same time? So maybe it *was* a bit more difficult than riding a bike! I gave Rose's neck a comforting pat in return for her patience.

"We'll take the dirt road to the Cabotts' place," Bree said. "Riley wants to meet up with us there, if that's okay."

"Is Riley part of my recovery program or yours?" I teased.

"He's a nice way to end the day." Bree shrugged but she couldn't quite hide her smile.

If I had to pick a word to describe Riley Cabott, it would have been *steady*. When it comes to guys, there are two kinds of steady—steady and boring or steady and intriguing. Riley was definitely in category two. He and Bree had come to the wedding together but I'd noticed he'd given her a lot of space. Bree was so independent I had a feeling she'd shake off any guy who made it hard for her to breathe. Riley must have known that, too, and that's what put him in the steady and intriguing column. A guy who paid attention.

I tried not to envy the easy way they laughed together. I'd never had a serious boyfriend, but it's not because I didn't want one. I just want the *right* one. Occasionally

I'd go to a movie or have lunch with one of the guys in my YAC group. YAC was an acronym for the Young Adult Class, which met for Bible study before the worship service on Sunday mornings.

I'd attended the same church all my life, so even though all the YAC guys were working full-time or were in college now, I still had a hard time moving past certain memories. Like all the years I'd been forced to listen to the obnoxious noises they loved to make. And the way they acted out Bible stories like David and Goliath by collapsing on the floor and letting red Kool-Aid dribble down their chins. Not exactly the kind of visuals conducive to a romantic date.

Maybe with the Lord's help I could have gotten past all that, but there was something else. And that something was The List. When I was a freshman in high school, the girls in my Wednesday night Bible study went on a weekend retreat—one of those camping experiences that put a dozen teenage girls in a dorm with one bathroom. The weekends are designed to promote friendship and bonding but instead they become a battle over who gets to plug her blow-dryer into the *one* outlet first.

The guest speaker talked about issues like modesty and respecting yourself and we politely yawned our way through her Friday night message. Most of us at the retreat were raised in Christian homes and we'd heard so many variations of her speech over the years we could have written our own.

On Saturday morning, though, she handed out paper and pens, sat on the arm of the couch, which I'd never

seen a guest speaker do, and told us to write down all
the qualities we'd like to see in our future husband.

A guest speaker that was *telling* us to think about
guys? This was something new. She didn't say a word
while we giggled over descriptions like *great looking*
and *drives a Porsche*. When we finished our assign-
ment, she told us to read through the list again and turn
it into a prayer request.

A prayer request?

There was an uncomfortable silence. I looked at my
list and immediately crossed off two things and added
three more. Out of the corner of my eye I saw the girl
sitting across from me crinkle hers up into a ball and
start over. There were no more giggles as we tackled our
lists again with the intense concentration we'd use to
take our SATs.

The really strange thing was that none of us shared
our revised list after that. I didn't. I tucked it in my
Bible in the Song of Songs, which was an appropriate
place not only because it's all about love and romance
but also because I figured no one who accidentally
grabbed my Bible to look something up would look up
something *there*. I'd blushed my way through that particular book a few years ago and can understand why
pastors don't quote verses from it with the same enthusiasm they do from 1 Corinthians 13.

After that, I started silently comparing any guys I'd
meet to The List. It got a little discouraging. It wasn't
like I was in a hurry to get married or anything, but
couldn't I meet someone who hit at least one or two out

of my Top Five? Was my list unrealistic? Even though I'd changed the *great looking* (yes, that was me) to *attractive,* maybe my expectations were still too high. But I'd comforted friends who'd lowered their standards to *warm and breathing* just so they wouldn't sit alone on the weekends. If God was presently molding a man to meet my specifications, all I had to do was wait patiently until He was finished. And obviously it was taking a while. But I was still convinced that waiting for Mr. Right was better than settling for Mr. Right Now.

"Still thinking about Mrs. Kirkwood?" Bree's voice floated over her shoulder, muffled by the soft thud of Buck's hooves against the road.

Rose had taken advantage of my momentary split with reality. When I snapped back to attention, she'd also taken a little side trip and was busy nibbling at the grass along the ditch.

"No, just decompressing after a horrible, no-good, very bad day." I tugged on the reins and Rose ignored me. In fact, I'm pretty sure I heard her laugh.

Bree twisted around in the saddle and saw my dilemma. "Give her a little kick with your heels. She's testing you."

And she gets an A plus.

I obeyed and exhaled in relief when Rose trotted to catch up to Buckshot. I didn't want Bree to think I wasn't a natural at this, even though my tailbone was wearing away like erosion on a riverbank every time it connected with the saddle.

There was a low growl behind me and Bree whirled Buck around. "Uh-oh."

I caught the look of concern on her face. "What's wrong?"

"I hear a motorcycle. Buck loves them. He runs to the fence whenever a Harley goes by, but Rose—"

"What about Rose?" I squeaked. The noise was getting louder and it sounded like someone was riding a chain saw.

"She might not like…" Bree lunged for the loop of rein a mere second before Rose decided she could outrun the horse-eating motorcycle. She must have figured she was close enough to home to make a break for it. So she did.

I just happened to be along for the ride.

Chapter Five

Describe your day. Use words.
(From the book *Real Men Write in Journals*)

Woe is me. (Dex)

Rose came in first, with Buckshot a close second, but Rose and I were the ones that rearranged the Cabotts' landscaping on the way in.

Rose downshifted from a full gallop to a sudden stop and if I hadn't been clutching the saddle horn, I would have somersaulted over her head. Instead I poured off the saddle like a bucketful of sand as the motorcycle roared past at warp speed.

Bree jumped off Buck and ran over. "Are you all right?"

My lungs weren't working. They pushed out short, hot gusts of air but refused to let any back in. I could feel my eyes begin to bulge.

"What a jerk!" Bree spoke the very words that were

going through my mind. "I can't believe he didn't slow down when he saw the horses."

Riley ran up with Dex—Dex?—right behind him. My brain couldn't quite process why *he'd* be at Riley's.

"Is she okay?" Riley looked at Bree and I was touched by his concern.

"I'm fine," I managed to wheeze.

"Poor baby," Riley murmured, dropping to one knee to examine Rose's feet.

Bree rolled her eyes and I realized I wasn't the one he was concerned about. She'd told me how attached he was to his horses so I didn't take it personally.

"Who *was* that?" she asked, frowning at the veil of dust still dancing in the air.

"Nobody from around here, that's for sure." Now Riley looked at me. "Are you okay, Heather?"

The adrenaline had subsided and I could inhale again. "Uh-huh."

"Shaken not stirred," Dex said under his breath.

I looked at him suspiciously, but he didn't crack a smile.

"Rose never bolts," Riley fretted. "I don't think you need to worry—"

"I'm supposed to get back on again, right?" I interrupted.

Riley and Bree exchanged approving looks, but I saw Dex frown.

"That's if you fall off," he pointed out.

Details, details. If I subtracted the heart-stopping terror of being held prisoner on the back of a runaway horse and focused instead on the exhilaration I'd felt when I finally got her to stop (okay, technically it was Mrs. Cabott's gazing ball that stopped her), all in all it had been kind of fun.

And it had helped me forget about the twins. And Mrs. Kirkwood. And The List.

Bree looked at Dex and then at Riley.

"Oh, sorry. Bree, this is Dex. Dad hired him to help with the barn chores once a week," Riley said. "Dex, this is Bree Penny. She lives down the road. And this is—"

"We met this morning." And I have the faucet-less bathtub to prove it. "You're working for the Cabotts, too?"

"I'm picking up a few jobs here and there." Dex shrugged. "Whatever comes along and pays a few bucks."

"Too?" Bree looked at me and I could tell she was wondering why this tidbit of info hadn't come up during our conversation over supper.

"Alex hired him to do some remodeling at the apartment this summer." I buried a sigh. "Some carpentry, painting. *Faucets*."

Dex didn't respond except to lift one shoulder and use it to nudge his glasses back to the bridge of his nose where they belonged.

"You never mentioned him… I mean *that*," Bree said. There was a funny sparkle in her eyes that warned me I was going to get the third degree later. How was I supposed to describe Ian Dexter? Narcoleptic handyman by day, sword-wielding treasure hunter by night?

"You can go riding with us if you want to, Dex," Riley offered. "We'll probably start a bonfire when we get back and roast some hot dogs."

I saw the color drain from Dex's face. "No, thanks. I have to get back."

"I could put you on Iris," Riley said, oblivious to the fear in Dex's eyes. "My four-year-old cousin rides her all the time."

Riley may have been sensitive to Bree, but obviously he needed a bit of fine-tuning when it came to dealing with other guys. Or maybe it was a test to find out where Dex's nerves were on the wimp-o-meter.

Come on, Dex, I silently urged. *Here's your next line: Iris? What is she, a Shetland pony? Don't you have something with a few more cylinders?*

He ad-libbed instead. "That's okay. I'll catch up with you some other time."

Riley might have pushed the issue but Bree must have felt sorry for Dex, too, because she came to his rescue with a simple but effective maneuver. She stepped in front of Riley, pulled her rain-straight blond hair off her neck and then let it sift through her fingers, completely short-circuiting Riley's thought process.

"It's warm tonight, isn't it?"

Riley nodded mutely. Oh, the power of the right haircut!

"We better get going. Daylight is aburnin', as Grandpa Will always said," Bree sang. She slipped her boot in the stirrup on Buckshot's saddle and he stood like a perfect gentleman as she swung her leg over his wide back.

I wasn't an experienced rider like Bree, so my attempt to get back in the saddle wasn't nearly as graceful as hers. To complicate things, Rose took a step to the side whenever I put my foot in the stirrup. I glanced over my shoulder to see if Dex would put his fears aside and help me out.

Nope, chivalry was truly dead. He was already halfway to his car—an ancient Impala the color of French dressing. I shuddered. Maybe he was color-blind.

Riley was the one who noticed I was having trouble and, like a knight in shining spurs, he held Rose still while I scrambled awkwardly into the saddle. I was a little nervous but instead of taking the road again, Riley led the way to the trails that meandered through a huge stand of maples on the back of the Cabott property. When I realized the trails were too narrow and bumpy to accommodate anything with an engine, I relaxed a little.

None of us said a word as the horses nodded their way through the woods. The setting sun filtered through the branches and formed intricate stencils on the ground under our feet. I closed my eyes and trusted Rose enough to go on autopilot for a few seconds while I soaked up my surroundings, lulled by the gentle creak of leather and the warm smell of horses and summer.

I talked to God a lot throughout the day and I tried really hard to listen, too, although it wasn't as easy. I wondered if He ever got impatient with my rambling commentaries.

Thanks, God, for getting me through my first day at the salon. And thank You for bringing me to Prichett. You knew I'd need a quiet place this summer to hear Your voice, didn't you? Well, I'm listening. Go ahead!

From the day Mrs. Holmes, my first grade Sunday

school teacher, rewarded my perfect attendance with a Bible (a cardinal-red hardcover with gold-tipped pages) to my high school graduation, when I'd received a plaque engraved with the verse from Jeremiah that promises God has a hope and a future for us, I accepted that God had a plan for me. And if He could create the entire universe in six days, eight weeks would give Him plenty of time to yank out the file marked Heather Lowell and let me in on it.

"Heather." I heard Riley's polite cough. "You probably should ride with your eyes *open*."

"Shh," Bree scolded. "She's praying."

I wasn't surprised she knew what I was doing. Bree is a believer, too. She brought God into our conversations as naturally as she did horses. Which meant she thought about Him a lot. I'd figured out that people tend to *talk* about the things they *think* about, which was another reason I was wary of the guys in YAC. Their conversations were dominated by *compare and contrast*. Comparing their scores on the newest version of a video game (pick one) and contrasting their cell phone plans. The only time God seemed to get worked in was during prayer time in small groups on Sunday mornings.

When we got back from our ride, Riley dragged out some rickety lawn chairs and started a bonfire large enough to bring a 747 in safely. Bree and I ended up round and drowsy from eating all the hot dogs and marshmallows he supplied us with. Finally, we saddled up the horses again and headed back to the Penny farm. By now it was past ten and the sun had slipped away, officially off duty.

"This is more peaceful than what you're used to in the city, right?" Bree asked as we started out. Now that the two horses were better acquainted, they walked shoulder to shoulder on the road.

"Peaceful?" She had to be kidding. The crickets and the frogs were belting out a chorus in the ditch at a volume level that rivaled my alarm clock. "Okay, maybe it's not sirens and honking horns but—"

"Not again." Bree groaned.

I heard it, too. And it was coming this way. The motorcycle. I felt Rose's shoulders bunch and I knew my nerves weren't up for another lap around the track. I slid off her back, hoping that if *both* our feet were on the ground she wouldn't be tempted to go AWOL again.

A headlight barreled toward us, but just as I braced myself to become a human windsock, the bike slowed way down and stopped a few yards away.

"Hey." The muffled Darth Vadar voice beneath the helmet was definitely male. I saw a tall shadow unfold. Now I wish I had stayed on Rose. I'd still be five foot six but at least I would have *felt* bigger. And I was about to get up close and personal with the guy responsible for re-creating the Kentucky Derby a few hours ago.

"Hi." *Why aren't there any streetlights around here?*

God must have heard my pitiful question because suddenly the moon rolled out from behind a cloud and lit up the area like a spotlight. It gave me courage to know He was keeping a watchful eye on us.

"You almost scared the horses to death," I said bravely, buying some time now so I could give the police a full description later. I started at the storm trooper helmet and memorized my way down the black leather jacket to the slashed blue jeans and heavy boots.

"Yeah. Sorry about that." Just before he reached me, he yanked off the helmet, releasing a ponytail that swung against his shoulder. But he didn't look threatening anymore. Maybe it's because he looked…well, drop-dead gorgeous. I heard Bree suck in a breath.

He smiled at us and shrugged helplessly. "I think I'm lost."

"Who are you looking for?"

He hesitated for a second. "A cow named Junebug?"

When Marissa Maribeau stumbled into the salon the next day, I almost performed a pirouette. Bernice had told me she'd been trying to coax Marissa into her chair for years but apparently she was a hairstylist's ultimate challenge—a self-trimmer. She had thick, waist-length hair, but the ends reminded me of frayed wire and the humidity was definitely not her friend. She must have come right from her pottery studio because she was wearing baggy khaki pants and a white T-shirt smeared with dried clay.

It didn't matter that she hadn't made an appointment. Bernice had warned me about the customers she referred to as Wild Cards. The ones who impulsively decided to get their hair colored, cut or styled and they wanted it done *now*.

I snapped a fresh cape open and held it up. Marissa skidded to a stop in front of me. I shook the cape and she took a wary step backward.

"My four-thirty canceled, so you can be my last customer of the day." I gave the chair a cheerful, game show hostess spin.

"I'm not here…" Marissa glanced in the mirror and her eyes widened. She reached up and pressed on her hair. Which promptly sprang back into place like a chocolate cake just out of the oven.

She groped for the arm of the chair and sat down. Hard.

Bernice wasn't going to believe this! The elusive Marissa Maribeau was now a Cut and Curl customer.

"You've got beautiful hair," I told her. "There's just way too much of it. Especially when you're fine boned. You want people to see your face, not your hair."

"I don't like to fuss."

"You'd have to fuss a lot less if it's shorter."

"How much shorter?"

Using my fingers as scissors, I made a pretend cut at her shoulder and ignored her low moan. "It'll still be long enough for you to put in a ponytail or tie in a scarf, but this will get rid of the split ends." *All ten inches of them.*

"I guess it would be all right."

That was good enough for me. I hustled her over to the shampoo sink and grabbed a bottle of industrial-strength conditioner.

She blinked up at me. Natural brunettes like Marissa usually had brown eyes, but hers were a striking bluish-gray. Tiny pleats marked the corners, indicating she wasn't as young as I thought she was when I'd met her at the wedding. Her skin was smooth and well moisturized, but some oil-free powder wouldn't be a bad idea for her T-zone…

"Uh-oh."

"What?"

"I know that look and you can forget about it."

"There was no look." I honestly had no idea what she was talking about.

"I'm an artist, remember? I throw a pot and I can see exactly what I need to do to finish it. What kind of glaze. Whether to etch it with leaves or flowers or just leave it alone." Marissa settled back comfortably in the chair. "I suppose it's the same for you when you've got someone's face in front of you."

I hadn't thought about it that way before. Didn't everyone pay attention to the shape of someone's face, the color of their eyes and whether or not their hairstyle flattered their features?

"You can't compare the two," I murmured, remembering the few pieces of Marissa's work I'd seen. She'd given Alex and Bernice a beautiful set of handmade dessert plates as a wedding gift. Each one had a delicate dandelion puff blowing across the center. I remembered wishing at the time that God had gifted me with an ability to create something like that.

"I'm not so sure. I walked in the door and right away you saw I had twice the amount of hair as a normal person. I've been looking at my face in a mirror for the past thirty-two years and missed it." Marissa crossed her arms under the cape and gave me a knowing smile.

That was because she was busy creating something beautiful *outside* herself. I didn't argue, though, because the customer is always right. My summer working at the Fun Fruit Factory had taught me that.

I picked up the scissors and clicked them above her head.

"Ready?"

Marissa closed her eyes. "Surprise me."

Half an hour later, I turned the chair around to face the mirror. "All done."

Marissa stared at her reflection. Instant panic washed over me when I saw her expression. I'd talked her into this and she hated it.

"What did you *do?*" Her eyes were wide with shock as they met mine in the mirror.

"I just…cut it." How was I supposed to explain this to Bernice? I definitely wasn't ready to go out on my own yet! "Your hair is naturally curly, but the length and the weight of it pulled most of the curl out. When you take that away, the curls find their original shape."

I'd also used enough anti-frizz gel to straighten the hair of an eighties' girl band, but no need to mention that. The overall effect was that Marissa's hair didn't dominate her face anymore. And I'd guessed that her curls, given the proper attention, were the beautiful corkscrew kind. And I was right. Normally I would have taken satisfaction in the final results, but not at the moment. Right now my stomach was tying itself into knots because I'd ruined one of Bernice's friends.

"I can see my face." Marissa touched her cheeks lightly with her fingertips.

"That was the plan," I said cautiously. "Look how big your eyes look now that you aren't hiding behind all that hair."

Marissa's mouth opened but nothing came out. She tried again. "This is going to take some getting used to."

At least she didn't pretend she loved it, like the first woman I'd practiced on at cosmetology school. She'd smiled and thanked me and then I'd heard her in the hall, frantically calling her usual stylist for an emergency appointment. The only reason I'd scraped up the courage to go back the next day was because my parents had already paid the tuition. Things had gotten better after that. Until now!

"No charge." Taking money would only add to my guilt.

"Why not?"

"You don't like it."

"I just said it would take some getting used to," Marissa corrected. She fingered the much shorter ends of her hair. "You did a great job, Heather, I'm just not sure I was ready to come out of hiding yet."

What did *that* mean? I saw her glance at her reflection again, but this time she smiled slightly. "Help me out here. I don't venture out into the real world very often. I'm supposed to give you a tip, right?"

"Make it a practical one instead. Please."

"That's easy. Don't let anyone talk you into joining a committee." She rolled her eyes. "I've got a temperamental art student named Jared Ward in my studio at this very moment who's insisting that Denise—one of the PAC committee members—promised him housing for the summer. That's why I stopped in, to see if you had a number I could call to get in touch with Bernice."

I had a swift flashback featuring the motorcycle maniac I'd met the night before. The one looking for Junebug. As soon as Bree had given him directions to Lester Lee's farm, he'd given her a polite salute and hopped back on his bike. It hadn't occurred to us that he was the one who'd been commissioned to create a statue for the park. A statue of Lester Lee's Holstein, Junebug.

I'd heard all about her from Bernice and over Easter break I'd seen the billboard with Junebug and Elise Penny's picture on it. A month ago, some mysterious benefactor had paid to recover it with a cute advertisement for the local 4-H. I can't prove anything but I think Alex was the culprit.

"I have no idea where to put him," Marissa said with a shake of her head. Which sent her curls into motion. She touched them and smiled again. "He showed up about an hour ago. Apparently Denise told him there was a vacant apartment on Main Street this summer that he could rent. Now Denise is gone to a weeklong crafting retreat and I have no idea whose apartment she was talking about."

As if on cue, something crashed above our heads and plaster dust sprinkled down from the ceiling like bits of confetti. I winced, half-expecting my bathtub to crash through the ceiling and take up residence next to the shampoo sink.

"Is someone in Bernice's apartment?" Marissa asked.

"It's my apartment now," I told her. "But I'm pretty sure Jared Ward thinks it's his."

Chapter Six

Heather (find out last name)
(Addition to Jared Ward's little black book)

"You're living in Bernice's apartment now?" Marissa ignored the sound of the vacuum cleaner that roared to life over our heads while I sent up a silent plea that Snap wasn't somehow involved in Dex's latest disaster. No wonder the poor thing hid under the couch when Dex showed up.

"She and Alex offered me the house, but I thought it would be better if I was closer to the salon." When I was nervous, my words tended to pick up speed and now they were practically rolling over the top of each other. "And it's so *cute,* don't you think? You'd pay a lot of money for an apartment like that in the Cities."

"Uh-huh." Marissa looked at me so thoughtfully I wondered if she'd somehow read my journal and discovered Reason Number Three. "That's the downside to being out of the small-town loop, I suppose. If Denise assumed Bernice's apartment would be empty, I can see her offering it to Jared. She already offered him the use of my studio."

I was dying of curiosity here. "Jared is…he's a student?" *Ponytail? Leather jacket? Motorcycle?*

Marissa must not have heard the question. "I've lived in Prichett for years and successfully avoided holiday open houses, sidewalk sales and the Prichett Advancement Council. I offer to help the committee with *one tiny detail*—choosing someone qualified to re-create Junebug the Cow in bronze—and what do I get? A homeless art student who was wolfing down the last of my granola when I left."

But does he drive a motorcycle? That's what I wanted to know.

"I have Jim Briggs to thank for this," Marissa grumbled as she gave her curls one last shake and headed for the door. When she pulled it open, she paused and looked up.

"What happened to the bells?"

I sensed that Marissa was the kind of person who valued honesty. So I confessed. "Mrs. Kirkwood."

Marissa nodded in complete understanding. "Thanks, Heather, for bringing me out of hiding. Now I have to call a certain excavator and find out if he has a guest bedroom."

Even if I hadn't heard the ominous sound of the vacuum cleaner upstairs, the sight of Dex's car parked in the alley behind the salon clued me into the fact that he was still lurking around my apartment.

My feet needed a soothing cucumber rub and a long soak in the bathtub that, by now, should have a faucet. I pushed open the door and my nose immediately twitched in response to the strange smell of Chinese food mixed with…burning rubber?

"Dex?"

I heard Snap's low, welcoming yowl from her hideout under the couch.

"You're early." Dex emerged from the bathroom. His hair was plastered against his head and his clothes were soaking wet. I suddenly remembered there were certain types of vacuum cleaners that sucked up both dirt *and* water.

"Actually, I'm late. Marissa came in just when I was about to close. It's almost seven."

"Seven?"

"What happened to—"

"I have to go." Dex grabbed his bucket of tools and charged past me, leaving a trail of wet footprints across the floor.

"What do you think, Snap? Should we make a onetime contribution to his mission trip and save the apartment while there's still time?"

At the sound of my voice, Snap crept out of hiding. I was touched by her loyalty until she rubbed her whiskers lovingly against the corner of the breakfast counter. Did I mention my nose had tricked me into believing that somewhere in the apartment was a container of sweet and sour chicken? Only it wasn't a trick. There was a note from Dex, signing over custody of the white cardboard carton to me.

"I forgive you, Dex," I said out loud. I grabbed a fork and shook the chopsticks to the side. They may be the authentic way to eat Chinese, but they weren't quick enough to suit my stomach—which hadn't had a deposit since a quick chocolate break mid-afternoon. I tap-danced my way back to the couch to find Snap already waiting there.

No way was I sharing. "I have one word for you. Indigestion. Go eat your kibbles."

Someone knocked on the door and I figured Dex had decided to come back to confess to whatever handyman crime he'd committed. Or he'd changed his mind and wanted to share my supper. Too late for joint custody, buddy!

"All I know is there better be a faucet…" I have a bad habit of starting to talk to a person before I can actually see their face. Suddenly I was cured. Because the guy leaning casually against the railing wasn't Dex.

"Heather, right? I'm Jared Ward."

I've never been the kind of person who gets tongue-tied around strangers. Ask my parents, who claim I did my own imitation of stand-up comedy at their dinner parties before I turned three.

Come on, Heather. You could say the words "want cake" when the kids in your weekly playgroup were still blowing spit bubbles. You can do this!

"I thought I'd come by and see the apartment I'm *not* going to be living in this summer and meet my closest neighbor." The teasing tone in his voice told me he had a sense of humor. The half step forward was my cue to invite him in.

"We're neighbors?" A gold star for my advanced communication skills!

"We are now. Marissa is letting me live in the garage behind the studio." He pointed over his shoulder and I could see his motorcycle parked next to a small concrete building at the end of the alley. He gave me a mischievous wink. "It ain't much, but it's home."

"I just got off work. Things are kind of crazy at the moment." Snap was probably finishing off my fried rice. And I still didn't know why Dex had looked like he'd been in a dunk tank.

Jared didn't take my not-ready-for-visitors hint. Instead, he ran a quick, appraising scan that started at my face and ended at my toes. I felt the heat from the blush that traveled along right behind it.

"You wear it well. Crazy, I mean. Not many people can pull it off."

He had no idea. It was all in the accessories. And of course having unlimited minutes with God. I was just about to give in to a moment of weakness (that may or may not have had something to do with his eyes—which were as blue as the ocean on a travel brochure) and invite him in, when he gave me an easy smile.

"You don't mind if I stop over when things *aren't* so crazy, do you?"

"No." That came out pathetically quick. He probably had girls fainting in a line behind him. Personality had always meant more to me than looks, but Jared Ward seemed to have been blessed with both. What was a girl to do?

"So, any idea when that will be?"

*In about five minutes. As soon as I see what Dex did to the bathroom...*but I couldn't say that without sounding like one of those desperate-for-a-Friday-date girls. And today *was* Thursday.

"The craziness tends to last a while." I was being truthful, not coy, and I couldn't resist the urge to test his confidence a little. "Like last night, when I was horseback riding with a friend? Some maniac on a motorcycle broke the sound barrier as he drove past us and almost sent the horses into orbit."

Jared's eyes widened, making them look even bluer. Not fair. "That was you?"

I wasn't offended. It *had* been dark when he'd stopped to ask directions. I tipped the brim of my invisible cowboy hat.

"I'm sorry, I'm a city boy. When I got on that flat stretch of country road I just had to open it up." Jared tucked his hands into the front pockets of his jeans, the kind deliberately created with worn spots and artistically placed rips. "When I saw the horses running, I thought it was on purpose. You looked like you had it under control."

How could I remain upset after that flattering—*but totally erroneous*—assessment?

"At least you slowed down the second time," I murmured. Forgiveness was an important part of my faith, after all.

"So, Friday nights aren't crazy, are they? What do people do around here on the weekends? Count tractors?"

He wasn't going to give up, which left me feeling flattered *and* flustered. "I'm not sure. I haven't been here very long, either," I admitted.

"Really? Let's figure it out together. What time do you get off work tomorrow night?"

"Five."

"Great." He bounded down the stairs and didn't stop until he reached his home-away-from-home at the end of the alley. I didn't realize I was still staring until he turned and waved at me. The wave I returned was limp with embarrassment and as soon as he disappeared, I lunged back into the apartment.

I was right. The take-out carton was lying on its side under the coffee table and Snap was cheerfully cleaning the last of the fried rice out from between her toes.

I fortified myself with a Tootsie Roll from Bernice's cache in the canister marked Tea, pretended I was a FEMA worker and bravely entered the bathroom. With my eyes closed. I turned toward the spot where my bathtub had been that morning. When I opened them, there was a faucet.

"Snap, I have a faucet. A real, live, normal-looking faucet!"

And a date for Friday night, an irritating little voice reminded me.

It's not a date. It's two people who are new in town getting together to see the sites. All two or three of them.

I decided to celebrate—the faucet, of course—with a long soak in the bathtub.

When my phone rang a little after ten, I hoped it was

Bree. She'd warned me she'd be putting in long hours helping her dad with the farm and there'd be times she wouldn't be able to talk to me until after dark. Which was fine with me because I did some of my best talking late at night.

"Does it work?"

"Dex?"

Silence. I took that as a yes. His question had been so uncertain I wondered what exactly had taken place while I was gone during the day.

"Yes, it works."

"I was late for another job."

"There aren't that many places to work around here," I said, daring to tease him. "Did Sally give you a job as a waitress?"

"No."

Obviously teasing Dex was like playing tennis when no one was on the other side of the net. Still, he'd made that "shaken not stirred" comment, so maybe there was a sense of humor buried in there somewhere. If someone had the patience to look for it.

"I'm not coming over tomorrow," he said. "I'll be back on Monday to start in the kitchen. Did you want me to replace the cupboards or paint them?"

The image of a crowbar and splintered wood sprang into my head. "Paint them. Definitely. And thanks for the Chinese—"

He'd hung up on me again.

"Food."

In the name of dessert, I grabbed another handful of

Tootsie Rolls, tucked my Bible under my arm and curled up in the chair by the window to talk to God.

Psalms was always a good place to hear His voice. Even though David was a guy, he tried to live honestly before God. There were times he praised Him, times he questioned Him and times he asked Him for things. And times he asked God—in no uncertain terms—to squash his enemies. Which, truthfully, made me a little squeamish. But after having met Mrs. Kirkwood, I was a little more understanding. David also asked God to direct his steps, something I was doing on a daily (hourly?) basis. We had a lot in common.

My Bible fell open to Haggai again. Not because a divine hand stretched out and turned to it but because there was a folded-up piece of paper there. A receipt for sweet and sour chicken from the grocery store. Scrawled on the back of it was a question.

What does it mean that the people earned wages and put them in a purse with holes in it?

Dex had hijacked my devotional time!

Panicked, I thumbed through my Bible, looking for the extremely personal poetry, musings and notes to God that I sometimes wrote on the back of church bulletins and making sure The List, safely hidden in the Song of Songs, hadn't been tampered with.

I breathed a sigh of relief when everything seemed to be in its rightful place. Not that Dex had been rifling through my Bible, but still…how had he known I was accidentally reading Haggai?

I skimmed through the verses and found the one he'd

questioned. Why did he think I knew what the *purses with holes* passage meant? I wasn't exactly a Bible scholar.

I did, however, know purses. They were kind of my specialty. And I was pretty good at finding shoes that matched, too. Encouraging him might not be a good idea, but I couldn't resist. I grabbed a pen, took out a fresh sticky note and wrote the first thing I thought of when I imagined a rip in my Juicy bag.

You might lose something important.

I put it back in Haggai, chapter one. A booby trap to see if I'd catch a snoopy handyman.

Chapter Seven

Likes children (and not just because he thinks you do)
(The List. Number 8)

No one had warned me that Friday was payday at Whiley Implements. There was a line waiting outside the Cut and Curl when I skipped downstairs. I had three walk-ins before I finally figured out why business was so brisk at the salon and that was because one of the women asked me to cash her check so she could get her hair cut.

I hesitated, not sure if Bernice made a practice of this. When the rest of the women lined up by the window noticed me staring at the check, they all came to her rescue and set me straight. Bernice *did* cash payroll checks but only the first two or three—then she'd remind everyone the Cut and Curl wasn't a bank and she'd pencil them in while they went to the drive-thru.

Payday turned the salon into a gathering spot for

women who hadn't had time to pamper themselves for two weeks. There were kids playing tag around my shampoo chair and by noon I'd made three pots of coffee.

At the end of the day, just when I was getting ready to indulge in some possible *first date* scenarios, Annie Carpenter, the youth pastor's wife, burst in. Her hair was in two loose Laura Ingalls Wilder braids and the yellow sundress she was wearing made her look like a daffodil.

I hadn't seen her since the gift opening on Sunday. I'd been thinking about her, though, because Bernice had made me promise I'd keep an eye on her over the summer. Annie was a first-time mom and having *two* babies had to be an adjustment. I'd loved Annie the minute I'd met her, which had been at Faith Community Church the day *after* I'd met Bernice for the first time. Bernice had told me later she'd never set foot in a church until that morning. It was through Annie and Elise's influence that Mama B had become a Christian, but she'd also said it had had a lot to do with the message I'd left on her answering machine. Which made me think of another one of Grandma Lowell's favorite sayings.

God's timing may not match ours, but it's always perfect.

"You're twin-less," I said as Annie wrapped me in a hug. She smelled like a combination of baby powder and men's cologne, probably from snuggling with her favorite three people.

"Stephen took the afternoon off so I could sneak out for an hour. When I left, he was practicing his Sunday school lesson on the twins, but he wanted me to invite you over for dinner after church on Sunday. He's going to grill chicken and I'm practicing potato salad this week."

Practicing potato salad?

"That sounds great. What can I bring?"

"We got an ice-cream maker on our last anniversary," Annie said. "The old-fashioned kind. I'll buy the ingredients if you figure out how it works."

The phone rang and I leaped toward the counter to answer it. That's another thing Bernice had forgotten to warn me—the boss and only employee of the Cut and Curl—about. I didn't know how she made it through the number of appointments scheduled in a day with the phone ringing constantly.

"Cut and Curl."

"You sound like you own the place," a teasing voice said.

"Mama B!" I'd been wondering if she'd call. I'd been dying to check in on her but she *was* on her honeymoon so I'd resisted the temptation. "Where are you?"

"I don't even want to tell you. It's too embarrassing."

"Can you see the Eiffel Tower?"

"Uh-huh."

I looked past Annie and saw Prichett's water tower in the distance. It was shaped like a giant Q-tip. For some strange reason, I didn't feel the least bit envious.

"Guess who's here? Annie." I said I was impulsive. Sometimes I even answered my own questions.

"Is that Bernice?" Annie crowded into my personal space but I didn't mind. All of us—Elise, Annie, Bree and I—missed Bernice already and she hadn't even been gone a week. I held the phone away from my ear so we could share the conversation.

"Hi, Annie. I'm glad you're there because I have a confession. I shipped Nathaniel and Joanna some things."

"From France?" The wonder in Annie's voice made me smile.

"Yes, France. And I think there's something from London, too. I'm losing track."

"Bernice, you can't spoil them like that." Annie made a face at the phone.

"Yes, I can. And we haven't been to Italy or Greece yet. I found a silk scarf for Esther today. If I tuck it into the next outgoing batch, will you make sure she gets it?"

Esther Crandall lived in the Golden Oaks Nursing Home. Another one of Bernice's friends I'd promised to check on over the course of the summer.

"Sure. Now I'm going to back out of this conversation so you and Heather can talk." Annie made a kissing noise into the phone and handed it back to me.

"How did you survive Mrs. Kirkwood?" Bernice wanted to know.

"I think the wounds are finally healing."

Bernice laughed. "I knew you'd charm her."

"Charm her?"

"Did she schedule another appointment?"

"Unfortunately, yes."

"There you go."

We talked a few more minutes and I told her about horseback riding with Bree and Marissa's haircut and Jared Ward coming to town. Bernice may not have raised me, but her next question proved that her Mom Alert was completely functioning. And set on high.

"Jared Ward? What's he like?"

Since I knew I'd have this exact conversation with Mom over the weekend, I figured I might as well practice. "He's about twenty-three or twenty-four."

"Really?"

Is he good-looking? Three…two…one…

"What does he look like?"

Close enough. "He looks a little like Orlando Bloom." *With a motorcycle.* "Denise told him he could stay in your apartment for the summer."

"What!"

"It's all straightened out." I probably should have mentioned that first. "He's living in Marissa's garage instead."

I heard Bernice whispering something to Alex. Maybe she was asking him to hire a private investigator to check into Jared's background. She and Alex could probably split the cost with Mom and Dad!

"Mama B, I should go now. It's almost closing time."

"Right. It's Friday night." Bernice sounded a bit wistful.

"What happens on Friday night?" I asked eagerly. Maybe there was something about Friday nights in Prichett I didn't know yet.

"Nothing that doesn't happen during the rest of the week," Bernice admitted. "It's nice to know that life in Prichett doesn't change, but I suppose it's going to be too quiet for you this summer. You're used to a lot more choices."

"I'll be fine," I assured her just before we said

goodbye. I *wanted* quiet. Prichett was my Go square. It was eight weeks of security before I stepped into my life. I'd traveled around Europe with a close friend and I'd lived apart from my parents for almost a year, but things felt different now. Even though I knew my family would always be there for me, I was going to be the one making decisions now. Like what to do with the rest of my life. The whole idea gave me a queasy feeling.

Out of the corner of my eye I watched Annie smiling blissfully as she smelled samples from a new line of shampoo I'd received earlier in the week. She was only five years older than me and already had five years of marriage under her belt. And she'd brought twins into the world.

I felt my twinge of envy bloom a little. Annie was off the Go square and moving happily down her God-chosen path. She was a wife and mother and, from what Bree told me, a mentor to the teenage girls in Stephen's youth group.

I was twenty-one and when it came to life, my major was still undeclared.

I'm listening, God! You point the way and I'm so there.

"Go ahead and pick your favorite," I told Annie. "You can tell me if it works."

She slipped one into the pocket of her dress and gave it a friendly pat. "Remember, Sunday after church."

"I'll be there."

Annie left and I turned my attention to the cash register. Money—the collecting and the disbursing of it—wasn't my gift. Another life lesson learned the hard way at the Fun Fruit Factory. I'd told Jared I was done with work at five o'clock, but we hadn't made any plans beyond that. Was he going to call? Was he going to stop by the apartment?

I heard a low purr outside and when I glanced up, Jared's motorcycle was parked right outside. He waved a helmet at me.

I swallowed my gum.

"I have to run up and change." They were the first words I could string together when he walked in.

"Oh, I don't think you need to change a thing."

Were there guys who could actually get away with lines like that? Yes, there were. And I soaked up the compliment like toner in a cotton ball.

Jared sat down in one of the squishy plastic chairs by the window and stretched out his legs. I counted the change in the till. For the third time.

"Marissa mentioned you're here for the summer."

"I'm helping out my…Bernice…while she's on her honeymoon." My relationship with Bernice and Alex was too complicated to explain to someone I'd just met. I was still protective of it. It was like a poem I wanted to finish before I could share it with someone else.

"So what else can you do? Besides cut hair?"

The question nudged me off balance. Was he wondering if I knew how to do a spiral perm or a French manicure? Or was he looking for something deeper?

"Let's see. I can actually make a piecrust from scratch—my grandmother would disown me if I bought the kind you *unfold*. I can play Mozart on the piano. And I can walk on my hands but since I haven't tried that since summer camp, you're just going to have to take my word for it."

Sounding a bit defensive, aren't you, Heather?

Jared pretended to wipe the sweat off his forehead. "Wow. All that and she's beautiful, too. Let's find out if you can paddle a canoe."

Our Friday night adventure to Marley Creek lasted less than fifteen minutes. We didn't even get the canoe in the water. The mosquitoes were hungry and saw an opportunity to devour the two unsuspecting outsiders that had naively wandered into their territory. As we raced back to the motorcycle, I wondered if anyone had thought of creating a designer perfume that included Deet. If not, I had first dibs.

"Plan B?" I shouted over his shoulder as he revved up the engine.

"You pick this time."

We ended up at Sally's Café just as Sally was about to close for the night. Jared talked her into staying open a few more minutes so he could ease the pain of the mosquito bites with a chocolate shake. She made the shakes and then kicked us out into the street.

"I need to sit down." Even the most comfortable shoes had an expiration date and I'd been on my feet for almost ten hours.

"I have a really great couch that looks like a sea serpent. It's got to be at least twenty feet long and the fabric is this

weird, shiny green. Vintage seventies' rec room. I hauled
it out of Marissa's basement this afternoon."

I wasn't really paying attention. My brain had stalled
right after the word *couch*. He wanted me to go back to
his…garage.

It wasn't that Jared gave off any creepy vibes that
made me feel uncomfortable to be alone with him. I'd
already learned a lot about him in the past few hours.
He loved city life and was hoping to end up in New
York or L.A. He described himself as a sculptor but
eventually wanted to own a gallery. He moved with
restless energy and talked with his hands. And he talked
more than I did. He wasn't anything like the guys I'd
met in the YAC group. His plans…his world…seemed
bigger. I was surprised at how much I wanted to keep
listening to him. Wanting to listen instead of talk—this
was a first for me.

"The couch sounds great but I've been inside all day."
I suddenly developed an annoying stammer. "Why don't
we find a bench in the park instead?"

Jared stared at me for a second, then shrugged. "Sure."

We crossed the street to the park, Prichett's miniature version of a green space.

"This playground equipment is new. My friend's
mom won the Proverbs 31 pageant last fall and the prize
was a donation to her favorite charity. With the money,
they replaced the slide and some of the swings. Bree told
me the Boy Scouts might build a gazebo this summer,
too." I sounded like a bad tour guide.

"Any idea where Junebug is going to go?"

"By the drinking fountain over there. For maximum exposure."

"I was hoping I'd have a little more creative input about the sculpture. I'm still hoping I can convince Marissa to get the committee to change their minds about a cow." Jared's foot suddenly shot out to stop a ball that came skipping toward us. With an apologetic grin, he kicked it back to the kids and then joined them in a game that looked like a no-rules cross between soccer and football.

He liked kids. This happened to be on The List. Come to think of it, so was outgoing. And creative. Character-*list*-ics were popping up everywhere and I'd only known him a few hours. I cupped my hands over my face so I wouldn't hyperventilate.

A few minutes later, Jared ran back over to me, rumpled and out of breath. And adorable. I scooted over and made room for him on the bench.

"What would you suggest for the sculpture?" I was curious. And a little uneasy. Bernice was vice president of the Prichett Advancement Council and she'd hinted they didn't exactly *embrace* change. In fact, she mentioned something about them fighting it, and I quote, *tooth and nail.* Jared was going to be in Prichett all summer and I didn't want him to make a bad impression in the first week.

Because they might fire him, right, Heather? And then he'd have to leave town.

To my amazement, Jared pulled his wallet out of his back pocket and thumbed through the contents until he found a piece of paper. "Something like this."

I studied the pencil sketch and resisted the urge to flip it around the other way. Just in case it was upside down. The three twisted spirals didn't look like anything that occurred in nature.

"What do you think?"

I think I felt the same way my mother felt when I'd bless her with one of my preschool art projects. In a burst of inspiration, I remembered her response.

"Tell me about it!"

I exhaled quietly when he smiled instead of dumping the rest of his milk shake over my head and stomping off to sulk the rest of the night away on his twenty-foot couch. I wasn't sure why Marissa had described him as temperamental.

"It's the land that gives back to the people who live here," Jared said, tapping his finger against the paper. "This is *the land.*"

It looked like a handful of corkscrew pasta to me. But what did I know? When my friends and I played Pictionary, I was the designated timekeeper because no one trusted me with a pen and paper. I drew a coat hanger once and everyone thought it was a swan.

"I'm not sure if they'll change their minds," I murmured, hoping he wouldn't be too disappointed when his dreams were crushed under Junebug's cloven hoof. "Why don't you run it by Marissa, first?"

"She says she isn't on the committee." Jared put the paper carefully back in his wallet and then slapped a mosquito on the back of his hand. "Looks like they found us again. We must give off tourist pheromones."

I realized we were alone. While I was studying Jared's sketch, our pint-size chaperones had raced home to beat their Friday night curfew. Crazy as it sounded, I wished I had one again. It would have given me the perfect excuse to avoid the subject I knew was about to resurface. All twenty feet of it.

This is no big deal. You watch a movie for a few hours. You go home. You're twenty-one years old. You don't need a chaperone.

This came from the rational, logical side of me. At least it sounded rational and logical. But if Jared didn't think I wanted to spend time with him, he'd find someone else to claim my spot on his shiny green couch. What made me nervous wasn't the *going* to Jared's house, but how much I *wanted* to. But I didn't want to get into a potentially uncomfortable situation, either.

"Do you want to come back—"

Jared's words were snuffed out by the soft but unmistakable sound of church bells down the street. I tilted my head back and saw a star winking at me, right above the trees. Reminding me that logical doesn't always equal smart.

So not funny, Lord.

"I think I'll go home—I have to work tomorrow morning." I held my breath right after I said the words. Here was Jared's next line: *No problem. When can I see you again?*

"Sure. If that's what you want."

I sighed. Why didn't guys memorize the script?

Chapter Eight

What did u do 2day? (Text message from Tony
Gillespie to Dex)

Dropd potato salad on my feet. (Dex)

Y? (Tony)

So I wouldnt have 2 share. (Dex)

"Heather, have you met Dex?" Annie's muffled words
greeted me when I stepped into her kitchen on Sunday
after church. She was cuddling a pink blanket—Joanna
Ruth—and Dex was standing beside her, holding a blue-
wrapped bundle—Nathaniel.

"We've met. Alex hired him to fix up the apartment this
summer." I was going to start repeating this in my sleep.

"Stephen invited him to have lunch with us, too."
Annie eased Joanna into my arms and ignored the desperate look Dex cast in her direction. "I'll get you two

some lemonade. Why don't you meet me in the backyard? Stephen is already out there messing with the coals."

"Hand him over," I sighed as soon as Annie disappeared. "You're holding him like he's a football and you're about to fumble him."

I didn't have to ask him twice. Dex tucked him into the crook of my arm and beat a hasty retreat. At least he had the presence of mind to pause long enough to hold the screen door open for me.

"Hi, Heather." Stephen waved a basting brush at me.

The entire backyard of the Carpenters' duplex was the size of the sunroom in the house I grew up in. I wondered where they were going to put a swing set and sandbox when the twins got older. Both Mom and Dad served on a lot of committees at church, so I knew pastors didn't make much money—especially in towns the size of Prichett. That Faith Community could even afford a full-time youth pastor told me a lot about their priorities. They were definitely in the right place.

I sat down gingerly on the edge of a lawn chair, shifting Joanna and Nathaniel into a more comfortable position in my arms. Joanna smiled at me but Nathaniel was as serious as a professor. He reminded me a little of Dex.

"They're quite an armful, aren't they?" The screen door slapped against the frame as Annie came out of the house, carrying a tray of picnic supplies.

"Flex for them, sweetheart," Stephen teased. "Show them the bulging biceps you're getting without an annual gym fee."

Annie looked at him in mock disgust. "Next thing you know, he'll be hiring me out to chop wood at Lester's place."

Stephen pretended to consider it and Annie pitched a plastic spoon at him. Then she turned to Dex and me. "Why don't you guys figure out this ice-cream maker while I put Jo and Nate down for their nap?"

Dex hadn't said two words to me and I was still trying to decide if he was stuck-up or just shy. He must have come right to the Carpenters' from church, because he was wearing wrinkle-free khakis (I can always pick out a polyester cotton blend from the real thing) and a junior executive white shirt with the cuffs buttoned at the wrist.

"We can figure this out, right, Dex?" I decided to give him the benefit of the doubt and went with *shy*. If necessary, I could talk enough for both of us. "There has to be directions in the box somewhere."

Stephen coughed lightly and I looked up.

"Don't count on it," he whispered with an anxious glance toward the house.

I blinked. "No directions?"

"Annie puts all the directions and warranties for stuff in a box. Which happens to be underneath the Christmas ornaments, which happens to be in the basement behind the hot water heater. You'll just have to wing it."

I slid the box toward Dex. "Winging it? Here you go, Dex. That's definitely your department."

For a second I thought I'd offended him. He stared

down at the ice-cream maker and his glasses slid down to the end of his nose. When he lifted it out of the box, his hands were shaking.

"Dex—"

He laughed, so suddenly and freely that it collided with the apology I was about to make and blew it into pieces. Then he muttered something that sounded like *distractions*.

"An ice-cream maker is a distraction?"

Dex ignored me as he dove headfirst into the box and then began lobbing pieces of the ice-cream maker at me. "Green is a distraction," he muttered. "Gold is a distraction."

Was he talking about the Green Bay Packers? Because that was the only green and gold distraction I knew about. Or maybe he was trying to figure out how to get to the next level. If that was the case, he needed someone to lead him back to the real world.

"It's a good thing we're making vanilla ice cream then," I said as gently as possible. "Because vanilla is *white*. Very harmless."

"The chicken is ready," Stephen called.

I sent a silent thank-you to God for the distraction.

"This is delicious!" Annie scooped up another helping of ice cream and dumped a handful of chocolate chips on top. Since imitation is the sincerest form of flattery, I sprinkled some on mine, too. "We got this last year for our anniversary and never used it because we were busy packing up to move to Prichett."

"Two weeks from now it will be five years," Stephen said.

"Are you planning anything special?" I tried not to look at Dex, who was stirring his ice cream into something that resembled the cooked cereal Mom had force-fed me as a child.

Annie laughed and wove her fingers into Stephen's. "Not yet. I can only plan things several hours in advance. I think the twins borrowed some of my brain cells when they were born."

"If I could convince her to let us hire a sitter for the evening, I'd take her out for a nice dinner. Something expensive. Something *hot*." Stephen gave her The Smile. The one reserved for couples who are truly soul mates. The one that makes girls with no significant other—like me—sigh with envy.

"*Hot?* Remind me again what hot food tastes like." Annie closed her eyes.

"You've got a whole youth group full of teenage girls," I pointed out. "I'm sure they'd love to babysit."

"And they're great," Annie said quickly. "It's just that the twins are only three months old—"

"But they go to bed at seven," Stephen murmured.

"And that's a lot of responsibility for someone."

"I'll do it." The words slipped out before I could completely think the offer through. Annie and Stephen gave so much of themselves to the youth group, they deserved to have some time away. It would be my gift to them to watch the twins so they could go out on their anniversary and eat hot food.

Annie squeaked and almost tipped the bowl of ice cream off my lap when she hugged me. Dex stopped stirring and stared at me in disbelief.

"You told me that you never babysat."

Annie and Stephen exchanged a worried glance. How dare Dex question my gift? And my credentials.

"I can change diapers and warm up bottles." And I'm sure there was a *Twins for Dummies* book out there somewhere if I needed a quick reference guide. I gave Dex a look guaranteed to refreeze his ice cream and then smiled at Annie. "We'll be fine. You just name the time and I'll be here."

The concern in Annie's eyes faded and she nodded happily. Stephen sent me a grateful look that inspired me to do another good deed.

"If you want me to, I can even come over a few minutes early and fix your hair."

Annie pursed her lips and blew a strand of sunset-red hair off her forehead. "That sounds almost as good as hot food."

"Great." I resisted the urge to cross my arms and give Dex a *so there* smile. Not that he would have noticed. He'd tuned out again and was stacking dishes on the tray as efficiently as a busboy.

"We've got a lot of leftovers," Annie said. "You guys should take some potato salad home."

That got Dex's attention. His eyes locked on the mountain of potato salad in the bowl on the center of the picnic table. Annie had told us she'd never learned to cook, so every month she picked out something new to try and practiced until she got it right. She'd confessed this potato salad was only her second attempt. Somehow the salad dressing had morphed into a gluelike substance that bonded the potatoes, celery and onion together like a chunk of concrete. I'd seen Stephen discreetly cutting it into bite-size pieces with his knife.

Annie handed Dex a small plastic container with a lid. My heart rate kicked into high gear when I saw him hesitate.

Dex, read your script. Don't you dare hurt Annie's feelings. Repeat after me: I'd love to take some home.

"Do you have a bigger container?" Dex asked her.

Not bothering to hide her delight, Annie covered the entire bowl with a piece of foil and presented it to him with as much ceremony as a queen would bestow knighthood on a loyal subject.

I dub thee Sir Dex of the First Order of Leftover Potato Salad.

I watched him blush and tried not to laugh.

"Heather doesn't have any," Stephen said.

I'd been hoping no one would notice.

"Maybe they can share it." Annie smiled her mega-watt smile.

Her comment triggered some kind of convulsive twitch in Dex, because he dropped the bowl and the potato salad ended up all over the grass at his feet.

Or maybe he'd planned it that way. As far as I was concerned, if a guy was willing to snoop in someone's Bible, he was capable of just about anything.

Dex left as soon as he finished directing the potato salad into Annie's marigolds with the garden hose. Annie didn't want to send him away empty-handed, so she made him take the rest of the ice cream home. Oddly enough, he hugged Annie goodbye, shook Stephen's hand…and wouldn't look me in the eye. Go figure. Maybe it was delayed guilt over the faucet.

The twins were still sleeping and I decided it was time for me to leave, too, so Annie and Stephen could have some time alone before Joanna and Nathaniel woke up for round two.

I'd ignored the cell phone chirping in my purse during lunch so I checked my voice mail as soon as I got into the car. There was a message from Bree, asking if I'd like to come out to the farm and go riding with her. I didn't bother calling her back—I answered in person when I showed up at the front door an hour later.

Elise sent me out to the barn, where Bree was already saddling up Buckshot.

"I wasn't sure you'd make it," she said, and tossed a brush at me. "I caught Rose for you, just in case."

"I didn't get your message right away because there was an incident with Dex and a bowl of Annie's potato salad." I slid open the door to Rose's stall and peeked in. She was peeking back at me.

"Dex was at Annie's, too?"

"Apparently Pastor Charles and Jeanne were in charge of an afternoon service at the Golden Oaks today, so Annie invited Dex over."

Bree had a strange expression on her face so obviously

I needed to explain the situation more clearly. "He's new in town and probably doesn't know many people."

"Mmm. Just like you."

I wasn't quite sure where she was going with this. "I guess so." I had a flash of inspiration. "Maybe they'll invite Jared over sometime. He's new in town, too."

"Did he call you last night?"

I'd told Bree all about Friday night when I'd called her during my lunch break the day before. CNN newsbreaks couldn't compete with the crucial information friends needed to share during the beginning of a relationship. Or a *non*relationship. "No. But his motorcycle was gone all day so maybe he was out at Lester's farm, dipping Junebug in bronze."

While I was talking, Bree saddled up both our horses. I couldn't spread cream cheese on a bagel that fast.

"But you're worried he didn't call because you didn't go back to his place."

Was I that transparent? But this was Bree, so the moment called for honesty. "I don't want to think he's—"

"A player? Shallow? Looking for some fun in the sun?" She tossed Rose's reins to me and walked Buckshot out of the barn.

"Bree!" I guess her moment called for honesty, too. I followed her into the yard, Rose kicking up dust behind me. She actually stood still for me this time when I vaulted myself into the saddle.

"I hate to say this, but if turning down that invitation is enough for him to lose interest, then *you* don't want to be interested."

"You're right." Depressingly right.

"I wondered about Riley last summer when he started hanging around. Mom freaked out because he's older than me and she was worried he was going to mess up my plans for college, but I was worried I was just a challenge."

"Aren't you?"

She grinned. "Sure. But that's not the point. It's kind of confusing, don't you think? There's one theory that says we should go out with a lot of guys and eventually we'll pick the right one, and then there's another theory that says it's better to look for friendship and hope at some point it develops into something more."

"But you have an idea what you're looking for." Did Bree have a list, too? Probably not. She was way too practical and independent…

"You have a list, don't you?"

"A list?" I decided to play dumb.

"You know, the Prince Charming list. The Mr. Right list." Bree wasn't fooled for a second.

"Do *you* have a list?" I turned this into a *What Would Jesus Do* moment and answered her question with a question.

Bree cleared her throat. "A believer. Helps my dad. Likes horses and isn't afraid of them. Has good personal hygiene. Employed."

Those were her Top Five? Bree *was* practical. Employed wasn't even on my list. In my defense, though, I'd written the list when I was sixteen and only updated it once since graduation. It wasn't too late to add an amendment.

"Okay, your turn. Spill it."

"Intelligent. Sense of humor. Loves to read. Adventurous. Not afraid to show affection." I took a breath after my Top Five and decided I might as well keep going. When Bree's eyes began to glaze over, it clued me into the fact that maybe my list was a wee bit longer than hers.

"You have the whole thing memorized?" Bree asked carefully when I finished.

"I may have forgotten one or two."

"Your list is really…detailed."

Wait a second. Did she mean detailed as in you've-put-a-lot-of-thought-into-this or detailed as in picky? Unrealistic? It's never gonna happen?

"It could be subject to change, I guess." I bravely straightened my shoulders. "Tell me the truth. Is one of them too extreme?"

Her slight hesitation told me there was more than one.

"The *he knows exactly what kind of gift to buy me no matter what the occasion?*" Bree bit her lip. "I'd let that one go, Heather. A guy who knows that wouldn't be the kind of guy who asks a girl to marry him."

Maybe she had a point. "And? Come on. I can tell there's more."

"This is *your* list. I'm not going to tamper with it."

"Bree!"

"All right. Maybe the *isn't afraid to wander into the purse department with me.*"

"Unrealistic?"

"Totally."

"I'm sticking to the *no pierced tongue.*"

"That's okay. I'm adding it to mine."

When we got back to the farm, Elise, Bree's mom, was waiting for us with a plate of brownies and a pitcher of lemonade. I told her about Bernice's phone call while we sat on the porch swing, but when Bree started yawning at the end of every other word, I knew it was time to go home. On the way to my car, I checked my cell. No messages. No missed calls.

Jared and I had spent only one evening together and I wasn't supposed to be this disappointed he hadn't called back.

When I got back to the apartment, my breath whooshed out of my lungs when I saw something propped against the door. A canoe paddle. Right next to it was an extra-large can of bug spray. I couldn't prevent a giddy smile, especially after I read the words he'd scrawled on the paddle in permanent marker.

Should we try it again? JW

Chapter Nine

The Word of the Day is:

Distraction: *The act of distracting or the state of being distracted. Distracted: to stir up or confuse with conflicting emotions or motives.*

   Green eyes are a distraction because of their visual impact.

(Dex—scribbled on page ten of the book *Real Men Write in Journals*)

Monday morning. Everyone complains about them, but Mondays hadn't gotten to me yet. Maybe it was because I'd only worked one. I had a full week at the Cut and Curl behind me and life had already begun to ease into a routine.

At seven forty-five I'd go down to the Cut and Curl and start the coffee. The three-minute brewing time gave me a chance to scoot over to Sally's and buy a raspberry Danish. When I got back to the salon, I'd turn the radio to WSON, which I could count on to provide a soothing background of uplifting praise and worship music. It also put me in the right frame of mind for the next thing on the agenda—listening to the messages on the answering machine. This usually meant I had to do some creative rescheduling of appointments. I was amazed at the drama that took place in Prichett between closing time on one day and eight o'clock in the morning on the next.

The messages the women left were usually long. And way too honest. They were rescheduling a haircut, not an international summit with world leaders. I didn't need to know that my eight-thirty had been up all night helping a cow (insert detailed description) give birth, my ten-o'clock was weaning her baby off breast milk and couldn't get her to take a bottle (okay, I know it's perfectly natural, *but still*) and my eleven-o'clock was experiencing a hot flash strong enough to "melt the polar ice caps."

Sometimes I think they forgot that I was the one listening to the messages instead of Bernice.

Sure enough, when I opened up the salon, the light on the phone was blinking. I ignored it because I was running a few minutes behind schedule. Maybe because I'd spent more time than I should have staring dreamily at the canoe paddle I'd propped next to the window. Now I had to sprint to Sally's if I wanted my Danish.

Dex was sitting at the counter when I walked in. I knew he saw me, because his eyes shifted in my direction but he didn't even say hello. What was it with this guy? Maybe he just wasn't a morning person.

"Hi, Dex. Kitchen cupboards today, right?" I sat down next to him and gave him a friendly smile. Burning coals, you know. It's biblical.

"I'm going to use one of these." Dex fished around in his pocket and dumped a handful of crumpled paper in front of me.

Paint samples. And every single one of them was a variation of the color beige. Sand. Linen. Wheatgrass.

Three strikes and you're out, Dex.

"I was thinking of something with more visual impact."

"Visual impact?" He blinked owlishly behind his glasses.

"Something a little more…jazzy."

"Jazzy?"

How to put this in words he'd understand? "Something with *color,* Dex."

"Sure." He rubbed his hand across his face in the same weary gesture I'd seen my dad use after he worked all night. Maybe Dex was rude and antisocial, but I felt a rush of sympathy for him. He had more part-time jobs than my aunt Jackie had Hummels.

Sally swept out of the kitchen and snapped a kitchen towel at me, her sentimental way of saying hello.

"Hi, Sally. The usual." This was something I had to tell my parents. I, Heather Lowell, had a usual. I didn't know this until I hurried into the café last Thursday morning and Sally asked if I wanted *the usual.* In the Cities, I'd gone to the same coffee shop for six months and ordered the same thing—a French vanilla latte—but every single time the girl behind the counter stared at me like she'd never seen me before.

Small towns were great. There was camaraderie. There was depth. There was loyalty….

"Sorry, Heather. You're running a little late today. I sold the last raspberry Danish to your friend here."

So maybe there wasn't loyalty. "Blueberry?"

Sally shook her head. "Marissa stopped in a while ago, muttering something about meals not being in the contract, and bought half a dozen. All I've got left now is prune."

Dex snickered into his glass of Pepsi. Now there was a palate-pleasing combination—raspberry Danish and soda.

"Prune's good for you." An elderly man one stool down from me suddenly leaned closer. "Keeps things moving."

Gross! That pearl of wisdom I could have done without.

"Um, no thanks, Sally. I'll just have a bagel and cream cheese. Please."

Dex and I ended up walking out of the café at the same time. He strode ahead of me even though we were going in the same direction. To the same place.

"What's your rush?" I couldn't resist giving him a hard time as I tried to keep up. "Are you late for your morning nap?"

He didn't even glance back at me. "I have to go to the hardware store and pick out some paint with *visual impact.* A guy shouldn't even know what that means."

I found myself laughing. Despite his evil snicker over the prune Danish. "It's good to expand your vocabulary. Think of it as your word for the day."

"Peace and quiet. How's that for a word of the day?" He veered off course and headed across the street where his Impala was parked.

"That's *two* words!" I shouted.

"So is visual impact," he shouted back.

Argh. He was right! I had this terrible habit of needing to get the last word in, but this time I didn't get the chance. Dex practically dove into the driver's seat and pulled the door closed.

"Chicken!" I huffed at the car's retreating bumper. "That's one word."

Amanda Clark was my last appointment for the day. She was so quiet I didn't even hear her come in but suddenly there she was, sitting in the chair next to the coffeepot. She looked like she was in her mid-to-late thirties but judging from the clothes she was wearing and the uneven blond stripes in her hair, she was still a hostage to the eighties.

"Mrs. Clark?"

She nodded and ventured over.

"I'm Heather Lowell. I'm managing the Cut and Curl for Bernice this summer."

"I heard that." She glanced at me once and then looked away.

"Sit down." I grabbed a plastic cape. "Did you have something specific in mind today? I have you down for a cut, but you are the last appointment…" This was a broad hint that I was willing to stay longer if necessary.

"I don't know." Amanda wouldn't look at herself in

the mirror and her fingers drummed nervously against her knees. "I have a job interview tomorrow."

"So you want to update your look." Maybe she hadn't said that *exactly,* but I could read between the lines. "We can do that. Where is your interview?"

"At Whiley."

Whiley Implements. It was tedious, repetitive work but I knew there wasn't much to choose from in Prichett. The truth was, she could probably get away with the same hair-style she had now, but it wouldn't hurt to boost Amanda's confidence a little. She looked like she could use it.

"Your natural color is auburn, isn't it?" I could see the pretty autumn tones hiding underneath the ten-dollar dye job.

"Kind of. Mostly it's just brown."

"What do you say we try an experiment? Go back to your natural color but add some gold highlights just to kick things up a notch?"

Amanda moved listlessly. "I don't care."

She didn't care? I had women who watched me mix up their hair color with the intensity of a chemistry professor grading a graduate student's final project.

Lord, what's going on here? Please let me know if there's something I can do for Amanda.

I hate to admit there are times I complain that God is slow to answer. I know He wants me to be faithful in prayer and that's why answers don't always come as quickly as I'd like them to, but in this case His response time was pretty good. In fact, it was *immediate*. There wasn't a mysterious hand jotting something on the wall or anything. Just a divine nudge that told me to look. So I looked.

Amanda was rubbing her ring finger. Only there wasn't a ring there, just a barren strip of white skin visible against her tan. Where a wedding ring must have been recently.

Panic set in. I had nothing. And I'd never watched Oprah or Dr. Phil so I couldn't even fake it.

Okay, God, I can see she's hurting, but what can I do besides give her some highlights and a ten-percent discount?

This time I didn't get the answer as fast. As a matter of fact, I didn't get one at all but I knew about faith. And faith meant that even when God was silent, He was still there. I wasn't in this alone. So I did what I could. Which was talk.

"I remember my first job interview," I said. "It was at the Fun Fruit Factory, a smoothie shop in Minneapolis. I was so nervous I changed clothes three times that morning, but when I got there I found out the newest employee had to wear the smoothie suit. They stuffed me into a rubber costume that looked like a smoothie glass, pushed a gigantic strawberry on my head and turned me out into the mall to see how many people I could draw in. Fortunately my mom was lurking around outside and pretended she was a customer or I may never have become one of the frozen chosen."

"How old were you?"

"Sixteen. I only had to wear the costume for a day because it turned out I had sensitive skin and the latex made me break out in hives."

"That's the last time I had a job, too." A smile flickered in her eyes. "Believe it or not, my first job was washing dishes at Sally's. Only her parents owned the place then."

"So you're a stay-at-home mom?" That would explain why she'd been out of the workforce all these years.

The silence that stretched between us was so long I didn't think Amanda was going to answer. Then she shrugged. "My youngest is leaving for college in the fall and my divorce was final last month. To tell you the truth, I'm not sure *what* I am anymore."

I said the first words that came into my head.

"That's easy. You're Amanda."

"It's only easy when you're what…nineteen or twenty?"

My eyes met Amanda's in the mirror and for the first time I saw some emotion in hers. Anger. Oh, well. Anger was better than numb and I got the feeling it wasn't directed at me.

"Twenty-one. And believe me, this isn't the easiest age, either. Everyone thinks I should know exactly what I want to do with my life."

"Aren't you doing it right now?"

Good question. And one I didn't have an answer for. Yet.

By the way—still listening, Lord!

"This is what comes easy for me, but I'm still not sure it's what I'm supposed to be doing. I keep asking God to show me where He wants me to go. I'm going to be like that widow in the New Testament who keeps bugging the judge until he answers her."

As soon as I said the words, I wondered if mentioning God was a no-no. This was where my tendency to talk first and think later got me into trouble. When Paul talked about spiritual gifts, I knew the gift of gab wasn't included on the list.

Amanda didn't seem offended. "I always thought it would be fun to own my own café. Not like Sally's—one of those cute little places with comfy chairs and books everywhere."

"There are foundations that help women start small businesses." I knew this because Mom served on the governing boards of several charities in the Twin Cities and she always kept me up to speed on what she was doing.

Amanda's entire body jerked like I'd poked her with a curling iron. "I'm forty-two years old. I can barely afford to send my son to college let alone go back to school myself."

"But you've got an interview with Whiley Implements tomorrow," I reminded her.

"There's only one opening." The weary look came back in her eyes. "And I heard there's over a dozen applicants. I probably don't have much of a chance."

You'll have even less if you can't look the interviewer in the eye.

The verse in Psalms about God being the One who lifts our heads unfurled in my memory. I wondered if Amanda had ever heard it, but she didn't know me so I wasn't sure how to tell her without sounding like an infomercial spokesman pushing health supplements.

Maybe I didn't know how to encourage her, but I

could make sure she stood out during that interview. God was the one who could influence Amanda on the inside; my specialty was the outside.

There you go, Heather. Changing the world, one haircut at a time.

I plunged back into the conversation. "What are you going to wear tomorrow?"

"Wear? I hadn't thought about it." She blinked down at her oversize T-shirt and gray leggings. Which she was wearing with plastic flip-flops. Shudder.

"Okay, we'll do a virtual inventory of your closet while we're waiting to rinse your hair. And don't leave anything out, not even the whitewashed denim jacket with the plaid collar and cuffs."

Amanda laughed out loud. "How did you know?"

"Mom refuses to part with hers. I'm going to start wearing it as vintage pretty soon."

Amanda dutifully recited the contents of her wardrobe and the number of pairs of sweatpants she owned didn't surprise me. By the time I dried her hair, we'd decided that the interview called for a man's tailored white shirt, a macramé belt (old-fashioned but still on the funky side) and a khaki skirt. I nixed the flip-flops but okayed a pair of leather sandals. No open toes, though, because she was in desperate need of a pedicure and there wasn't time.

I spun the chair toward the mirror, hoping she liked the results. "Ta-da."

"Heather, you're amazing." Amanda looked at her reflection in the mirror for the first time since she'd come into the salon. I considered that progress. And the expression of shock on her face was the same one I'd seen on Marissa's face after I'd cut her hair. Why were these women so surprised they were beautiful?

"Look what you gave me to work with." I refused to take the credit. I'd just brought out the best of what she already had. Just like I'd done with Marissa.

"My grandmother always said you can't make a silk purse out of a sow's ear."

"Grandma Lowell says a girl should make the most of what God gives her. Which is what we just did. And you know, she wasn't just talking about what's on the *outside*." *Attitude, Amanda. Lift up that chin!*

"I like your grandma better."

"What time is your interview tomorrow?" I was going to pray for her. Highlights were great, but they could only get a girl so far.

"Ten o'clock." Amanda pulled out her checkbook. "How much do I owe you?"

Color: forty dollars. Haircut: eighteen dollars. Giving Amanda Clark back some of her confidence: priceless.

"Just for the haircut." I cut her off when I could see she was about to argue with me. "The rest is compliments of the Cut and Curl—just let me know how the interview goes, all right?"

"I will." She looked me in the eye when she said it.

Chapter Ten

Adventurous
(The List. Number 4)

I took a deep breath before I went into the apartment. I'd been so busy at the salon I hadn't had time to think about what was happening right above my head. Who knew what Bernice's kitchen was going to look like? It occurred to me that I should have told Dex I wanted to okay the paint sample before he started. After all, the color of his Impala had already given me serious doubts as to whether he could find the number five, made up of little green dots, hidden in the background made up of little red dots. Yet I'd trusted him to go to the hardware store alone.

I blamed the canoe paddle.

The smell of fresh paint hit me when I cracked open the door, and there was no escaping the inevitable.

"Dex? Are you still here?" I hadn't seen his car parked outside, but that didn't mean anything. Maybe the police had hauled it away for disturbing the peace.

No answer. The coward. He was like those graffiti artists who ran away after they painted the side of a train.

Snap bounded up and rubbed against my ankles, which gave me a reason to look at the floor instead of the kitchen.

"Okay, Snap. Tell me that Dex doesn't think fuchsia has visual impact." I forced myself to look up.

Wow.

The cupboards were green. Not leprechaun-green or pea-soup-green but a pretty, subdued ivy-sort-of-green guaranteed to instantly lower a person's stress level. And it brought out the earthy red and gray tones in the brick in a way I wouldn't have expected.

It had to be a fluke.

"Knock, knock." Jared's voice came through the open door. Followed by Jared. My heart returned his greeting with a joyful skip. *Down, girl!*

He hopped over the stack of paint cans. "I saw you on the landing so I thought I'd make sure you got my message."

"I got it but I should point out that a sticky note is much easier to deal with than a canoe paddle." Wait a second. Did I bat my eyelashes? Jared's teasing dared my inner flirt to come out and play.

Jared grinned. "I'll try to remember that. What are your dinner plans?"

"Chicken salad."

"Sounds good. Got enough for two?"

"I do." Did I really say that? See Heather blush.

"Why don't we eat at my place? It has less atmosphere but at least we'll be able to breathe."

I hesitated.

"Or we can eat in the park." Not a drop of sarcasm in the suggestion. He was too good to be true.

"The park sounds great."

"Good color choice." Jared nodded toward the kitchen cupboards. "I think Marissa spent an hour at the hardware store this morning with that guy... I can't remember his name."

"Dex," I murmured. "*Marissa* helped him?"

"He came to the studio this morning and asked her opinion on some paint samples. She closed up the place and they took off together. I didn't realize it was your kitchen he'd been commissioned to paint, though."

"My...Alex hired him to do some remodeling this summer," I explained. Quickly. There'd been a question in his voice that called for immediate clarification.

"Marissa mentioned she hired him to clean the studio twice a week after closing," Jared said. "I wonder when the guy sleeps."

Oh, I'm sure he fits it in somehow.

"I need a few minutes to put things together." Including myself. "I'll meet you over there."

After Jared left, I went into the kitchen to give the cupboards a closer inspection. I probably should've been glad that Dex had asked Marissa for advice, but I was disappointed. Maybe I'd hoped the color he'd chosen was an indication there was some creativity underneath the surface. Something…interesting. A hidden ability that went beyond outsmarting two-headed dragons.

I piled the chicken salad onto the croissants I'd bought over the weekend and tossed in two peaches just to show him I understood the importance of a healthy diet.

Jared was waiting for me on our—correction, *the*—park bench when I crossed Main Street. There was a cooler at his feet and when I glanced inside, I saw two bottles of water and something wrapped in foil.

"My measly contribution. Not half as good as what you brought to the table."

Did I tell him it was from the grocery store deli? Mom had taught me how to cook but I was still trying to find a balance between running the Cut and Curl all day and having enough energy to drag something out of the refrigerator when I got home. Lately, prepackaged was in the lead.

"You worked late tonight, didn't you?" Jared balanced his sandwich on one knee while he reached down and grabbed a bottled water. Which he handed to me.

A series of little bells went off in my head. Ding, ding, ding. Major points for Jared Ward!

"A little." More than a little, but it had been worth it to see the spark of life in Amanda's eyes.

"I spent the day up to my elbows in clay, reconstructing Junebug." Jared said. "Marissa and I cleaned out a storage room in the back of the shop so I'd have enough room to work. Her studio upstairs is pretty cramped."

"How long do you think it'll take to finish the statue?"

"I'll be here all summer, but the grant covers the entire project no matter how many hours I put in."

"Then what?"

"I've got one more semester of grad school left and then who knows? Italy sounds good. Or I could work in a gallery. Maybe apprentice with another sculptor. At our age, life is a buffet. We can wander through and pick out what we like best. We can even skip the salad and go straight for dessert if we want to."

"You're talking about having a lot of choices." At least that's what I *hoped* he was talking about. Otherwise there was a great big helping of *it's all about me* in that philosophy.

"I guess so." Jared shrugged. "I may not know exactly what I want to do yet, but I know what I *won't* be doing—making soup bowls and coffee mugs."

"Are you talking about Marissa?" The shock in my voice didn't seem to faze him.

"She's talented but she's wasting it here. She might make a living selling dessert dishes but as for making a *life,* sorry, not seeing it."

"Maybe it's what she *chose* to do. You know, off the buffet." It was snarky to throw the buffet analogy back at him but Marissa was a friend of Bernice's so I was feeling loyal on her behalf.

"There's choosing and then there's settling," Jared argued. "My dad settled and he was miserable his whole life. All he wanted to do was play jazz guitar and he wound up teaching music lessons to whiny rich kids after school instead."

I didn't know Marissa well enough to argue that she wasn't miserable, but when I'd seen her in church on Sunday, her eyes closed and her hands lifted in worship, I remembered thinking how serene she'd looked. She didn't look like someone who'd been given a handful of celery sticks from the salad bar of life.

"Look at you. You're helping out a friend this summer, but I'm sure you wouldn't be fulfilled if you stayed here and cut hair the rest of your life."

"Maybe I would." I lifted my chin. If that's what God wanted me to do, wouldn't I be happy doing it? Or didn't *happy* matter? Maybe sometimes a girl had to accept the plan God had for her, like she would a dose of liquid cold medicine.

Jared stared at me intently for a second, and then he draped his arm over my shoulder and leaned closer until we were almost nose-to-nose. "There's more to life than a steady paycheck, Heather. Ask my dad."

It wasn't fair that sometimes chemistry won. My brain heard the words but my heart ignored them and chose to focus on his blue-lagoon eyes. What had Jared said about dessert first?

I moved a fraction of an inch away from him and Jared sat back. "I have something for you." He retrieved the foil package from the cooler and unwrapped it carefully, exposing a raspberry Danish in perfect condition. "I heard these are your favorite."

A double hit. Blue eyes and my favorite pastry.

"I…" *Can't form an intelligent sentence to save my life?* "Do you want half?" Saved by good manners. Mom would've been proud of me.

"It's all yours. I'm going to go back to the studio to work a few more hours. My muse usually comes out late at night, but I couldn't pass up a chance to see you."

I inhaled a chunk of frosting as I tried to process that information. He. Wanted. To. See. Me.

"Oh, that's—" Unbelievable. Incredible. Amazing. "—nice."

The kind of lukewarm response guaranteed to puncture a permanent hole in the male ego. *I didn't mean it! I can come up with a better word!*

"So, we're going to give the canoe another try Friday night, right?"

Obviously Jared had a sturdier ego than most guys. Or maybe he thought I was playing hard to get. *Was I playing hard to get?* I wasn't sure. I'd never *played* at anything before. And I'd never had a guy interested in me who was burning through every characteristic on The List, picky detail by picky detail, either. And we barely knew each other.

I silently scrolled through each blank square on my calendar. "I think I'm free Friday night." Did I flutter my eyelashes at him? *Stop! You're doing it again!*

"Great. Come by the studio sometime this week to check out Junebug. I'm going to be putting in quite a few hours, so I could use an excuse to take a break."

I could so be an excuse.

"Sure. I'd like to see it." *You.*

"What are your plans for the rest of the night?"

"I'll probably go horseback riding with my friend, Bree."

Jared winced. "The one who already hates me for scaring the horses that night?"

"That's the one."

"So I suppose she wouldn't let me go along with you two sometime?"

Hadn't he just set up a Friday night canoeing date? And now he was filling in the empty spaces on my social calendar with coffee breaks and horseback riding?

"She would. If Bree can get someone on a horse, she's a happy camper. Have you ever ridden before?"

"City kid. Remember?" Jared grinned at me and shook a swatch of hair out of his eyes. "But I'm up for it."

Had I mentioned that *adventurous* was in my Top Five?

Bree was out with Riley when I called her, so I switched my plan. I called Mom and filled her in on what was happening in Prichett. I told her about lunch with the Carpenters, about Dex painting the kitchen cupboards and a very quick mention that Jared and I had supper together in the park. Mom wasn't a worrier by nature, but I adhered to the unspoken rule between moms and daughters. Information was strictly on a need-to-know basis. If I mentioned our upcoming canoe trip on Friday, there would be questions. And the first question would be *where does he go to church?* Which made me suddenly wonder if moms had a list for their daughters' future husbands, too. Scary. I was going to have to investigate the possibility. Mom was a prayer warrior in the truest sense of the word and I didn't want her many fervent prayers to crowd mine into a corner of the throne room.

After we said goodbye, I straightened Dex's paint cans and cleaned up the kitchen. Snap decided she'd had enough alone time and wandered into the kitchen, so I retrieved a wad of masking tape out of the wastebasket and turned it into a kitty toy. We chased it along the floor on our bellies and that's when I saw it. The canoe paddle. Only it didn't look quite the same as it had when Jared had left it at the top of the stairs. Six inches of the handle was covered in green paint. This was a mystery I didn't need to hire a detective to solve.

Dex had used it as a stir stick.

"Dex!" I grumbled his name, even though he couldn't hear me. I mean, it wasn't like he'd drawn a mustache on the *Mona Lisa* with a Sharpie, but the paddle didn't belong to me. I was pretty sure it was the equivalent of a coupon—I had to turn it in for my date with Jared. Now it had been vandalized. This would indicate I couldn't be trusted with the care of a simple, inanimate object. Maybe guys remembered things like that when you wanted to borrow their iPods.

It wasn't until later that I found out that that wasn't all Dex had done. When I picked up my Bible, I noticed a scrap of color peeking out of Haggai again—a sticky note plastered over the one I'd left. I'd given Dex my interpretation of the *purses with holes* verse and he'd written back a cryptic message.

Or it could mean what they're putting their time, energy and abilities into something that doesn't last.

I chewed on the end of my pen while I tried to find a hidden meaning in the words he'd written. Was he talking about me? He had to be. Easy for him to criticize. He was going into the mission field and everyone knew a person hit the top of the spiritual measuring stick with that one.

Jared said Marissa had a gift she wasn't using to its full potential. That she was making a living, not a life. The beautiful dishes she made might end up shattered on the floor or packed away in someone's attic. Did that mean she was putting her time, energy and abilities into something that didn't last? And did that mean I was doing the same thing? Hair grew. Hair went gray. Nail polish chipped. Over time, gravity won against firming creams, sunscreen and Botox. Yet this was what I was planning to put my life into. And if I wasn't supposed to, then why did I have to be so good at it? And enjoy it so much?

I wrote down one question, because I knew Dex literally needed things spelled out.

Are you talking about me?

On Wednesday morning, while I was waiting patiently for my raspberry Danish, Sally limped out of the kitchen.

"Sally, what happened?" I blurted out the question, not realizing it would momentarily suspend conversation in the entire café.

"Arthritis. It's always there, some days it just clamors for more attention, that's all."

"Your ma worked in the kitchen until she was seventy-two," one of the men reminded her. "Can't remember anything slowing that old gal down."

"Maybe she didn't have arthritis," I pointed out in Sally's defense.

"She didn't." Sally poured coffee with one hand and kneaded her hip with the other. "Dad did. I thought for years his bum knee was an excuse to lie on the couch and read Zane Gray westerns, but now I'm not so sure."

"Ain't it about time for you to retire, anyway, Sal?" one of the men in a nearby booth cackled.

There was an immediate flurry of activity in response to his question. He was attacked and beaten from all sides with the flyers from the Sunday newspaper.

"Who'd take over the place?" Sally's scowl swept the length of the counter. "I barely make a living as it is. The whole bunch of you howl like a pack of coyotes if I raise the cost of a cup of coffee a few cents."

She wrapped up a Danish and slid it across the counter to me. "Here you go, kiddo. Pencil me in for a dye job, would you? Saturday afternoon? I'll try to close up early."

A chorus of discontented murmurs rocked the café. Sally's eyes narrowed. "Oh, for mercy's sake! I'll cook your eggs, but then you all can go home and tell your wives to throw a roast beef in the oven. Or better yet, do it yourselves."

I tried not to laugh as the grumbling subsided and the men hunkered low over their plates of eggs and bacon.

"Trouble is, I had two girls quit on me. There's a rumor the gas station on the highway is going to be open twenty-four hours and they might add on one of those sub sandwich shops. One of the girls applied there and the other one just got hired at Whiley." Sally had lowered her voice, but one of the men overheard us.

"That sandwich place might give you some competition, hey, Sally? Maybe force you to lower the price of your BLT a little."

"I lower the price any more and I might as well come to your house every day and fix your lunch for free," Sally shot back.

"One of them got hired at Whiley?" I thought about Amanda and wondered if it was the job she'd interviewed for.

"Yesterday. I can't match their hourly wage."

"Amanda Clark mentioned she's looking for a job," I said hesitantly.

"Guess I'm not surprised," Sally said under her breath. This time no one heard her but me.

"Maybe you could give her a call." I held my breath. Sally and Bernice had known each other for years and their friendship was the only thread that connected Sally and me. It probably wasn't enough to give me the privilege of expressing my opinion.

"I thought Bernice said you were a city girl." Sally speared me with a sharp look. I was a busybody. That's what she was thinking.

"I am."

"You sound small town to me." Sally gave me an approving nod. "I'll give Amanda a call today."

A call. Hearing the words reminded me it was the

middle of the week and I still hadn't summoned the courage to stop in to see Jared at Marissa's pottery shop. I'd seen the lights on in the garage and heard music rolling out of the windows in the evening, but I hadn't talked to him since our impromptu picnic, and the Friday canoe outing was getting closer.

I decided to use my lunch break to say hello. What I didn't know was that I was going to have to stand in line. A cluster of teenage girls roamed the shop while Marissa stood behind the counter, wrapping up a platter for another pair of girls who were closer to my age.

"Are you having a sale today?" I wandered over to her after she closed the cash register.

Marissa snorted softly. "What I have is a graduate student that every girl in this town between the age of sixteen and sixty has a crush on. You'd think Michelangelo was working in the back room."

I could feel the heat that crept into my face. "Oh."

"What can I help you with, Heather? I've been selling so much this week I haven't had a chance to put out any new pieces."

"I don't need—"

"Hey, Heather. It's about time you decided to stop by. I was beginning to think you don't support the arts." Jared appeared in the doorway just behind the counter, grinning, and immediately the girls hovering by the vases inched closer.

One of them sighed. Not that I blamed her. Jared took ripped blue jeans and a plain white T-shirt to a whole new level.

I saw the flash of surprise in Marissa's eyes and then something that looked like...*disappointment?*

"Never mind. I guess you found what you're looking for."

Chapter Eleven

Likes musicals. Tolerates musicals.
Knows there's a section devoted to them at the
video store
(The List. Revised. Number 17)

"Come on back." Jared motioned to me and I scooted around the counter in a cowardly attempt to escape the angry glares of the girls who stood watching us.

"I only have half an hour." I followed Jared into his makeshift studio, where an enormous mound of clay, molded in the rough shape of a cow, stood in the center of the room. Next to it, Jared had pinned a series of black-and-white photos of Junebug to an easel.

"The tricky part will be getting her out of here. We might have to take the service doors off." Jared walked over to a deep sink attached to the wall and scrubbed off the clay on his hands.

"I've heard rumors about Junebug. Is she really the diva everyone says she is?"

"She insists on having her own trailer—with fresh flowers—and ten gallons of Evian water. Or else." He stretched out the hem of his T-shirt, which looked like a prop from *Jaws*. "Lester insists it was a love bite."

"Mmm. Maybe she's the president of your fan club." Was he going to deny it? Seriously, when did teenage girls start spending their money on *pottery?*

"Musicians. Artists. It's all part of the mystique." He winked at me, then snagged a thermos on the floor next to Junebug and used it to nudge me toward a backless, red velvet sofa. When I plopped down on the cushion, a cloud of dust rose into the air.

"Another piece of history from Marissa's basement," Jared said. He perched on the edge of the sofa and gave it an affectionate pat, raising another dust cloud. "Not quite as cool as the sea serpent, though."

Which I still hadn't met. But maybe other girls had. Now that I was sitting next to him, I felt awkward. Probably the aftershocks of a major reality check. A guy like Jared Ward was a novelty in Prichett. A gorgeous, unattached novelty.

He poured our coffee into a pair of Marissa's hand-made mugs and gave one to me. "I can't believe there are still towns like this. I talked to a guy in the café last night who's never traveled outside a three-county area."

"Maybe Prichett is like Brigadoon."

"Who?"

"Brigadoon isn't a *who,* it's a movie about a village

in Scotland that only appears for a single day, every hundred years." I'd seen the movie at least half a dozen times. It was one of Grandma Lowell's favorites.

"Never heard of it."

Maybe likes musicals was another one of those unrealistic qualities Bree had hinted at.

My cell phone suddenly began to dance in my pocket and I saw Annie's name on the screen.

"Do you mind?"

Jared shrugged. I took that as a *no*.

"Hi, Heather. I hope I'm not interrupting anything." As usual, Annie's voice was full of laughter, as if she had a secret she was willing to let you in on if you asked.

"No, this is fine. I'm on my lunch break." I didn't mention *where* I was taking it.

"I was wondering if you're free this evening. The senior high girls are having a going-away party for Greta. We're going to do the typical girl's night out thing—watch a movie, eat chocolate. I thought maybe you'd like to come."

I couldn't say no. Bernice had a soft spot for Greta Lewis and I knew she'd want me to be there to cheer her on. Greta was leaving at the end of the summer for college in New York, where she planned to major in fashion design. The evening gown Greta had designed for Elise to wear in the Proverbs 31 pageant was the reason she'd been accepted into the program.

"What time should I come over?"

"Seven. That's when the twins go to bed."

I tried to imagine keeping a group of teenage girls—

who'd been devouring large amounts of chocolate—quiet. "Annie, why don't you bring them over to my apartment? That way we won't keep the twins awake and Stephen can have a quiet evening."

There was such a long pause that I flipped my phone over to make sure we hadn't been cut off. "That's exactly what Bernice would say," Annie finally said. "Are you sure?"

"Positive."

"We'll be there!"

"Big plans for tonight?" Jared asked when I tucked the phone away, still basking in the warmth of Annie's compliment.

"That was my friend, Annie Carpenter." I hadn't been sure about Sally, but I knew I could safely claim Annie as a friend. "We're going to watch a movie tonight with the girls in the youth group."

"Sounds like fun." He crooked an eyebrow at me and the sarcasm registered. Without thinking, I elbowed him in the side.

"It *will* be."

Jared chuckled. "I don't think I've ever met anyone like you, Heather Lowell."

"Hairstylists," I demurred. "It's part of the mystique."

But I spent way too much time that afternoon trying to figure out what he might have meant by that.

After I closed up for the day, I ran upstairs to do damage control. Dex had been loose in the apartment and I couldn't remember what the next thing on his list was.

Easing my way into the apartment, I discovered a new maze of paint cans; only these were filled with varnish. He hadn't stripped the hardwood floor yet, which was a good thing, because it's hard to entertain if all your furniture is crowded into a galley kitchen.

I checked my watch. An hour would give me time to vacuum, dust and make a pan of brownies. I tackled them in order of importance. Which meant brownies first, dusting last. I collected the ingredients and ignored the recipe on the back of the box. The brownies were supposed to be fat-free but by the time I added pecans, white chocolate chips and half a container of caramel ice cream topping, I think I successfully defeated their original purpose.

In the name of multitasking, I pushed the vacuum cleaner with one hand and dusted with the other. When I got close to the sofa, where Snap was napping, she gave me the evil eye. She was sprawled in the center of Bernice's afghan, which I distinctly remembered folding into a neat square before I went to work that morning. Unless Snap had figured out a way to *unfold* it, I could only assume Dex had been the culprit.

"He was sleeping on company time again, wasn't he, Snap?"

Snap yawned, refusing to rat him out. I *knew* the catnip mouse I'd found under the coffee table had been an attempt to win her over.

Bree was the first arrival. Annie hadn't mentioned she was coming to the party, too, and I happily reeled her inside to help me get things organized. It also gave me a few minutes to tell her about my lunch break with Jared.

"I wouldn't worry about all his groupies," Bree said when I took a breath. "Not when he keeps making plans to spend time with you."

"I keep waiting to find something *wrong* with him."

"You can't find anything?"

"Nothing. It's…scary."

Bree didn't crack a smile at my description. "Because he might be the one?"

I was amazed she could put my confusion into words. "When you meet someone while you're in high school, you know in the back of your mind that it probably isn't going to last. But then you get to a certain point and suddenly, it could. He could be the *forever* and that makes it different. It makes it—"

"Scary."

Now we both laughed but mine faded into a sigh. "You have to get to know him, Bree. He's great. I think my dad would like him."

"You said he wanted to go riding. Bring him over. Horses are a great judge of character."

"I thought that was dogs."

"So we'll introduce him to Clancy and the Colonel."

A knock on the door interrupted us and before I could open it, Annie's girls burst into the apartment, armed with videos and enough junk food to stock their own vending machine.

"Stephen says thank you," Annie whispered as she handed off a grocery bag to Greta's best friend, Melissa.

"I don't think giving the twins a bath and putting them to bed was as terrifying as a living room full of girls watching *Sense and Sensibility*."

Ooh, one of my favorites.

Everyone crowded into the living room and sprawled on the floor but gave Greta a place of honor on the sofa next to Snap. Halfway through the movie, Alicia scooted closer to me.

"Can you braid my hair, Heather?"

I nodded because it would give me something to do with my hands other than scooping up salsa and tortilla chips. "You don't have much for me to work with," I teased her.

Alicia knew what I was talking about and she grinned. Last December, she, Greta and the other girls in the youth group had had their heads shaved to convince Melissa, who was undergoing chemotherapy, to come to the senior Christmas tea. I'd driven to Prichett to help Bernice at the salon that day but hadn't told her I was coming.

She wasn't as shocked to see me as Alex Scott was.

Bernice hadn't told me anything about my birth father up until that day. Sometimes in our conversations I could hear the tension in her voice and I sensed that if I followed it to its source, *he* would be there. So I'd never asked. I told myself it was enough that I'd found Bernice after twenty years. I didn't need to know *him,* too. But her silence made me uneasy. If she'd had a relationship that had produced a child—me—then why couldn't she talk about him? Maybe I was the child of an abuser. Or a drug addict. My imagination had conjured up different scenarios but none of them came anywhere near the truth, which I discovered that day at the Cut and Curl when Alex had decided to surprise Bernice, too.

After the girls left, I'd gone into the back room to get us some chocolate. When I came out, Alex was standing there. I remember telling him he looked like Alex Scott. Instead of laughing, he got the same expression on his face that Devon Ross had had when his partner pulled a gun on him in *Streets of Gold*. But it wasn't his expression that answered all my unspoken questions. It was Bernice's.

I was the child of an actor. A celebrity. The man whose face I occasionally saw on magazine covers at the grocery store. The man who played the part of Devon Ross in a series of espionage movies that were favorites in my video collection.

I hate to admit it, but I immediately assumed that Alex had dumped Bernice when he found out she was pregnant with me. Later that night, she told me that she was the one who'd left. I didn't quite understand what happened between them, but she'd never told Alex about me. She thought he'd want to meet me, but a month went by and I didn't hear from him. Until the end of January. He contacted my parents and told them he'd like to meet me but he understood—given the situation—if I didn't want to meet him.

I'd talked to Mom and Dad about it. Prayed about it. Lost sleep over it. And then I made my decision. Someone who'd hurt Bernice, I could have gone a lifetime without knowing. Someone who'd loved her—who I was pretty sure *still* loved her—I wanted to get to know.

"Heather, are you falling asleep? There's a line forming in front of you!" Greta's voice rose over the hum of conversation and brought me back to reality. The movie was almost over and the girls sat in an uneven row behind Alicia, eager for me to do their hair, too. I didn't mind, because it gave me a chance to get to know them better…and give them some subtle tips on basic hair and skin care.

If you go a little lighter on the eyeliner, it actually makes your eyes look bluer and you want people to notice them, not the eyeliner.

You don't need to buy an expensive face peel. I have a recipe for one and your mom has everything you need for it right in the kitchen. Remind me to jot it down before you leave.

I talked one girl out of getting her lip pierced and another out of chemically straightening her naturally curly hair. *Anti-frizz gel. It's your best friend.*

Annie noticed me trying to hide a yawn.

"Okay, girls, Heather has to open up her *other* salon early in the morning. Before we leave, though, I'd like everyone to come over and stand in a circle around Greta. I have something for her."

"Grace graffiti!" All the girls shouted the words.

I knew what they were talking about. Bernice had told me about the scripture verses Annie wrote on three-by-five cards and gave to people to encourage them.

Bernice had taken the habit to heart. Since I'd moved in, I'd discovered a few of them sprinkled throughout the apartment. One in the medicine cabinet. One taped to the inside of the closet door. I'd even found one skewered on a wire hanger in the closet.

Annie put her hand on Greta's shoulder and the laughter in the room subsided. It got so quiet I could hear the second hand on the kitchen clock ticking.

"Greta, you are *so* loved. A light in the world. Chosen. Gifted." Annie's words may have been for Greta, but silently I claimed them, too. "The Lord bless you and keep you. The Lord make his face shine upon you and be gracious to you. The Lord turn his face toward you and give you peace. The Lord gift you and make you prosper."

I wasn't sure why I started to tear up. Maybe it was the expression on Greta's face. Or the gentle fire in Annie's eyes as she gave Greta the blessing. Maybe it was because I'd heard that verse from Numbers before but it had never touched me the way it did now.

After the girls left, more quietly than they'd come in, I flopped down on the sofa. I couldn't help comparing what Annie had offered the girls—prayer and a special blessing—to what I'd given them. Makeup tips and a hairstyle that wouldn't survive the night.

Her words came back to me. Gifted. Chosen.

But for what, Lord?

Chapter Twelve

What did u do 2day? (Text message from Tony Gillespie to Dex)

Evacuated an apartment. (Dex)

When I ran down to Sally's on Friday morning, Amanda was behind the counter. Strangely enough, the place was almost deserted. The television was off and classical music drifted from the radio near the cash register.

"Hi, Heather." Amanda surprised me by leaning across the counter and giving me a one-armed hug. "I'm glad you came in. I wanted to thank you for telling Sally I was looking for a job."

The two men who were sitting a few stools down stopped talking and stared at me. I smiled. They didn't smile back.

"How is it going?" I asked the question even though I had a hunch what the answer was going to be. Amanda looked better than she had the day she'd come into the Cut and Curl. She was wearing a white polo with the café's logo on it, a pair of checkered capris and snazzy orange canvas slip-ons. And she'd created a headband out of a yellow scarf. The biggest difference, though, was in her smile.

"Couldn't be better." Amanda looked at the men. "More coffee, Stan? Bean?"

Stan shook his head and wrapped one hand protectively around his cup. The other man, Bean, glowered at me and didn't respond. I noticed right away they weren't drinking coffee out of the generic white coffee cups that filled the open cupboard behind the counter.

"Those look like the cups Marissa makes."

"They are. Sally and I ordered them especially for the café. It's actually like getting a cup and a half right from the get-go."

"And she raised the price, too," Stan muttered.

Amanda ignored him. "Would you like to try a cup? Today we have double mocha mint truffle."

"Sounds like a box of Valentine candy," Bean said to no one in particular. "And where's the newspaper?"

"I brought in some magazines—they're in that wicker basket right over there." Amanda pointed to a white basket the size of a laundry basket on the floor at the end of the counter. "And some books, too. Classics. *Moby Dick. Treasure Island. The Call of the Wild.*"

Uh-oh.

I slanted a look at Stan, who was still scowling into his cup. There'd been some changes since Amanda started working at the café. I hoped they didn't have anything to do with the empty booths this time of the morning.

"Um, where's Sally, by the way?"

"She had a doctor's appointment this morning," Amanda said, grabbing a towel and wiping down the spotless countertop. "Her hip is still bothering her."

"Maybe *she'll* turn on the TV," Bean butted in, tempting me to remind him not to skip his daily dose of fiber.

"Music gives the café more of an atmosphere, doesn't it?" Amanda closed her eyes, her shoulders swaying in harmony with the soft instrumental music wafting from the radio.

Stan looked like he was about to voice his opinion on that so I jumped in. "The coffee smells great. I'll take one to go. And a raspberry Danish if you have one left."

I made a point of closing my eyes and sniffing appreciatively as Amanda filled a foam cup. *Expand that palate, Bean!*

"We don't have Danish anymore. We're serving biscotti now. White chocolate apricot or pistachio."

Bean echoed Stan's grunt.

"I'll take the pistachio." Biscotti, classical music and handmade coffee mugs. Was this my fault? I glanced at Bean and Stan, who were watching me with suspicion. Apparently they thought so.

Mayor Lane was waiting outside the Cut and Curl when I bounded up to the door. Two minutes late for duty. I had to admit Candy was intimidating. She ran both Prichett and the feed store on the edge of town but wore one uniform for both duties—a pair of overalls over a faded T-shirt, hiking boots and a dusty baseball cap.

"Good morning!" Was I supposed to call her Candy? Ms. Lane? Ms. Mayor?

"Is it?" One eyebrow rose, disappearing under the brim of her cap.

This had to be a trick question. I could already tell the day was going to be one of those perfect summer days—sunny and warm with a light, fragrant breeze.

"Do you want to make an appointment?"

She followed me into the salon. "I want a decent cup of coffee. Something that doesn't taste like the candle in my bathroom smells."

"Help yourself. I just made it." If a person is accountable for what they know, I was going to pretend I didn't know anything. Technically, I wasn't responsible for the changes at Sally's. I'd only told Sally that Amanda was looking for a job. *I'm innocent, I tell you. Innocent!*

The frown that had plowed three little rows between Candy's eyebrows didn't disappear until her third swallow of coffee. "There's a PAC meeting the first week of July. Tuesday night. Seven o'clock."

"Oh." I nodded politely even though this had nothing to do with me. The Prichett Advancement Council was the committee that had hired Jared. Bernice had been the vice president for ten years and she'd confided in me that she was hoping to be demoted to treasurer. The town's entire budget was so small she figured it would be easier to manage than her checking account.

"So, we'll see you there." Candy poured herself another cup of coffee and sauntered toward the door.

"Me?" I squeaked the word. Bernice hadn't said a word about attending the PAC meetings while she was gone.

"With Bernice gone, we're an opinion short and it seems to me like you're pretty interested in what's going on in town." She gave me a wicked smile. "Enjoy your biscotti."

The day went from bad to worse. The phone rang so many times I started to let the answering machine pick up the calls. By three o'clock, my perfect summer sky was being infiltrated by puffs of harmless-looking gray clouds. By four o'clock, they'd taken over and called for reinforcements. When I turned the key in the door to close up for the day, the sky opened up and canceled my canoe trip with Jared.

No, no, no.

On cue, my cell phone rang.

"Did you order this?" Jared didn't sound as disappointed as I felt. *Why not?*

"I thought the creek looked a little low the last time we were there." My measly attempt at humor to prove I was the kind of girl who didn't get upset by life's unexpected curve balls.

"Where are you?"

"Standing under the awning of the Cut and Curl." Which leaked. I dodged another miniature waterfall that cascaded through a weak seam in the canvas above my head.

"I guess we'll have to take a *rain check*." He laughed at his own joke. Which might have been funny if I was in the mood for one. I scowled up at the clouds and a raindrop made a direct hit in the center of my forehead.

"I guess so." But hey, my middle name is *flexible*. Dinner? A movie at the theater in Munroe? I'd even try bowling.

"I'll talk to you later, then."

"Sure." What was happening? When was *later?* What did that mean in guy-speak? Later tonight? Tomorrow? Never? The guy who couldn't wait to schedule his next date with me was suddenly leaving me with an open-ended weekend.

Fortunately, when guys disappointed you, there were best friends. I immediately dialed Bree's number, figuring the rain had messed up her schedule, too.

"This is a summer shower," Bree said when I told her about the canceled canoe trip down Marley Creek. "Look at how thin the clouds are on the horizon. This will blow over in an hour or two. Come over and we'll go riding or watch a movie." I could tell by her tone that Jared had been temporarily relegated to wimp status. Maybe I needed to remind her that he drove a motorcycle.

"Give me an hour so I can clean up and change my clothes. I smell like a coconut."

"Okay, but don't eat dinner. Mom's making lasagna and I know she'll want to wait for you."

She didn't have to tell me twice. I bravely faced the downpour and darted into the alley behind the salon, taking the stairs two at a time to the landing. It didn't matter. By the time I got there, my hair was plastered to my head and my Tommy Hilfiger polo was soaked. I lunged toward the door. Only I couldn't get to it. There was a grid of yellow police tape stretched from railing to railing, warning me *not to cross the line.*

My first instinct was to panic. Maybe Dex had committed a crime other than falling asleep on the job. Maybe he'd discovered a skeleton buried in the wall… I put the brakes on my runaway imagination. There were no sirens. No police cars. No detectives waiting to interrogate me. There was only Dex. Somewhere. Hopefully close by so I could get into my apartment. And maybe yell at him.

"Dex? Are you in there?"

"I'm down here."

I twisted around and saw him standing at the bottom of the stairs. Looking worse than I did. "What's going on?"

"You can't go in there. At least, not without some kind of protective breathing apparatus."

First the rain had drowned out my canoe trip, now Dex was trying to sabotage the rest of the evening. "*What* are you talking about? Did you put this tape here?"

"Yes—"

"That's all I need to know." I started pulling the tape down. "Even though you work part-time practically everywhere in this town, I happen to know a person needs special training to be a cop. Which you don't have. Which means this isn't official police tape and I don't have to pay attention to it."

He vaulted up the stairs and tried to restick a piece of the tape to the railing. "There's been an…incident."

Visions of faucetless bathtubs danced in my head. "What did you do?"

"The varnish I used to strip the hardwood floor was pretty strong." He glanced at the door in a way that made me very nervous.

"Dex, do I still have a floor to walk on?"

"Of course you have a floor. It's strong *smelling*." He sounded irritable, like I should know this. Excuse me, but I wasn't about to assume anything when it came to Dex's skills as a handyman. Maybe it was time to have a talk with Alex about delaying the remodeling. Until September.

"I think I'll be fine. Some days I'm practically marinated in perm solution, you know." He had to be overreacting. I turned the doorknob and opened the door a crack. Then slammed it shut again. There was breathing in perm solution and then there was being dropped into a vat of chemicals that had the potential to rearrange the DNA of any children I might have in the future.

"Where's Snap?" I gasped.

"I dropped her off with Aunt Jeanne a little while ago. Mr. Bender at the hardware store told me the fumes should dissipate in forty-eight hours."

Forty-eight hours. That was the entire weekend. I was soaking wet and now I didn't have an apartment to seek refuge in. And the person I could blame for a third of this fiasco happened to be standing right in front of me.

A stationary target.

No, an opportunity for grace.

I hated it when Grandma Lowell barged into my thoughts like that. My emotions were jerked back and forth like a chew toy being claimed by two German shepherds. *Target. Grace. Target. Grace.* Dex had relocated my cat without my permission, turned me into a homeless person and still hadn't apologized. Didn't this give me the right to let him know what I thought about the situation?

Probably. But I took a deep breath and chose grace. Only because Grandma Lowell was patiently tapping her foot, waiting for me to make the right decision. Rats. "You're okay, aren't you?"

Dex just stared at me. Maybe the fumes had melted his brain cells. There was a drop of rain suspended on the end of his nose and I tried not to smile. He reminded me of a soggy puppy. Which brought out my inner animal shelter volunteer.

"Do you feel dizzy? Do you have a headache?" I stepped closer and tried to see if his pupils were dilated but his rain-spotted glasses obscured my view. Without thinking, I plucked them off and he cringed like I'd just stripped him of his superpowers. "Take it easy and let me see those baby…" *Blues*.

Wow. They *were* blue. Not a stunning tropical-beach-blue like Jared's but a soft, comfortable-pair-of-blue-jeans blue.

"Just a sec." I took a deep breath, held it and darted into the apartment. I came back with one of Bernice's fluffy towels and draped it around his shoulders, using one of the corners to wipe off his glasses. He hadn't moved. The dazed look on his face had me worried.

"Dex?" I prompted. How could a girl find out if

someone's brain had been adversely affected by harmful vapors when she wasn't sure if *the someone* had a firm grasp on reality to begin with?

"What day of the week is it?"

"Friday."

"Month?"

"June."

"President of the United States?"

"Harrison Ford."

I decided he was fine. Two out of three wasn't bad. And *Air Force One was* destined to become a classic. "Bree Penny is expecting me to come over anyway tonight, so I'll hold my breath long enough to throw some things in an overnight bag and go over there."

While I waited for the apology that should be ready for processing, Dex turned and jogged down the stairs. Was I the only one willing to take the high road here?

"You can keep the towel," I called down to him.

He yanked it off his shoulders and I giggled when I saw his expression. There was a four-foot-tall penguin wearing a polka-dot bikini printed on it. Which seemed to spark some brain activity. Which should be followed by an *I'm really sorry, Heather. I'm going to call Alex and tell him I'm just not cut out for this line of work....*

"I'll take care of the cat."

There was no way I was leaving Snap with him for forty-eight hours. Not when I had a front-row seat to see the way Ian Dexter took care of things.

"I'll be over in ten minutes to get her. Bree loves cats."

He gave me a *whatever* shrug and jackknifed his soggy body into his waiting Impala.

Hold on, Snap. I'm coming to rescue you.

I kept my cell phone in my pocket on vibrate all evening—just in case—but Jared never called me back. I tried not to dwell on the list of reasons why. Reasons that *if* I chose to dwell on them would be that a) he'd let our date—the one he'd seemed to be looking forward to—slip by without rescheduling it for another time because he really *hadn't* been looking forward to it and b) every single twenty-something in Prichett thought he was the most attractive item in Marissa's shop and he was keeping his options open. Which was linked to reason c), definitely the worst one. He'd found someone who wasn't skittish about his stupid couch.

Fortunately—because of Elise—I barely noticed the comatose phone in my purse. She took advantage of the evacuation and decided she would spoil me rotten for Bernice's sake. While Bree and I played Scrabble, she made a butter pecan layer cake with waves of home-made frosting and a pitcher of raspberry iced tea.

"I'm down to two *x*'s and a *j*. I forfeit." Bree saluted me with her fork. "I knew it would stop raining. Do you want to take the horses out for a quick ride?"

"A quick ride…like over to the Cabotts'?"

"Maybe."

"Sure." I'd packed an old pair of jeans just in case. And something I'd found in Bernice's closet. A pair of turquoise-blue cowboy boots with shiny silver tips across the toes that were as eye-catching as a French manicure.

Bree whistled when she saw them. "Not too shabby."

"I hope Bernice won't mind that I borrowed them," I said, doing a foot pop straight out of *The Princess Diaries.*

"Are you kidding? She'll have them bronzed. Just like Mom did with my baby shoes."

Bree was probably right. My relationship with Bernice was a blessing I hadn't expected when I'd made that first phone call to Prichett a year ago. Bernice had been so…generous with me. Ever since we'd met, she'd shared her thoughts, her feelings, even her struggles while she figured out what it meant to follow Jesus. She'd given me the keys to her apartment and to her business. She trusted me to take care of her friends while she was in Europe. The only secret she'd kept was Alex, and that was only because she thought she'd been protecting me.

Elise suddenly appeared in the doorway with a digital camera. "Hold that pose."

Of course when she said that I started to teeter. My ballet teacher would have confiscated my toe shoes if she'd been in the room. Bree jumped in to steady me just as Elise took the picture. The result was something that looked like a circus act.

"I'm e-mailing it to her right now." Elise disappeared into the study.

"Let's get out of here," Bree whispered. "When Mom gets out the camera, she goes a little crazy. And life around here has gotten too weird since I taught her how to surf the Net."

It didn't take us long to saddle the horses. There were pockets of blue sky over our heads. The rain had coaxed a buffet of scents out of Elise's flower gardens, so every breath I took was like shopping in an exclusive bath and body store. Only better.

When we got to the Cabotts', Jill met us on the front steps and told us Riley was cleaning out the barn. She let Bree go but took me as a hostage.

"How do you like small-town life?" Jill poured a glass of water for me and pressed it into my hands. Then she pulled a chair out from the table. My cue to sit down and stay a while.

"I'm getting used to it." *Except when it comes to everyone knowing everyone's business. Still working on that one!*

"I can't believe the number of young people migrating to Prichett this summer," Jill said. "You. That artist. Pastor Charles's nephew. Old Dan—that's my husband—hired him to help out a few nights a week with barn chores. It's easy to get behind in the summer and Dex is such a personable young man."

Wait a second. Did she just say Dex?

"Personable?" I sputtered.

Jill looked uncertain, like maybe she'd used the word wrong. "He sat in the same chair you're sitting in right now and talked to me for almost two hours last week."

"Dex talked to you? *Dex?*"

"Uh-huh. My boys were never big on conversation. It would be a treat if Riley kept me company like that sometimes." Jill exhaled in motherly frustration. "Honestly, sometimes I think his entire vocabulary revolves around the contents of the refrigerator."

Something was wrong here. I'd been around Riley. He was outgoing. Confident. And he could completely hold his own in a conversation with me and Bree. But Dex? *Friendly? Talkative?* She had to be kidding.

"What did you talk about?" I admit it. It was a trick question.

"He was telling me about the mission work he's going to be doing in September. I'm going to talk to Old Dan about supporting him even though I know what I'm going to hear. *We've got enough people in Hollywood that need to be saved. Why don't we send missionaries there instead of Africa?*"

I swallowed a laugh at her interpretation of Dan Cabott's gravel-strewn voice.

Maybe that explained why Dex had come out of his shell. To raise money for his trip. I knew that wasn't very charitable, but being displaced from my apartment for the weekend and being denied a heartfelt I'll-make-it-up-to-you-in-chocolate apology will do that to a girl.

"And he's a big C.S. Lewis fan, just like me," Jill went on. "We must have talked for over an hour about the *Screwtape Letters*."

Which I *knew* hadn't been made into a video game, so maybe Dex did do something else in his spare time.

"Heather!" Bree's voice echoed in the scrape of the screen door. "We're ready to go."

I hesitated but Jill shooed me away. "Go on. Have

fun. And tell Riley to bring you both up to the house when you get back. I'll have some snacks."

When I walked outside, Bree was holding the horses' reins and Riley was walking up the driveway with Mr. Personable himself.

I was about to take advantage of the moment and ask Dex if he had an identical twin lurking around somewhere when I heard a familiar sound. The beautiful music that could only be created by a motorcycle engine.

"I wonder who that is." Bree smiled at me as Buckshot danced in place beside her and Rose gave an unhappy snort.

"It's just a motorcycle," I said. Casual words, heart cranking up to fourth gear. I knew that helmet. And those vintage-washed jeans.

While we watched, the motorcycle shot up the driveway and skidded to a stop a safe distance away. I was going to play it cool. As soon as he was in range I was going to give him The Look. The look that said *I have a life. I have friends.*

Jared stripped off his helmet. "Finally. I've been looking everywhere for you."

And he was looking at me when he said it.

"Really?" Was that my voice? Because it came out in a squeak. There was no way I could pull off *cool* now.

"It looks like I'm just in time for my first riding lesson."

Chapter Thirteen

Pretend your day was on a scoreboard. What would it say?
Cowboys—1   Missionaries—0
(Dex—page 15 of Real Men Write in Journals)

Bree wasn't about to let him off the hook that easily. Not when she knew he'd blown off our date because of a little downpour. "I think Buttercup, the Shetland pony, is free this evening."

"Do you have something that goes as fast as my motorcycle?" He grinned at her and Bree looked at me. By mutual agreement, we switched to nonverbals.

She fanned her face with her riding gloves. *Wow.*

I raised an eyebrow. *What did I tell you?*

"Are you sure you don't want to go riding with us, Dex?" Riley asked.

Everyone's attention was now on Dex. The bottom

dropped out of my stomach. We had to go through this again, only now Jared was there to witness Dex's fear of horses.

"*Carpe diem,* dude," Jared said, giving Rose's neck a pat.

Dex may not have been high on my list of favorite people at the moment but I didn't want him to be humiliated. He was perfectly capable of doing that himself whenever he started a new project. And a person shouldn't be pressured into doing something he was afraid of.

"*Carpe diem.*" Dex looked confused. "Didn't he win the Kentucky Derby a few years ago?"

"It means *seize the day,*" Jared said, with a glance at the rest of us that judged Dex completely clueless.

"Oh. Right." Dex's expression never changed, so why did I have the sneaking suspicion that he knew exactly what it meant?

"Dex!" Jill poked her head out the door and greeted him like a long-lost friend. Or maybe she felt sorry for him. "Old Dan wants to know if you have time for a game of checkers?"

"Sure." Dex brushed past me and disappeared into the house.

No one said anything for a few seconds, then Riley shrugged. "Let's go. Carp a dime."

Bree gave Riley a tender look. Knowing Latin must not have been on her list.

We came back to the house when the mosquitoes went into full attack mode, but none of us were in a hurry to end the evening. Riley suggested a bonfire and while Bree and I put the horses in the round pen and brushed them out, Jill came out with a huge bowl of popcorn and root beer floats. We pushed the lawn chairs aside and spread horse blankets out on the ground to sit on. I was feeling very country.

Bree and Riley paired up on an expedition to find more kindling, leaving Jared and I alone. He scooted closer to me. "I'm sorry I canceled our canoe trip."

He smelled really good. Was it all right to notice that? Or more importantly, was it all right to *enjoy* it?

"It's kind of hard to canoe in a monsoon." He'd looked all over for me. He was so forgiven.

"That was only part of the reason."

Uh-oh. I held my breath, waiting for the rest.

"I had a crummy day today. I've never done a sculpture this size before and it's more of a challenge than I thought. Except I can't tell anyone that." He nudged my knee with his. "I was licking my wounds in private. It's hard to explain to people who don't understand the creative process."

And apparently a hairstylist would be one of those people who wouldn't understand the creative process. Is that what he meant?

"I understand when things don't work out the way you plan."

He smiled. "Anyway, I got through it. I know you work tomorrow but how about doing something with me on Sunday?"

Yes! "I'm free after church."

"You still go to church?"

This was a strange question. A question to which there was only one response. "Uh-huh."

"With your parents?"

Which ones? Answering that question would be way too complicated and I still wasn't sure I was ready to share it.

"I'll probably go with Bree and her family since I'm staying with them." I'd told Jared about the quarantine on my apartment but didn't mention Dex's name. He already had to live down choosing checkers over horseback riding.

"My parents had the philosophy that if God's out there, it was up to me to find Him. I'm glad they did it that way because then it's something I chose instead of something that was forced on me."

I wasn't sure about his parents' philosophy but I could see his point. Everyone needed to discover their own personal relationship with God. There were kids I went to school with at His Light Christian Academy who seemed to be going through the motions because they had to. Once they graduated, they left their faith behind. Like a protractor. Maybe they were wondering how often they'd use it in the real world.

"Mom and Dad always told me to ask questions," Jared said, his eyes intent. "Most religions don't want you to do that—they just want you to accept their idea of right and wrong. I mean, if they're so sure what they believe is true, they shouldn't be afraid of questions. If there is a God, He should be able stand up to a little scrutiny, don't you think?"

I'm sure the question was hypothetical but he was

right. That was the way I'd been brought up. Mom and Dad had never been intimidated or gotten defensive when I'd asked tough questions but they had warned me there was a place where questions stopped and faith began. I knew that was true. If God were easy to figure out, He wouldn't be God.

Mom liked to say that faith was taking one step forward and meeting God on the second. Just when I was about to ask Jared what he believed about God, Riley and Bree came back.

"Hey, you two are letting the fire go out!" Riley tossed in an armload of kindling and sent up a spray of red sparks.

"Sorry. We were talking." I grabbed the closest stick and tossed it on the fire.

"Yeah. That helped." Riley winked at me.

"So. Sunday," Jared murmured in my ear.

Sunday.

But first I had to get through Saturday. Twenty-four hours and counting!

In the morning, I gave up my raspberry Danish, oops, my biscotti, because Sam—Bree's dad—made us buttermilk pancakes for breakfast. And because I was a coward. I couldn't face all those empty booths at the café again.

What I'd forgotten was that Sally was my two-o'clock.

I decided to avoid bringing up the subject of Amanda as long as possible.

"So, you closed up for the day?" I gently pushed

Sally against the back of the chair and she sprang forward like she was attached to a rubber band. This was worse than I thought. She was so tense her neck and shoulders felt like a relief map.

"No, I left Amanda in charge."

And the subject was avoided for a record ten seconds.

Sally stared at herself in the mirror. "I'm a dinosaur, Heather. Straight out of the Stone Age. A dinosaur. And the café is a dinosaur, too. Soon to be extinct."

Extinct, because I'd encouraged her to hire Amanda Clark. She was losing business because Amanda was trying to turn the café into Prichett's version of Starbucks.

"You have a lot of loyal customers."

"Loyal customers who can't tell you which president is on a fifty-dollar bill because they've never seen one," Sally scoffed. "I know the truth. The only reason I've kept the place going all these years is because the café hasn't had any competition. Not since the Blue Light Lounge stopped serving lunch fifteen years ago. Now, with a Bucky Burger coming in, that'll be the end of the café."

I'd missed something. A Bucky Burger?

"That new gas station they're building on the highway was supposed to put in a sub sandwich shop. That would have been all right with me. Subs are fine if a person's on a health kick but, eventually, everyone goes back to beef. It's just the way it is. But I can't compete with those frozen hamburger patties they can turn out a mile a minute, and loyalty goes out the window when it's up against fast and cheap. If they put in one of those soft-serve ice-cream machines, I may as well move to Yuma and join my sister's water ballet class at the senior center."

Somewhere during Sally's verbal avalanche, I figured out this wasn't about Amanda. Which should have absorbed all the guilt I was feeling, but Sally was so upset I had to come up with something to encourage her.

"Sally, the café is practically an institution. You have something that Bucky Burger doesn't have."

"All-you-can-eat spaghetti and meatballs?"

Okay. Two things. "Atmosphere. People don't just come to the café to eat. They come to talk, to hang out with their friends and family. They want to do that in a comfortable place where they can linger over their meal, not zoom through the drive-thru and eat in their car."

Sally collapsed in the chair like a blown-out tire. "A drive-thru. I never thought about a drive-thru."

"There might not be a drive-thru," I said quickly, but from the expression on her face, the damage was done.

Just keep spreading that sunshine, Heather!

"Amanda's got so many new ideas I was getting excited about the café again," Sally said. "She even came up with international night once a week. We've been looking at recipes all morning for Thai Tuesday."

Maybe there were some hard-core curry fans in Prichett. Anything was possible. But hadn't Sally noticed that the retired farmers lining the counter had jumped ship since Amanda came on board? I wondered if there was a recipe somewhere for Thai meat loaf.

Maybe that would bring them back. But then again, probably not.

Sally sighed. "According to Jim Briggs, they won't break ground for the Bucky Burger until next spring, so I have some time to figure out what I'm going to do about the café."

"You can't just give up, Sally. It's okay if people have a choice where they want to eat. Bucky Burger may be fast and cheap but it's also loud. And…impersonal. You've known your customers for years. It's like eating with your family—"

The telephone rang right in the middle of my passionate speech.

"Cut and Curl. This is Heather, how can I help you?"

"Hi, Heather." A cheerful voice—that I couldn't quite place—greeted me like a long-lost cousin. "This is Audrey Cooke down at the Golden Oaks Nursing Home. I've got a note on my calendar to call you about tomorrow afternoon. Does three o'clock work for you?"

"For…" Fill in the blanks for me, Audrey.

There was an astonished gasp on the other end of the phone. "For Paint the Town Red Day. You're going to be here, aren't you? That's all they've been talking about all week."

What was Paint the Town Red Day and who were *they?*

"Audrey? I have no idea what Paint the Town Red Day is." Honesty was always the best policy. Even if it did make you look like the dullest pair of scissors in the drawer.

"It's makeover day at the nursing home. The residents can get their hair styled or their nails done. Get sassy with some red lipstick. Have some P&P. It's a big hit here."

She was going to have to walk me through this every step of the way. "What exactly is P&P?"

"Pampering and Popcorn. Once they're all dolled up, the staff puts in their favorite DVD and pops up a few bowls of popcorn. It's kind of like a movie night out— only *in*. Anyway, Bernice was all signed up to do makeup and we assumed you'd be taking her place since she's on her honeymoon." A giggle followed the word.

Bernice *had* asked me to visit her friend Esther over the summer. Plus, it sounded like a sweet thing to do for women who didn't get out much. "Sure. I'll be there. Do I need to bring anything?"

"No. One of our aides sells Mystique Makeup on the side, so she always donates free samples. I'll see you then!"

I hung up the phone and walked back to Sally. The fight had gone out of her and she was now staring, trancelike, at her reflection in the mirror.

"A brunette dinosaur is still a dinosaur."

"First of all, you aren't a dinosaur, you're a business woman who's respected by everyone in the community. Embrace it."

I fluffed Sally's hair and studied the gray that was battling for dominance. I knew that if Sally went au natural, she'd have that eye-catching shade of silver that didn't age a woman, just made her more fascinating. And I told her so.

Her mouth dropped open. "You want me to voluntarily turn into my mother?"

"I want you to consider giving nature six months to take its course and see what happens. If you don't like it, I'll break out Burnished Brown Number Nine."

"All right. You talked me into it." Sally was morose again. "I'm a dinosaur, no sense hiding it anymore. It's not like I'm fooling anyone."

I wasn't going to argue with her. In six months she'd see the results of her decision and then I could smile and say *I told you so.*

It wasn't until I was closing up for the day and heard the growl of a motorcycle on Main Street that I remembered Jared. And that I'd told him I'd do something with him after church on Sunday. But I understood when he postponed our Friday date because of a little rain (at least I did after he tracked me down at Riley's) so I was sure he'd return the favor and understand why I had to postpone our date.

I locked up and went to get my car to take to Bree's. The Penny hospitality was going to have to extend another night. I'd snuck up to the apartment bright and early before opening the salon and saw that Dex had been busy. He'd put the police tape back up, creating a web so thick I'd need an electric hedge trimmer to break through. But just in case I tried, he'd left a note on my door.

NOT YET.

That was Dex. A man of few (very few) words. I was tempted to rip the note down and give it to Jill Cabott as evidence.

On the way out to the farm, I called Jared.

When I heard him say hello, I had to admit he had a great phone voice. Kind of low and rumbly. Like his motorcycle when it was idling.

"Hi, it's Heather. What are you up to?"

"I'm still at the studio, trying to capture Junebug's essence."

"You're what?"

"A quote from Lester Lee. Who, by the way, spent most of the afternoon watching me work. I had to redo Junebug's ear three times until he gave me the thumbs-up. Apparently her left ear curls at the tip and if I didn't get it right, no one would believe that Junebug was the model for the statue."

I laughed, expecting Jared to join in. He didn't.

"What are you doing?"

"I'm on my way to Bree's house. By tomorrow night I should be back in the apartment."

"So what time are you free tomorrow?"

"That's why I called you. Bernice had volunteered to help at the nursing home tomorrow and they assumed I'd be filling in for her. It'll only be for a few hours."

So, do you want me to call you when I'm done? This was the question I couldn't ask. We weren't at that stage in our relationship yet. Everyone knew that the beginning of a relationship consisted of two people trying hard not to be the one to fall *first*. That made you vulnerable. But I wasn't used to those games and I didn't like them.

"Whatever. I'll talk to you sometime tomorrow, then." His voice sounded distant. He was upset. Or not.

Maybe I was reading too much into it. I thought he was analyzing the future of our relationship but he was probably tying his shoe. Or wondering how late the gas station was open.

"I'll probably be home by six." Big hint.

"Have fun."

I hung up the phone, leaving me to conclude that men weren't from Mars: they were from another galaxy entirely.

Chapter Fourteen

Did u talk 2 her yet? (Text message from Tony
to Dex)

Whats Latin for not going 2 happn in this
lifetime? (Dex)

"Heather! Audrey said you'd be here. It's so good to
see you." Esther Crandall was waiting for me in the reception area and I gave her a hug.

"Hi, Esther. Where do I report for duty?"

"In the atrium. I'll show you where it is." Esther caught
my hands in hers and took a step back to study me. "Small-
town life agrees with you. The salon is keeping you busy?"

"It is. But I love it." We fell into step together as we
walked down the corridor. She reminded me of a hum-
mingbird—tiny and vivacious. Or a pixie queen. Her
silver hair was braided into a crown around her head and
the blush of color in her cheeks had a hint of sparkle in it.

"We appreciate you giving up your afternoon to come down here and put some color in our day. We're a lively group—I've seen some of the men turn off their hearing aids until we're finished and most of them won't venture from their rooms until the staff brings out the popcorn."

Esther was right. I could hear the Beach Boys blaring from a room at the end of the corridor. There was a cluster of women, all wearing colorful plastic leis, waiting for us in the atrium. Esther introduced me to everyone. I recognized some of the volunteers from Faith Community, including Jeanne Charles, the pastor's wife. She had a grass skirt on over her conservative brown pants.

"Tropical theme today," Esther whispered. "It gives us an excuse to do the limbo."

I choked back a laugh when she winked at me.

"I'm first." A woman in a wheelchair, wearing sunglasses and a bright silk scarf around her neck, waved to get my attention. "It's my birthday today."

"It's Tildie's birthday every day," I heard one of the women grumble.

I hid a smile. "Happy birthday, Tildie. What's your favorite color?"

"I'm wearing it, sweetie."

Fire-engine red. A shade or two brighter than her hair.

I looked at the card table scattered with samples of Mystique Makeup and the hopeful faces of the women who'd gathered around me. I put a plastic lei around my neck and pushed up my sleeves.

"Let's get started."

* * *

It was almost ten o'clock when I got back to the apartment.

Before I went home, I stopped out at Bree's to pick up Snap and tucked her under my arm while I sprinted up the steps. When I was almost to the top, I could see a shadowy figure waiting for me.

"Don't tell me I can't stay here tonight!" I groaned the words when I realized it was Dex standing on the landing.

"Everything's back to normal."

I wasn't going to touch that one.

"That's a relief." I pushed open the door and released Snap, who dove out of my arms in a graceful arch and promptly went to check out her food dish.

Dex followed me inside. "You look…content."

It was a strange thing to say but fit the way I felt. I'd had a great time with the ladies at the Golden Oaks. And Esther hadn't been kidding about the limbo. "Thanks, Dex."

He looked at me like I'd gone from content to delusional in the space of a few seconds. "For kicking you out of your apartment for the weekend?"

When he put it *that* way…

"I had a great weekend with Bree at the farm. The next time Alex calls, I'll tell him the floor looks great."

"Alex Scott calls you? Why?"

Oh, please. "Because he's my dad."

Dex looked so stunned he couldn't possibly be faking it. I exhaled slowly, wondering what it would mean to him. I was still trying to figure out what it meant to me.

Bernice had had a run-in with the paparazzi a year ago and one of the things Alex had warned me about if he and I were seen together that my private life might be under scrutiny. I'd decided to take the chance, but it didn't mean I always felt at peace about it.

"I thought you were just the renter."

"Nope. I'm the daughter."

I could picture the wheels turning in his head, like he was playing Memory and searching for a match. "So Bernice—"

And we have a winner!

"Is my biological mother." I finished the sentence. I didn't like the word *biological*. It sounded so clinical. And it didn't begin to describe the woman who had been alone and confused but had loved me enough to bring me into the world.

"But they just got married."

I smiled, remembering their wedding day. "It was about time. They split up before I was born but they never stopped loving each other. If I hadn't found Bernice, they might not have ever found each other."

"Semper fidelis."

I'd heard the expression before. "What does that mean?"

"Always faithful."

It fit. "You're right. Neither of them ever married."

Dex shrugged. "I was talking about God."

Sometimes I forgot that Dex was going into the mission field. Maybe because he didn't seem like the missionary type to me. If there *was* a missionary type.

What I couldn't figure out was why I'd told Dex about Alex and Bernice when I still had a hard time talking about it with anyone else. I mean, missionary or not, he didn't exactly have that warm, fuzzy, you-can-tell-me-anything type of personality going for him. So why were we having this conversation?

Then my thoughts jumped their track and went down a completely different path. "Wait a second. *Semper fidelis.* That's Latin."

His eyebrows rose above the dark frames of his glasses like two crescent moons to ask the eternal question, *so what?*

"I *knew* you knew what *carpe diem* meant."

He gave me a long look. "The varnish is still kind of tacky. You better take off your shoes or they might get ruined."

Ha. He only *thought* that would distract me. "Come on. Admit it."

"I don't know what you're talking about." He crossed his arms.

"Fine. I'll see you tomorrow, Dex." For the next episode of *Home Makeover: Nightmare on Main Street.*

Dex's smile came and went so fast that I was sure I'd imagined it. *"Deo volente."*

At the risk of validating every blond joke I'd ever heard, I couldn't resist teasing him. Just to see if there was another smile in there. "Seize the violin?"

No smile. No response. Nobody home. Dex's internal alarm clock must have gone off, telling him it was time to leave. He took a few cautious, sticky steps away from me, picking up speed as he got closer to the door. I decided I wasn't going to be ignored. Again.

"Conversations are like doors, Dex. You can't just leave them wide open." I had to shout the words, because I could hear his cowardly feet running down the stairs. But I took comfort in knowing he'd heard me.

He'd left the door open.

I went to close it and saw lights on in Jared's garage. He was probably upset I'd canceled on him. Or worse, he thought this was my way of getting revenge for canceling on *me*. That's why he hadn't returned my call. He thought *I* was playing hard to get. So now he was playing harder to get.

Maybe I should call him again? No, that was cell phone roulette. One call was acceptable. Two calls in the same evening (less than two hours apart) shrieked desperate. And if he didn't answer that second call, I'd still get a message. And it would be: I'm-busy-and-have-a-life-too-you-know.

"Heather? Is that you?" Jared was standing in the alley.

Great. Now he was going to think I was a stalker. Was this better than desperate? I slunk down the stairs. "I just got home a few minutes ago."

Jared met me halfway. He must have been working on Junebug because he'd stripped off his shirt and draped it over his shoulder. There was a smear of clay across his bare chest and that was all I was going to let myself notice.

"Heather, did you ditch me tonight on purpose? Are you getting ready to deliver the *let's just be friends* speech? Because I have to tell you that I like spending time with you. I like *you*. But if you don't want to hang out together, just tell me. Wondering what you're thinking is messing up my muse."

I was messing up his muse. It was the best compliment I'd ever gotten.

Honesty. It was what I'd wanted. And it would take us one giant step forward into…into *what?* Uncharted relationship territory, that's what. I needed clarity. I needed some road signs. *Take a right. Turn this way. Warning: Temptation ahead.* I liked him, too. He'd taken a risk and now it was my turn. Why couldn't I say the words?

Don't forget he's burning his way through The List, Heather.

Except for the most important one.

"No speeches. I like hanging out with you, too." Honest but wimpy. It was the best I could do. I'd wanted signs. Right now there was a great big yellow light blinking in my head. *Caution!* I wanted to find the plug and yank it out.

"Great." He gave me a lazy smile. "I'll see you tomorrow after work. I'm feeling inspired again."

On my way back to the apartment, I got a text message from Dex. Deo volente. *God willing.*

I thought about Jared and sighed. I really hoped He was.

Call me a coward, but I avoided Sally's again the next morning. I knew my picture was on a dartboard somewhere. My consolation for missing out on Amanda's biscotti was the piece of butter pecan cake Elise had sent home with me. I was just about to take my morning break and dig into it when someone pushed on the door so hard it bounced off the rubber stopper on the wall.

A teenage girl charged in, towing a smaller replica of herself by the hand.

"Do you have any openings for a cut?" she choked.

One glance at the younger girl and I knew why her sister sounded so panicked. She'd tried to give herself a haircut. With a pair of those blunt-tipped scissors favored by kindergarten teachers everywhere.

I knelt down so I was at eye level with her. "Were you playing beauty shop?"

The little girl grinned at me. Which I took as a yes. "What's your name?"

"Whitney Darnell." Then she held up four fingers before I asked, proving she'd been through the drill before.

"Let me get the elephant chair for you, Whitney."

"Can you…fix it?" her sister whispered.

"Sure." Hair emergencies took priority over cake. "It's okay. Take a deep breath. What's your name?"

"Kaylie…Kaylie…Darnell."

Judging from her ragged breathing, it sounded like she was about to pass out on the floor right in front of me. For the first time I noticed she had a large, reddish purple birthmark on her face. Her hair was long and straight so the way she angled her head partially concealed it.

"Have a seat. And some cake. I'd skip the coffee, though, if I were you."

Kaylie gave me a nervous look. "I don't drink coffee."

"I was teasing you."

"Oh." Kaylie found a chair by the window and I

swung Whitney up into the elephant chair to get a close-up of the damages. Whoa. One side of her hair was choppy but the other side was almost bald. Any shorter and she'd look like she was on her way to boot camp.

"What's wrong?" Kaylie was on her feet in a flash, panic making her eyes the size of cupcakes.

"Nothing." I flashed her my confidant stylist smile. The one that said I was one with my scissors.

She dragged her hair across the birthmark and twisted it around her fingers. "I was supposed to be watching her but I was reading. Whit asked me if I wanted to play with her and I told her no." It was obvious she regretted *that* decision. "The next thing I knew, she dumped a handful of…hair…on my book."

"I did the same thing to my hair when I was about her age," I said. "And to three of the girls in my play-group." And Mom had the pictures to prove it.

"My mom is going to kill me," Kaylie moaned. "Will it grow out by the time school starts? Picture day is the first week."

By my estimation, Whitney's hair would be two inches long by the end of August. Maybe three. I didn't tell Kaylie this. It fell in the TMI category. Too much information. "Everyone's hair grows at a different rate." That was safe.

Whitney hummed happily while I worked out my strategy. She hadn't left me much to work with but I evened it out the best I could.

Kaylie inched her way over again. "What can you do to the other side?"

"Absolutely nothing."

She looked terrified. "Nothing?"

"There's no hair there to do anything with," I pointed out gently. "Little kids and scissors. This happens all the time. Last week a mom brought in her six-year-old who'd poured red food coloring on her hair because she was pretending she was a movie star."

"What am I going to do?"

"You can take comfort in knowing that her eyes are so beautiful, no one is going to notice her hair…or buy her a really cute baseball cap."

"Pink," Whitney announced.

Kaylie groaned again.

"You're all done." I unclipped the cape and helped Whitney down. "You can pick out a sucker for sitting so well."

Kaylie's face suddenly turned white. "I forgot my purse. I don't have any money with me. I can't pay you."

"That's okay. No big deal." I felt like I was talking the poor girl off a ledge. "Don't rush back. The salon is open all week, just stop by whenever you can."

"Thanks—"

"Heather."

"You're Heather? Annie mentioned you."

"You know Annie?" It didn't surprise me. Annie was like the Pied Piper of teenage girls.

"I'm in her youth group…sometimes." Kaylie pulled her hair across her face again. I didn't think she was even aware she was doing it.

"I help her out once in a while, so I'll probably see you again."

Kaylie ducked her head and didn't answer. "Whit, it's time to go."

Whitney raced up to us and wrapped her arms around my knees. "I'm pretty."

"You are." Even with the freshly shorn baby lamb look she had going.

"You look like you've been scalped," Kaylie muttered. "Let's find you a hat so people don't stare at you."

She sounded resigned. As if she knew what it felt like to have people stare. I'm glad she knew Annie. If anyone could bring Kaylie Darnell out of her shell, it was Annie.

Amanda poked her head in the salon mid-afternoon, waving to get my attention. "It's Moroccan Monday today. You *have* to have supper at the café."

How could I pass up Moroccan Monday at Sally's? "I'll be there." *Incognito.*

Amanda gave me a thumbs-up and strolled past the window.

God, Sally is upset enough about the Bucky Burger. Don't let her regulars bail out on her now. And forgive me for being such a busybody. I'll quit. I promise.

After I'd cleaned out the comb drawer, swept the floor and rearranged the bottles of shampoo and conditioner on the shelves (twice), I couldn't delay the inevitable anymore.

Sally's was quiet when I slipped in, but every seat at the counter was occupied.

"Hi, Amanda—"

"Shh!" The half-dozen men sitting at the counter all

made a hissing noise that sounded like air escaping from a tire.

I froze.

Amanda waved me closer with the book she was holding. "Don't mind them. Sit down, Heather. We're just finishing up."

I inched over to the counter and perched on the edge of one of the stools, just in case I had to make a quick getaway. Sally came out of the kitchen and made her way over to me.

"It's the book club," she whispered.

"Book club?"

"Caffeine and the Classics. Amanda started it. She's been reading a chapter of *Treasure Island* every afternoon. It's been a big hit so far. If you're in the club, you get a bottomless cup of coffee and a free biscotti."

Which made me wonder if it was the book or the free coffee that appealed to Sally's customers. But either way, the men were back. It didn't matter what bait Amanda had used to lure them in. I was in awe. As a team, Sally Repinski and Amanda Clark could end up owning the Bucky Burger franchise. At the very least, they'd give them a run for their money.

"Thanks for hiring her, Sally."

"I should be thanking you, kiddo. She's got a lot of ideas. I'm not sure Prichett is ready for all of them, but we'll ease 'em in a few at a time. If Bucky Burger sinks us, at least it'll be a fun ride to the bottom."

The door opened and another customer walked in, earning the same loud *shush* that I'd been greeted with.

The man slunk to a booth by the window and Sally saluted me with the coffeepot. "I'll be right back. He's new—must be here for Moroccan Monday."

Amanda finished reading and closed the book. "That's it for today, fellas. How about one more round of java before I break out the lamb kebabs?"

There was a chorus of baritone grunts and half a dozen handmade pottery mugs were lifted in the air.

I had entered the Twilight Zone and its name was Sally's Café.

"Here try these." Sally thumped a plate down in front of me.

"Is it really lamb?" I looked down at the plate of kebabs and couldn't get past the visual of little white lambs frolicking in the grass.

"No, it's beef. Lamb sounds more authentic. No one's going to know the difference. And if I throw in a free piece of pie with every kebab platter, believe me, no one's going to care."

Chapter Fifteen

Isn't too proud to say he's sorry (preferably with chocolate)
(The List. Number 14)

"I hope you don't have plans for Saturday night, because I've got plans for you." Jared grabbed my hand and wove his fingers through mine.

"Plans?" That sounded wonderfully mysterious.

And I was ready to have plans. We hadn't been able to spend much time together. He'd been hard at work on Junebug every day and into the evenings so I'd finally gathered the courage to stop by the studio to say hello after I closed up the salon on Wednesday.

The expression in his eyes when he saw me made me kick myself for not coming by sooner. Even after our conversation on Sunday night, this was still uncharted territory I was venturing into. Ordinarily I blazed a trail into new situations but this was different. There was someone else I had to consider. Jared. I wasn't the world's greatest expert on dating, but I'd watched enough of my friends either a) have their hearts broken or b) break someone else's heart, so I knew it wasn't something to be taken lightly.

"I don't…" Have plans, I was going to say. But then I remembered I did. Annie and Stephen's date night. "I'm babysitting Annie's twins on Saturday night so she and Stephen can celebrate their anniversary."

Jared frowned. "Can't she find someone else? Today's only Wednesday, it's not like you'd be backing out at the last minute."

"Maybe you and I could do something Friday night instead." *You're pathetic, Heather.*

Jared shook his head. "I could only set it up for Saturday night."

I was dying of curiosity now. Maybe if I explained the situation to Annie, she could find someone to take my place. Maybe if *two* girls from the youth group would be willing to stay with the twins for a few hours, Annie wouldn't worry about them. Hot on the heels of that reasoning came the voice of my conscience, telling me I was kitchen mold.

"I'm sorry." Understatement! "Annie and Stephen haven't had a night out since the twins were born and I promised I'd be there."

"Haven't they got a whole congregation who can help them out?" Jared asked. "How did you get volunteered?"

The tone in his voice scraped against my nerves. I

shifted and pulled my fingers away from his. "Um, because *I* was the one who volunteered me? They're friends of mine and I don't mind helping out."

"You don't mind helping out a lot of people, do you, Heather?" Jared stood up and walked over to the window.

"Is there something wrong with that?"

"I don't think it's wrong to look out for yourself once in a while, that's all. If you keep giving, people keep taking. It's a natural law."

Now there was a topic for a daytime talk show. And that law sounded *unnatural* to me. At least from what I'd always been taught.

"I won't cancel on them. They deserve a night out."

Jared's shoulder lifted slightly—the signal that ended our conversation. The minute of silence that followed felt like an hour. Frustrated, I grabbed my purse and walked past him on my way to the door. Slowly. Just in case he wanted to reschedule.

He didn't.

By the time Saturday came around, it was obvious Jared and I had entered a contest to determine which one of us could out-stubborn the other. I just wasn't sure who was winning. I used my executive power to close the Cut and Curl early that day so I had time to fix Annie's hair.

The second I got out of my car I could hear Joanna's wail. It had permeated the walls of their apartment and stretched all the way to the sidewalk at a decibel level I'd only experienced in the front row of a Skillet concert.

"I don't think Stephen and I should go tonight." Annie greeted me at the door, still in her pajamas and holding Joanna, whose little body stiffened and rose out of the blanket like an unhappy jack-in-the-box. "Joanna has been fussy all day…I haven't even had time to shower or get dressed yet."

Panic set in. I'd been expecting happy babies. Sleeping babies. Not babies who'd been so demanding they'd sucked the wind out of the buoyant sails of the S.S. Annie!

I caught a faint whiff of sour milk and saw the faint shimmer of moisture in her eyes. There was no way I was going to run for cover. If Annie could do this all day, I could put in a three-hour shift. I took a deep breath and forced a smile. "Of course you're going. Let me hold Joanna while you shower. There'll still be time to do your hair before Stephen gets home from work."

Annie wavered for a second but I gave her a playful nudge. "Come on, Cinderella. It's time to go to the ball."

A faint sparkle came back in her eyes. She eased Joanna into my arms and darted into the bathroom.

Lord, I'm going to need your help! Please have your heavenly choir up there strike up a lullaby.

The heavenly choir must have had another engagement because Joanna continued to cry so hard she woke her brother up. He was upset at having his nap interrupted and decided to change Joanna's soprano into a duet. I jiggled them around the tiny living room so by the time Annie emerged from her room, wearing real clothes again, I'd calmed them down enough to convince her we'd be fine for a few hours.

I dried Annie's hair and coaxed it into a French knot. Not quite the elaborate style I'd been hoping to create, but it was all I could manage in the time it took for the twins to feverishly drain the contents of their bottles.

When Stephen came home from work, I met him at the door while Annie was busy looking up the phone number of the restaurant they'd chosen.

"Don't even take time to comb your hair," I whispered. "Joanna is cranky and Annie is this close to changing her mind about going out."

Stephen's eyes flashed once in sympathy for the evening ahead of me before he retreated. "Tell her I'm waiting for her in the car."

He may have been concerned about me, but he wasn't going to let it ruin an evening alone with his wife.

I was definitely adding that to my list.

After Annie and Stephen's car disappeared down the street, I propped the babies in their infant seats. In less than fifteen minutes I went through my entire repertoire of nursery rhymes, silly faces and breakfast cereal jingles. Nathaniel's eyelids drooped and there was a sweet half smile on his face that told me he appreciated my off-key attempt at karaoke. Joanna, however, refused to be won over. She must have sensed there'd been a change in command because her ear-piercing cries had faded into a heart-wrenching combination of gasps and hiccups.

I picked her up and walked her around the room, cheerfully pointed out the interesting use of color in the trio of Thomas Kinkade prints above the couch. She obviously didn't appreciate the arts, because the gasps increased in intensity.

"Joanna." Her tears reduced me to a level I'd promised myself I would never be reduced to—putting on the pleading, singsong voice that adults thought children responded to. I knew it wouldn't work, but at the moment I was willing to try anything. "Please don't cry. Mommy and Daddy will be back in a few hours. Don't you want to play with Auntie Heather for a while?"

No. I swear she said it. I put her back in the infant seat, picked up a rattle shaped like a dinosaur and made it dance. Nathaniel kicked his feet in glee. Joanna scrunched her eyes closed and drew in a deep, ragged breath. Oh, no. She was increasing lung capacity—

The doorbell rang.

I jogged to the front door—backward—so I could keep an eye on the twins. "Coming!"

"Did you know you're currently exceeding the acceptable level for noise pollution?" Dex peered over my shoulder. "What did you do to her?"

Why couldn't it have been someone who liked children? Someone like…no, I wasn't even going to let myself *think* his name.

I scowled at Dex. "I didn't do anything. Annie said she's been fussy all day. This is the night they went out for their anniversary."

"I know. That's why I stopped over."

"To prove I'm a failure at babysitting?"

"You keep my secrets, I keep yours." He stepped around me and went straight for Joanna. "Hey, Stinky."

Oh, that was going to win her over. I rolled my eyes at his back. Now I had three kids to keep an eye on.

Joanna stopped crying. She even gave him a tearful smile. And a slushy-sounding hiccup.

"That's my girl. I bet you're cutting a tooth." Dex picked her up and offered his finger, which Joanna clamped down on like a pit bull on a postal worker's leg.

I hoped his hands were clean.

"Is she drooling a lot?"

Suddenly exhausted, I slumped into Stephen's recliner. "It's kind of hard to tell with all the other bodily fluids she's been creating."

Yuck. Did I actually say that out loud? But Dex didn't bolt toward the door. "It'd be early for a tooth, but you never know. Kids are as different as fingerprints."

I looked at him suspiciously. "I thought you didn't like kids."

"When did I say that?"

"You didn't. I just…assumed. When we were here for lunch that day, you looked like you were holding a live grenade."

"Never assume."

I gave him a teasing salute because he sounded so serious. "Yes, sir."

Dex loped the perimeter of the room with Joanna while I slid to the floor to entertain Nathaniel. When I stopped shaking the dinosaur rattle, I could hear Dex singing softly to Joanna. The hiccups had subsided and her eyes were almost closed.

"You're good." I had to give credit where credit was due.

"I have five younger sisters and brothers."

"You do?" Why that surprised me, I'm not sure.

"Seventeen, sixteen, thirteen, twelve and nine. Three sisters and two brothers. Mom worked when they were young, so I took care of them during the summer." He paused. "And the rest of the year, too, I guess."

"You must be pretty close, then." I tried to imagine taking care of a troop that size. "I'll bet they miss you."

He didn't answer. No surprise there. Didn't he know his reluctance to talk about his family only spiked my natural curiosity to find out why? I picked up Nathaniel and followed him into the kitchen. "Aren't you going into the mission field?"

"Short term. Two years."

That didn't sound so short-term to me.

"Doing what?" Getting Dex to string together more than a few sentences at a time was a challenge I wasn't sure I was up to.

"Whatever they need me to do. I have to raise my own support, but I'm hoping to leave by the beginning of September."

Hopefully they weren't expecting someone who could fix faucets.

"Are these chocolate chip cookies?" he asked.

It was ridiculously easy to divert my attention with food.

I made a note to finish our conversation after a quick chocolate fix.

"I brought them over." Somehow I'd known that an evening of babysitting would demand sugar. "Go ahead and have one." *Or five.* I watched in amazement as Dex swooped in low and snagged a handful without disturbing Joanna.

Nathaniel sighed and I traced my finger over the plump curve of his cheek. Babies were really cute when they were sleeping. "Do you think we should put them to bed now?"

"Nate's ready. Joanna's not quite down for the count yet."

Joanna looked to be as sound asleep as Nathaniel. "And you know this…how?"

"Patience you must learn," Dex intoned.

"Say good-night to the Jedi master, Nathaniel." Which only proved that, in spite of the mocking scorn I'd injected into my voice, I knew exactly who he was imitating. Which made me a walking *Star Wars* trivia-bot, too. Which meant I had something in common with Dex. Now I had to rent a foreign film over the weekend to make up for it.

After putting Nathaniel in his crib, I found Dex and Joanna stretched out on the floor in front of the television, tuned into the Weather Channel. Humid and in the high 80's for the rest of the weekend. I felt sorry for all the women with naturally curly hair.

I sat on the chair and pushed my hands through my bangs. "No wonder Annie has Philippians 4:13 stenciled on the wall over the changing table."

"It doesn't get any easier."

"You don't have the gift of encouragement, do you?"

"I have the gift of reality."

Sure you do, Yoda.

I dropped to the floor a few feet away from Dex and

wondered if the Weather Channel was the fluke of a dying remote control or if he'd turned to it on purpose. Just as the weather person pronounced that San Francisco was going to be hot and Chicago was going to be breezy and pleasant, Dex rose slowly to his feet.

Joanna was officially asleep.

I wasn't sure if he knew you were supposed to put a baby to sleep on its back so I trailed behind him into the twins' bedroom, just to make sure he did things right. He did. In fact, he did a fancy maneuver with Joanna that I was going to have to copy if I ever babysat again. Instead of awkwardly repositioning her in order to lay her down, he kind of let her slide down his arm like a magician would shake a card out of his sleeve.

"Where's her blanket?" He twisted around to face me.

"I think it's still in the living room. I'll go get it."

My mission only took a few seconds and when I came back into the nursery, Dex had started up the mobile attached to the headboard. Even after watching him in action, I still thought he was insane to send musical butterflies dancing above a sleeping baby's head.

"Won't that wake her up?" I moved closer to tuck the blanket around her and Dex stepped to the side.

"At this point, a helicopter landing on the roof wouldn't wake her up," Dex whispered.

We ducked out of the room and I braced myself for the awkward moment that was about to descend. Or for Dex to walk out the door without a word. Instead he sat down on the floor and picked up the toys that were strewn around.

"Thanks for coming over to help." I perched on the edge of the chair and noticed that the long-range forecast for the Midwest predicted thunderstorms.

"I'm going to order a pizza."

I blinked. "Pizza?"

"The cookies were only an appetizer. There's a pizza delivery around here, right?"

I had no idea. I checked the phone book and found out that the Blue Light Lounge delivered pizza with fast, friendly service on the weekends. I called it in and returned to find Dex in the same exact state I'd left him. Focused on the Weather Channel. *Now* it was awkward.

"Is there a movie on?" Hint, hint. Now that I knew I should bring an umbrella to work on Wednesday, it was time to move on to something a little bit more lively. Like a golf tournament.

"This is the only station that comes in. He reached for a wicker basket near the couch and fished around inside of it. "I could read *Goodnight Moon* to you. Or, there are some games in here."

"Trivial Pursuit?" I edged closer. I was terrible at the Sports questions but unbeatable in Arts and Entertainment.

"Nope. Looks like our choices are Candy Land and Twister. Which one?"

"Um…*Candy Land.*" There was a no-brainer. Joanna and Nathaniel were a little young to play. It had probably been a shower gift from someone who liked to plan ahead. Way ahead.

"Candy Land hasn't been opened yet, but the shrink-wrap on the Twister game has definitely been tampered with. What do you think that means?"

"I have no idea," I said primly. Even though I did. Annie and Stephen didn't indulge in PDAs but I'd seen some of the looks that had passed between them over the barbecued chicken during my last visit. Sigh.

"We probably shouldn't open Candy Land," Dex said. He slapped the Twister game between us. "I'll let you spin first."

"Dex, I don't…" The faint gleam of laughter in Dex's eyes cut off my air supply. Was he *flirting* with me? Impossible. Guys like Dex didn't know how to flirt. To flirt meant there was *chemistry*. And guys like Dex didn't have chemistry. They were like flour in the pantry. They added stability, not spice.

The doorbell rang and I scrambled to my feet. Whoever was at the door was going to get a hefty tip for perfect timing. Even if the pizza was cold.

"Hi."

It was Jared.

Chapter Sixteen

"Hi." The word squeaked out like I'd spent the evening sucking helium.

"Can I come in?"

"Sure." I glanced over my shoulder and saw Dex standing a few feet behind me, a wad of money in his hand. The awkward silence I'd felt with Dex was a party compared to this. "You two know each other, right?"

"Dexter. You actually have a night off from your broom?" Jared laughed.

"No." Dex was back to monosyllables.

"I thought you might want some company," Jared said, his eyes catching mine again. "I've got three videos to choose from—every one of them chick flicks—and the only thing chocolate I could find at the grocery store at eight o'clock on a Saturday night."

For the first time I noticed he was holding a cake. It was a double chocolate layer cake decorated with pink roses. Across the top, in flowing white icing, were the words, *I'm sorry I was such a jerk.*

Jared might have had a stubborn streak, but he sure knew how to make it up to a girl.

Now what? Do I invite him in to share a pizza with Dex and me? Do we watch the Weather Channel together? Or play Twister? Maybe Dex would bow out gracefully to the "three's a crowd principle"?

"This is great. Now we can split the cost of the pizza three ways." Dex stuck his wallet back in his pocket. When Jared and I came into the living room a few minutes later, Dex was planted so firmly in Stephen's recliner he needed to be mulched.

While we watched the movie, Jared communicated his irritation using his own brand of Morse code— which meant shooting a series of weighted glances in Dex's direction. Dex was oblivious. He plowed through most of the pizza and half the cake.

When Annie and Stephen tiptoed in half an hour earlier than expected, they didn't look surprised to see Dex and Jared providing twin support.

"How were they?" Annie whispered as Stephen went straight to the twins' room. "Stephen was a basket case all evening. I finally had to drop a Philippians 4:6 bomb on him."

Do not be anxious for anything…

"They were fine. Dex thinks Joanna might be getting a tooth," I whispered back. "Enjoy the rest of the evening. And feel free to finish off the chocolate cake."

"Thanks so much, Heather," Annie whispered. "We

really needed a few hours to laugh together. I mean, we love being parents, but I don't want to forget what it's like to love being a couple."

"Anytime," I said, and meant it.

Jared was waiting for me by the door, but there was no sign of Dex. I felt a stab of frustration because I'd wanted to thank him again for helping me with Joanna. When you didn't want him around, he stuck by like gum on the bottom of your shoe and when you did, he pulled one of his disappearing acts.

Jared started to say something but my yawn drowned out whatever it was. "I guess that answers my question. Can I take you out for breakfast tomorrow morning?"

I could tell he wanted to make sure things were okay between us. And with Dex there, we hadn't had a chance to talk.

"I have church in the morning." *Don't you have church in the morning?* Not that going to church meant a person had a relationship with Christ, but at least it might give me a clue we were looking for answers in the same book. The only time Jared had talked about God was that night at Riley's. I'd replayed that conversation in my mind and realized he hadn't actually come right out and said he was a believer. But he hadn't said he *wasn't,* either. I was willing to give him the benefit of the doubt, especially since there was an invisible picture of his face on the top of The List.

"I'll call you around noon, then." He started to

walk away but then turned back, pulled me against him and kissed me.

Slightly off the mark but close enough to count. When I came to, Jared was halfway down the block and Dex's car was pulling away from the curb.

I couldn't remember driving home. I staggered up to the apartment and flopped down on the bed, trying to make sense out of what had just happened. Jared didn't seem like the type of guy who considered kissing a recreational sport and he hadn't pushed the *come over to my place and check out my couch* issue for a while. I'd convinced myself that he was being careful because he respected me…and himself. That he wasn't one of those guys who viewed relationships the same way they did their favorite video game, where it was all about moving to the next level.

I touched the side of my mouth, where Jared's misplaced kiss had landed. What was *that* about? There hadn't been much emotion there. It reminded me more of a timber wolf marking his territory than something to write about in my journal—if I kept one. The thought crossed my mind that maybe the kiss had been more for Dex's benefit. Which was crazy. Jared wouldn't see Dex as a threat. Which proved how frazzled I was and how much I wanted life to be simple again.

God, I can't read Jared's mind but show me his heart, okay? I don't want to make a mistake.

All my chaotic thoughts tangled together that night while I was sleeping. In my dream, I was pushing a stroller with (gulp) three babies in it. Junebug came to life in Marissa's studio and took out a shelf of pottery. But the scariest thing was the kiss. It wasn't Jared who'd pulled me against him. It was Dex.

I woke up gasping for air, with Snap purring away on the pillow next to my head. When I realized it was a dream, I talked myself back to reality. Annie had twins, *not* triplets. A clay statue could *not* come to life. And *Jared* was the one who'd kissed me.

Since both my thoughts and dreams were ganging up on me, I got up and did something guaranteed to bring focus back to my life. My nails. I was a few minutes early for the church service, so when I saw Annie unloading baby paraphernalia from her car, I changed course and went to help.

The door opened before we reached it and I glanced up to thank our knight in shining armor. Dex. Of course it had to be Dex. I felt myself blush, remembering the dream. He had Joanna tucked in the crook of his arm.

"Did you lose Nathaniel?" I asked the question to accomplish two things: take the focus off my red cheeks (which I wasn't about to explain) and because I really wasn't sure that Dex hadn't misplaced one of Annie's twins.

He pretended to look around. "There's a Nathaniel?"

Annie giggled. "Stephen has Nate. Thanks, Dex. There's some potato salad in my fridge with your name on it."

"I'll stop by after the service."

"Are you free after church, Heather? We're having some people over for lunch."

"I…ah, have plans."

"Oh. You can invite Jared, too. We've got plenty of food."

Annie was a mother, all right. A young mother, but still a mother. Nothing got past her.

"I'm not sure what our plans are. But I'll mention it."

"Great. But if it doesn't work out this time, we'll understand."

Dex and I trailed behind her in a lumpy caravan on our way down the hall to the nursery. Stephen met up with us just outside the door, Nathaniel cradled in his arms.

"Sorry I'm a few minutes late, I had to meet with the kids about the Fourth of July celebration next weekend." Stephen looked at Dex and me and I knew what was coming next. "Are either of you interested in helping out? We usually run some games for the teens—a pie-eating contest, maybe some karaoke."

"Sure." Dex didn't hesitate.

"I don't know what my plans are yet." Lukewarm words. Yuck. They put a bad taste in my mouth. But maybe Jared wanted to do something with me. And if he did, I had a hunch it wouldn't be organizing games for the youth group.

"The local businesses are going to donate prizes. Maybe the Cut and Curl could offer a free haircut or something," Annie said.

"No problem." I latched onto Annie's suggestion and pushed aside the irritating voice in my head that told me I was taking the easy way out.

"Let me know what you need me to do, Stephen."

Dex tucked a corner of Nathaniel's blanket in, gave his toes a little squeeze and took off.

"Is something wrong with Dex?" Stephen frowned.

"That's just Dex. He's a now-you-see-him, now-you-don't kind of guy." I was surprised they hadn't figured this out by now. "The antisocial type."

"Dex isn't antisocial," Annie said, laughing. "It was his idea to start a summer Bible study for the guys in the youth group. They've been having a great time."

I watched Dex pause at the end of the hall, where two little boys ambushed him. Dex got them both in a headlock and mashed their faces together.

The guy had no people skills. He lacked what Grandma Lowell would have called *social graces.* If that didn't put Ian Dexter in the antisocial category, then he must have an evil twin somewhere—an evil carpenter twin—because I couldn't pry more than one or two sentences out of him.

"I think he's still dealing with a lot," Annie said, nuzzling Joanna's silky red hair. "He spends a lot of time in his head. Sifting through the junk. I did the same thing."

"Dealing with what?" Maybe exhaustion, considering how many jobs he was trying to hold down.

"Annie, I think it's time to get the twins settled." Stephen gave her a meaningful look and Annie made a face.

"Oops. I was thinking out loud again."

The prelude was starting, but I didn't want to abandon Annie and Stephen. We lugged everything into the nursery and the nursery worker who hurried up to help was Kaylie Darnell. Even though she was a teenager and it was July, she was shrouded from chin to ankle in beige twill. There was a fine line between thrift-store chic and great-grandma's attic and she'd crossed it. Maybe she tried to pick out clothes that helped her blend into the woodwork.

"It looks like you've got your hands full this morning." Annie counted babies and arms with the speed of a calculator. The results she came up with made her frown slightly.

"The other person scheduled to work with me had car trouble this morning. She should be here in about fifteen minutes."

"You and Stephen go ahead. I'll stay and help Kaylie until reinforcements come," I offered. "We'll be fine."

Stephen was already putting Nathaniel in an infant seat on the floor. "Thanks, Heather."

Now Annie handed Joanna over with a smile. "See you two later! Come and get me if they're fussy."

"They'll be fine," Kaylie promised, cuddling Joanna against her.

When we were alone, I dropped to the floor in front of Nathaniel's infant seat, made sure he was comfortable and wiggled my eyebrows at the other baby who was drooling in the next chair. "Who's this little charmer?"

"That's my brother, Adam," Kaylie said. "He screams if I'm out of his sight."

Which gives you a really good excuse not to be in Sunday school with other people your age.

"He's a cutie, too." I offered my finger, which Adam latched onto and tried to maneuver into his mouth.

Kaylie carried Joanna over to the enormous quilt that hung on the wall by the changing table and started pointing out colors to her.

I know I'd told God I wasn't going to be a busybody anymore, but did prying Kaylie Darnell out of her shell fall into that category? I hoped not. "Annie mentioned there's going to be a Fourth of July celebration in the park next weekend. Are you planning to go with the youth group?"

"No."

I stood up and wound the baby swing, where another apple-cheeked pixie was dozing. Time to try another route. "Are you going to be a senior this fall?"

There was a long silence. Déjà vu. It was like talking to Dex. "Yes."

"Any plans after that?"

"I'm still praying about it."

"Me, too."

Now she looked at me. Skeptically.

"Hey, sometimes it takes a while to figure out what you want to be when you grow up."

"You're managing the Cut and Curl."

"Just for the summer. Once the end of August rolls around, I have no idea. I keep waiting for God to unveil the plan. And I've been out of high school almost three years. Most people are well on their way to *something* by then."

"What did you do after you graduated?"

"I went to Europe with a friend of mine for a year. When I came back, I signed up for cosmetology school. Which surprised a lot of people. Especially my parents."

"You went to Europe? For a *year?*"

"Not quite a year. More like nine months."

Kaylie suddenly sat down in the rocking chair with Joanna and leaned over to nudge up the volume on the kids' praise tape that was playing.

I think it was to drown me out.

Jared was waiting for me on the stairs when I got home. After our misunderstanding, I expected he'd want to talk. Instead, he dangled a key in front of my face.

"Let's go for a ride."

Cruising country roads on a motorcycle didn't exactly lend itself to meaningful conversation. But it was fun. When we got back a few hours later, he pulled into the alley and parked next to Marissa's garage instead of my apartment.

"Come on. I've got a surprise for you. Since we couldn't go out last night, this is the next best thing."

I figured I owed him that much. Especially when he'd apologized with chocolate cake. I followed him inside and the first thing I saw when I walked inside was the couch. It wound through the center of the room and the slippery green fabric did look sort of serpentlike. I shuddered, imagining Snap sliding in between the cushions, never to be seen again. Or Dex. Mmm. That was a more pleasant thought.

"Well? What do you think?" Jared smiled at me and

I tried to think of a nice way to tell him that his couch creeped me out.

"It's…" That's when I noticed he wasn't looking at the couch but the lopsided card table in front of it. He'd covered it with a red-and-white-checkered cloth. And it was set for two. Between the plates was a taper candle set in one of those old green bottles, coated with drips of colorful wax.

He came up behind me and put his hands on my shoulders. "I wanted to take you to Madison last night. It was the grand opening of The Yellow Door, a new Italian restaurant. Invitation only. One of my friends is a chef there so he got us a table—or would have. It's all about who you know. Since we couldn't go, I talked him into giving me the recipe for his portobello ravioli instead."

"You made dinner?" Chocolate cake with an apology written in frosting would have been enough. Ravioli was overkill. Not that I was complaining.

"I can do more than open a can of pork and beans."

Somewhere inside that statement was a dig directed at the male population of Prichett, but I was too touched by the trouble he'd taken to reenact the Saturday date-that-wasn't to look for it.

"I'm sorry we couldn't go last night." I meant it, but I still wouldn't have backed out on Annie, even if Jared had told me what he had planned. "It would have been fun. But this is better."

Way better. Creative. Thoughtful. *Romantic*.

It wasn't until the middle of dinner that I got up the courage to mention the upcoming Fourth of July

Frolic. Except I called it a *celebration*. No point in scaring the poor guy.

"Sounds like the perfect time to skip town," Jared said. "You don't have to work, right?"

"I'm working until noon on Saturday. Some of the women who are in the parade want updos, so I decided to open the salon. Annie and Stephen need some help running games for the youth that day, but I haven't told them I would yet…." I left the sentence open, hoping he'd take the hint.

"It sounds like you want to stick around." He pushed his plate away and leaned back in the chair.

"They could use all the help they can get." *Not very subtle, Heather.* I couldn't believe it. Was I *testing* him? That was a big no-no in all the books on relationships. Because it wasn't fair to set up a test, especially since— according to the books—guys never knew when something was a test. Apparently guys didn't even know there *were* tests. So, it wasn't a test. I was simply trying to *discern* (a much more mature term) what his thoughts were about being with me at the Fourth of July Frolic or being without me doing…whatever.

Jared was looking at me like I was from Mars. No wait, that was supposedly *his* home planet. "Then you better help them."

"Don't you want to help, too? It'll give you a chance to get to know some of the people in town." I inched my way out onto that particular limb.

"Like that's at the top of my list." Jared actually laughed at me. "No thanks."

Crash.

It was a good thing it wasn't a test. Because Jared would have just gotten a big fat F.

Chapter Seventeen

How beautiful you are, my darling…Your hair is like a flock of goats…

What worked for King Solomon doesn't cut it today.
(Dex—written in the margin of *Song of Songs*)

I was surprised when Kaylie came into the salon the next afternoon. She didn't say anything, just took a seat by the window and picked up a magazine. I had a cranky toddler named Chloe in my chair, two walk-ins in a race to drain the coffeepot and a phone that wouldn't stop ringing.

When the first baby curl drifted onto little Chloe's shoulder, she burst into tears. Her mother tried to cheer her up by pressing her doll into her arms, but Chloe sent it sailing across the room, where it smacked against the door.

"Cut and Curl. This is Kaylie. How can I help you?"

I heard the words over the wailing and saw Kaylie on the phone. My phone.

"What can I do for you?" She flipped through my appointment book and grabbed a pencil. "We've got several openings after three o'clock on Friday. Four o'clock? Great. Heather will see you then."

"Is it going to be much longer?" One of the walk-ins marched up to me.

"Ten more—" Chloe had peeled a piece of vinyl off the arm of the chair and held it up like a trophy "—minutes."

The phone rang again. My scissors slipped and I nicked my finger. Chloe saw the drop of blood that spattered against the cape and started to howl again. Manic Monday. Now I knew why people called it that.

"Cut and Curl. This is Kaylie. How can I help you?"

Two hours later, I sank into the shampoo chair and closed my eyes. "You saved my life, you know."

I wasn't sure why, but Kaylie had taken over as my receptionist, fielding phone calls as efficiently as a press secretary. Her shyness completely disappeared when she was talking on the phone. I'd even heard her banter with some of the customers while she was setting up their appointments.

"I brought you the money to pay for Whitney's haircut."

"But you didn't have to stay."

Kaylie lingered by the counter, fiddling with a pen. "I was rude to you yesterday. I wanted to say I was sorry."

"Don't worry about it. I should be the one apologizing. I was being nosy. I like to think of it as *curious* but sometimes they end up looking alike."

The phone rang again and Kaylie reached for it, and then drew back with a guilty look.

"Go ahead, you're on a roll. I'll even pay you." I was joking but Kaylie's eyes widened.

"You'd hire me?"

"You'd *want* to work here?"

"Yes."

"Then…yes."

Kaylie grinned and picked up the phone. "Cut and Curl. This is Kaylie."

Now I had to find the courage to break the news to Bernice that she wasn't the only employee anymore.

Because of Kaylie, I was out the door a lot sooner than usual. Jared had text messaged me, asking me to stop by the studio after work. I waved at Amanda as I walked past the café's window. She waved back with her copy of *Treasure Island*. Moroccan Monday must not have gone over as well as she and Sally had hoped because there was a sign on the window announcing Mexican Monday. All-You-Can-Eat (Beef) Tacos.

I slowed down and savored every step. It felt good to actually *feel* the sunshine instead of watching it out the window. When I turned the corner, Jared's motorcycle was parked in front of the pottery shop. There was no sign of Marissa when I went inside, so I tiptoed past the counter and peeked into the studio. Jared was on his knees, brushing a layer of hot wax on one of Junebug's hooves.

"Hi." Every time I saw Jared was a fresh reminder of how good-looking he was. He looked better in rumpled clothes than most guys did in a tux.

"Hi." He barely glanced at me. Maybe it was time to

remind him that he was the one who'd asked me to stop by. "You texted?"

He was drawing a blank. I could see it in his eyes.

"Two o'clock. I believe the exact words were, *Heather, stop by.*" Ringing any bells here?

"I meant later tonight." Jared tossed a metal tool into a bucket of gray water. It hit the side with a sharp clank and sank. At the moment, I could relate.

Awkward pause here!

"Hi, Heather." Marissa poked her head in the doorway. "Can you come upstairs a sec? I want to show you something."

I glanced from her to Jared. "I'll be right back."

Jared didn't answer.

"The Boy Wonder is in a mood today." Marissa's voice was low but her eyes were twinkling. "Lester is making him spend the evening at the farm because he said Jared isn't capturing Junebug's expression. He thinks they need some bonding time."

That explained it. I knew how Jared felt about Lester's interference with his sculpture. And Junebug. The last time they'd "bonded," Junebug had altered the design of his shirt.

We reached the top of the stairs and Dex was standing there. His nickname should be Visa because he was everywhere I wanted to be. At the moment, he looked like he'd been making mud pies. When it came to Dex, I couldn't rule anything out.

"I thought you were working at the apartment today."

"Until noon." He rubbed his thumb against his nose

and left a smear of clay. No sense mentioning it. He'd figure it out. Eventually.

"Don't quit, Dex, you're doing great." Marissa veered around the potter's wheel and walked toward the back of the studio. "I got a letter a few days ago asking if I'd donate some pieces to a charity auction and I could use your opinion, Heather."

I wasn't always qualified, but I always had an opinion. I had the feeling, though, that Marissa had only come down to rescue me from Jared's bad mood.

Dex glanced at me and then sat down, where a misshapen lump of clay huddled on the potter's wheel. Fascinated, I stopped to watch him.

"You might not want to get that close," Marissa warned. "It gets messy."

I inched closer, waiting for Dex to do something. Something other than sit there like the lump of clay he was supposed to be doing something with.

The wheel began to hum and he pressed his hands against the clay. Slowly it began to take shape under the pressure of his hands. Until one of the sides caved in.

"Again?" Marissa clucked her tongue.

"That's nine." Dex scraped his palms against his thighs.

"Your pot flopped nine times?" Did the term glutton for punishment mean anything to him?

"Not counting yesterday," Marissa said. "Yesterday was…how many, Dex?"

"Six."

"Can I try?" It looked like fun.

Dex's pot flopped again. "You'll ruin your clothes."

I grabbed a smock off a hook on the wall.

"And your shoes."

I kicked off my sandals and pushed them under a chair.

Dex gave in. He stood up and I took his place at the wheel.

Marissa was trying not to smile.

"Now what?"

"Dex can walk you through it." Marissa leaned against a shelf and folded her arms.

"I should go." Dex's voice sounded strangled.

"Come on." I flashed him an impatient look. "You can spare a few minutes. Think of it as making up for the deadly fumes you subjected me to."

"Fine. Put your hands on the clay."

"Like this?"

"No."

"Then *show* me." I jiggled up and down, already imagining the cute planter I could make for the window of the apartment.

Dex started the wheel and put his hands over mine.

I squeaked. "It's moving too fast."

"Put your fingers here and guide the clay."

"Do you guys mind if I get my camcorder?" Marissa asked.

"Yes!" Dex and I said it at the same time.

The pot wobbled from side to side while I did my best to keep it under control. It wasn't as easy as it looked.

"It'll work better if you get your hands wet." Dex pointed to the bucket next to the wheel. I leaned down and plunged one hand into the warm water.

The pot flopped again and I moaned. "Ten."

"You can't add that to my score. You have to start your own."

"Then I get to keep this one when it's done."

"Be my guest." Dex put his palm against the side of the pot to shore it up. Muddy brown water sprayed my arm. "Keep your hands on it. The more you touch it, the easier it is to work with."

Marissa grinned. "That's what I love about being a potter. There are a thousand sermons in a lump of clay."

I knew exactly what she meant. It was the same with people. The more people let God get His hands in their life, the more they saw how faithful He was and the more yielding they became.

"But we have this treasure in jars of clay." I murmured the verse that came to mind. I'd been on the Bible Quiz Team for four years in school but I was still surprised when one of those dormant verses suddenly came to life and zipped around inside my head like a shooting star. Usually right when I needed it.

"Hard pressed on every side but not crushed." Dex spoke the words close to my ear, stirring my hair. Challenging me.

I struggled to remember the rest. *"Perplexed but not in despair."*

"Persecuted but not abandoned."

"Struck down but not—" The sides of the pot caved in like a cheese soufflé.

"Destroyed." I was laughing so hard my ribs hurt.

In the midst of our recitation of 2 Corinthians chapter

four, I saw Jared standing at the top of the stairs. But he wasn't laughing.

"If there's ever stand-up comedy night at the church, you two would win first prize," Marissa said, wiping tears from her eyes with the tips of her fingers.

Dex's hands were still covering mine. I eased them away and he twitched like he'd been zapped with an electrical current. Or maybe our little competition had overloaded his memory circuits.

"Let me show you how to do that. If you need a lesson on how to mop the floor, you can get Dexter to help you." Jared's words were teasing but Dex didn't smile. It wasn't the first time Jared had made fun of Dex. Maybe he hadn't forgiven him for single-handedly eating half the cake at Annie's that night. Or maybe— I remembered the kiss and felt my cheeks heat up—for being there in the first place.

"Thanks, Dex." I verbally stepped in between them. "Are you sure you don't want to finish it?"

"Go ahead. I already have one."

"Where is it?" I didn't think he'd show me but he picked something off the shelf. It had already been fired and the final product was a lopsided bowl in emerald green, shot with tiny bursts of gold.

"This is *great*." I turned it over in my hands and noticed something written on the bottom. Dex tried to take it away from me but he wasn't fast enough. I saw the word etched roughly in the hardened clay.

Fireflies.

The strange thing was, I could *see* them. They came

to life in a wild dance against a field of fragrant green grass. "Did you copy one of Marissa's designs?"

Dex didn't answer so Marissa did. "I can't take the credit. He came up with that on his own. I may have to borrow it."

"Mine isn't going to look this good."

"No offense, but it's going to look better." Jared pulled up a stool and sat beside me. I tried to give the bowl back to Dex. He didn't budge. Go figure. Ten seconds ago, he was trying to wrestle it away from me.

"You can keep it."

"Really? Because—"

"It reminds me of your eyes."

The rest of the words I was going to say got stuck in my throat. I must not have heard him right. My mouth opened and closed several times, like a pump trying to coax water from a well.

"Your eyes. Fireflies in a field."

Jared snorted and I said the first thing that came to mind to cover it up. "They're just…green."

"No."

He sounded so certain that I felt a flash of irritation. I was pretty sure I knew what color my eyes were. I'd been looking at them in the mirror every day for years.

"They're green, dude." Jared was my witness.

Dex didn't argue with him. He grabbed the broom that was propped against a chair and followed Marissa downstairs.

"Someone's been around the Pine-Sol too long." Jared started up the wheel. "Ready?"

I took a deep breath and nodded, but what I really wanted was a mirror.

When I got back to my apartment later that night, I pressed my nose against the mirror and studied my eyes. I was right. They were green. Green…with microscopic flecks of gold so tiny I couldn't figure out how Dex had noticed them.

But *fireflies?* If Dex hadn't said it, it would have been almost…poetic.

"Mayor Lane wants to talk to you." Kaylie mouthed the words, pressing the phone against her chest.

"Just a sec." I clipped one of Mrs. Christy's snow-white curls in place and bounded over to the counter. I'd scheduled Mrs. Christy as my last appointment, just to end the day on a good note.

"This is Heather."

"PAC meeting tonight. Seven o'clock."

Was this a recorded message? "Mayor Lane?"

"We're meeting at the community building. You don't have to give the vice president's report tonight—"

That was a relief. I wouldn't have a clue what to put in it.

"—we'll wait until next month."

"Okaaay." The last time I'd been the vice president of anything was when I was in fifth grade. I'd run for president, assuming the entire class would *want* full-length mirrors in the bathrooms. Instead, Kenny Ikeman's promise of ten new red rubber playground balls cost me the election. Solid evidence that way too much emphasis is put on sports.

"Kaylie, please hold my calls for the rest of the day." I handed her the phone.

"Yes, Miss Lowell."

We giggled.

I finished up with Mrs. Christy and she paid in one-dollar bills so new they crackled like autumn leaves when she counted them out. Then she dug around in her purse for my tip. This time it was a doily as fine as a spiderweb. And a pat on the cheek.

"I have something for you, too." Mrs. Christy dug deeper and presented Kaylie with a huge caramel wrapped in wax paper. It looked homemade. I knew the difference and I could almost smell the butter and brown sugar.

When the door closed behind Mrs. Christy, I was ready.

"I'll trade you."

"Not a chance."

"Then you're fired. Pack up your personal belongings but leave the caramel."

"I'll share."

"It's a deal."

I hadn't known how much fun it would be to have Kaylie working with me during the day. When she answered the phone, her voice was cheerful and confident, but she was painfully withdrawn when there were people around. If she had to talk to someone, she'd position her head so they were looking at her profile. Which meant she wasn't looking the person in the eye— she was staring at the floor. It was like watching someone with a split personality. Which one was the real Kaylie Darnell?

I put the Closed sign in the window and we collapsed in the chairs under the dryers. Kaylie twisted the caramel into two pieces.

"You did great today. I can't believe how much I get done when I don't have to answer the phone every five minutes."

"Can I come in every day?"

We hadn't formally discussed her hours. Which a responsible employer would have done. But not me. Nooo. I'd hired her without Bernice's permission and now I had to set up a work schedule. One that wouldn't cut Bernice's salary in half.

"I'm busiest in the mornings. Why don't we say eight until one. Three days a week? You probably want your weekends off."

"I don't need weekends off." Kaylie looked away, but I'd seen the expression on her face. And kicked myself.

"You don't want to work Monday through Friday, do you?"

"I'll work as much as you want me to. I need the money."

"To save for college—"

"Surgery."

"Surgery?" The first thing that raced through my mind was that she had some sort of rare disease. Maybe there was some way to sign her up for major medical...

"On my face." Her next words came out in a rush.

"Don't tell anyone, okay? I haven't even told my mom yet."

Red flags began to pop up in my head, waving frantically to get my attention. "She knows you're working here, right?"

"She doesn't want me to get a job. Everyone around here knows that—that's why no one would hire me."

Everyone except the clueless girl from Minneapolis. Who had.

Chapter Eighteen

Each one should use whatever gift he has received to serve others, faithfully administering God's grace in various forms.
1 Peter 4:10
(Grace graffiti—written in lipstick on Heather's bathroom mirror)

"**D**on't cut those brownies." Candy strode in with a box balanced on one shoulder.

I dropped the knife and it clattered down the table. "Why not?"

"Denise gets kind of persnickety if someone tries to take over her duties."

Cutting brownies was a *duty?* What was her job title? I wanted it.

"Pass these agendas out. There are seven of us. Eight if Jim Briggs talked Marissa into making an appearance."

"I really don't know what I can contribute. I don't know anything about Prichett. Or its advancement."

Candy rubbed her chin. "How's international night going at Sally's?"

"I don't think the lamb kebabs were a big hit. They switched to Mexican Monday. All-you-can-eat tacos. Sally was right when she said everyone goes back to beef—the café looked pretty busy yesterday."

"How's Amanda doing with the book club?"

"They're starting *The Call of the Wild* next week."

"Really." Candy arched an unplucked eyebrow at me.

I'd fallen right into her trap. So maybe I knew *a little bit* of what was happening on Main Street. It was hard not to. All the businesses stood shoulder to shoulder like a chorus line. Which made me uneasy. How long would it take for word to get out that Kaylie Darnell was working at the Cut and Curl? According to Bernice's conspiracy theory, news traveled so fast she suspected there was surveillance equipment wired into the streetlights. For my own peace of mind, I'd have to sneak a look at the town budget for any suspicious electrical bills.

"Half an hour. That's all I have time for." Marissa swished into the conference room, wearing a multicolored sundress with a handkerchief skirt. She'd wound a bandanna around her head like a turban but some of her curls had escaped, giving her a stylish, Gypsy look. Right behind her was a man about my dad's age, with sun-streaked brown hair and an appealing smile. Jim Briggs. I'd seen him at the wedding reception.

Candy muttered something under her breath about tortured artists.

Over the next few minutes, the rest of the PAC drifted in.

Denise from the variety store. Mr. Bender from Bender's Hardware. Sally and Amanda. There were a few more people whose names I forgot as soon as I heard them. What I didn't expect was that everyone knew who *I* was. They sat down and greeted me like a long-lost cousin, and peppered me with questions about Bernice and Alex.

"We're going to get started." Candy's voice cut through the hum of conversation like a chain saw. "Old business?"

Old business dragged on for close to an hour. Hadn't old business been new business last month? Which meant it had already been talked about. I was beginning to understand Bernice's frustration. Robert's Rules didn't apply at PAC meetings. They'd been replaced by Candy's Rules, which she seemed to make up as she went along.

"New business." Candy used her stapler like a gavel, shutting down a lively conversation about weekly garbage pickup.

Denise raised her hand. "I have new business to discuss."

A low moan took a lap around the table.

"Not again," Sally muttered. "This is like a prerecorded message."

Denise ignored her. "I know it's only July, but we have to plan ahead. The Main Street Christmas decorations need to be replaced."

"*Like I've said before,* there isn't money in the budget for new decorations." Candy scowled at Denise. "And the decorations are in perfect condition. Aren't they, Jim?"

Everyone looked at Jim, who slipped two inches lower in his chair. "I wouldn't say…perfect."

"See." Denise looked smug. "If a *man* notices they aren't in good condition—no offense Jim—it means they need to be replaced. With snowmen. Snowmen are very popular."

"Snowmen are expensive. Bells are free. Because we already *have* bells."

"You're the mayor—there must be money available somewhere." Denise must have sensed she was losing ground because she sounded a little desperate now.

"The street department has been whining about the potholes at the corner of West and Jackson for two years. How am I supposed to explain that I came up with money to buy snowmen we use one month out of the year instead of fixing a road people use every day?" She answered the question by banging the stapler against the table. "Next."

Denise looked dejected. I raised my hand before I realized what I was doing. Wait a second. What *was* I doing?

"Heather. You have new business?"

"No…I just wanted to comment on the Christmas decorations."

"That's old business now. You have to wait until next month."

"But—"

"Candy, let Heather say something." Marissa, who'd been as motionless as one of her handmade pots for the past hour, came to my rescue.

Candy crossed her arms. I took that as my signal to continue. "The money for the decorations doesn't have to come from the city budget, right? The PAC committee could *raise* the money."

Denise straightened in her chair like a neglected houseplant injected with fertilizer. "That's a good idea."

"It is?" Candy's eyebrow spoke a language all its own. And right now it was speaking to me. "Raise the money *how?* By selling cookies door-to-door?"

A not-so-subtle hint that I was young and had no idea what I was talking about. Now I had to at least pretend I did. "We could host a community celebration. Have food. Music. And use the proceeds for the decorations."

"There's the Fourth of July celebration in the park this weekend." Amanda spoke up.

Candy shook her head. "This is Tuesday. We don't have enough time to plan and we'd be competing with the organizations who count on the Fourth of July weekend to get them out of the red."

Denise looked at me. In her eyes was a clear message. *You're onto something—keep it going, girl.*

"Something else then." I glanced at Marissa and had a burst of inspiration. "What about a community celebration to unveil the statue of Junebug? Sally and Amanda could cater the food—"

"*Junebug?*"

"And we could have a parade." Jim winked at me over Marissa's head.

Candy's expression changed. "A parade?"

Amanda and Sally put their heads together, whispering, and then Amanda raised her hand. "It would be a great opportunity to get everyone in town together."

Go, Amanda!

Mr. Bender cleared his throat and his arthritic fingers tapped against the table like a drumroll. "If we had it at the end of August before school starts, more people would come. We'd probably have a better turnout than we do for the Fourth."

"Fine. We'll do it." Candy nodded at the woman sitting next to her who was taking notes. "Heather's in charge of the August event."

The words *Heather's in charge* momentarily cut off my air supply. "I can't be in charge, I don't know anything about organizing something like this."

"It's the way we run things, Heather. If you come up with an idea, it's your baby. You're automatically in charge." She smiled. The enjoy-your-biscotti smile.

"But this was Denise's idea!" I couldn't help it. I didn't want to be the head of the committee. I wanted to be the girl who smiled and poured lemonade. For a few hours. And then went home.

"It was my idea to get new Christmas decorations. It was *your* idea to raise money to buy them." Denise smiled at me, too. The traitor.

"This is a committee, right?" Marissa's eyes touched each person at the table but skipped right over

Jim Briggs's head. "That means we all work together on a project."

Jim was smiling at her. I noticed that even though Marissa wasn't looking at *him,* her cheeks were pink, like she knew he was looking at *her.* Very interesting.

"*All* of us?" he asked.

Now Marissa looked at him. "I can help with this *one* thing."

The stapler whacked against the table again. "Next *new* business item on the agenda."

"It's going to be raising money for a new conference table if she doesn't quit abusing the poor thing," Amanda muttered.

Denise inched the brownies closer. I hoped that meant they were the next item on the agenda. They weren't. The meeting dragged on until almost nine, when Candy combined the last few items on the agenda so she'd make it home in time for her favorite television show. Thank goodness for the Agriculture Channel.

I caught up to Marissa as she made a beeline for the door after the meeting. "Thanks for offering to help me."

"I owe you one for the haircut. I'd been looking for a way to lose five pounds without having to wear spandex."

A thought suddenly occurred to me. "Do you think Jared will be done with the statue by the end of August?"

"He should be finished by then but it depends on how fast the foundry can cast it."

"Does that usually take a while?" When I'd come up with the idea for Junebug's unveiling, I hadn't thought about possible complications. Now I was swamped with them. What had I gotten myself into? What had I gotten *Jared* into? And would he forgive me? He didn't exactly hide his disdain for Prichett. Which made me question why he'd taken the job in the first place.

"It can take a few months." Marissa must have walked to the meeting, too, because she didn't veer toward the parking lot when we reached the end of the sidewalk.

"Months?"

"Don't worry. I'll check into it tomorrow."

Great. "I better warn Jared."

Marissa's steps slowed as we reached the corner across the street from the Cut and Curl. "Are you two dating?"

Dating was such an old-fashioned word now. I wasn't quite sure how to label it. "We've been spending time together."

"So you like him." She sounded surprised.

"He's different from the guys I know. It's hard to explain, but he isn't afraid to talk about important things."

Like life. Even though I didn't always agree with Jared's perspective, I could appreciate that he *had* one. He had a sense that there was a bigger picture. I felt the same way—and I was anxious to be part of it. To find my place in God's plan.

"Do you have time to stop over and have a cup of tea with me? We never did figure out what I should donate to the auction." Marissa changed the topic and I was relieved. I wasn't sure I wanted to talk to her about Jared. Not when I sensed disapproval. But maybe it was sharing her studio for the entire summer that she had a problem with, not Jared.

"Sure." After my impromptu pottery demonstration with Dex—and then Jared—that afternoon, I'd totally forgotten to help her.

We walked in silence to her studio. There were no lights on, which meant Jared was done for the day.

"He finished up before I left for the meeting."

She'd read my mind.

I tried not to look as disappointed as I felt. Jared had gone out to Lester Lee's the night before so we hadn't seen each other. He'd called me during lunch, but when I mentioned I was going to the PAC meeting, he hadn't had much of a response. I was falling more in love with Prichett every day, but I could tell that Jared could barely tolerate small-town life. He said it was as exciting as watching grass grow, but I had to disagree. The messages my customers left on the answering machine were proof that life in Prichett wasn't as dull as he thought it was. He just had to look beyond the surface.

Marissa turned the lights on and we went upstairs to her studio. "I'm finally catching up. Sally ordered another dozen coffee mugs and Alex told me that he wanted eight more place settings of the dishes I gave them as a wedding gift. Here, take a look at these."

Behind an Oriental painted screen was a table filled with colorful vases. Some were short and chunky but the one that drew my attention was vibrant red and looked like a tangle of plant roots. "I love this one."

"So do I."

I ran my fingers over the glossy surface. "Aren't you tempted to keep it?"

"Imagining someone else enjoying my work gives me a better feeling than hoarding it. Not to mention I don't have the cupboard space to keep everything I like."

We picked out three more vases to donate to the auction and while Marissa made a pot of tea on a tiny two-burner camp stove by the window, I decided to explore.

It wasn't my fault the studio brought out my inner Indiana Jones. It was like a rabbit warren—small but full of interesting nooks and crannies that Marissa had created with shelves and painted screens. I rounded one of those screens and the toe of my sandal kicked something. Fortunately, I regained my balance without taking out any of Marissa's pottery. There were times when I could look back on ballet class with fondness and this was one of them—Miss Holt had disciplined the klutziness right out of me and half a dozen other six-year-olds. Whether I liked it or not, I was destined to be graceful.

I rubbed my bruised toe against my calf and studied the thing that had just tried to kill me. It was a sculpture—a large block of clay glazed in browns and blacks that had no distinguishing characteristics. Maybe it was an accident. Or a doorstop.

Then I saw a nose.

"Heather, do you like lemon or honey?" Marissa called.

"Both." They helped kill the taste of the tea. I knelt down and stared at the sculpture. There *was* a nose. And a chin.

"It's ready." Marissa's voice at my shoulder made me jump.

"I'm sorry, I was just looking." Looking. Snooping. Take your pick.

"Genesis." Marissa knelt down and ran her hand over the outline of something that suddenly took on the shape of a man's rib cage. "I did this one a few years ago."

"It's Adam, isn't it?" One by one the features of the man hidden in the clay began to appear. The slant of his jaw. The slope of his shoulder. It was amazing. Marissa could create something like this, but she spent her days making mugs and plates. Maybe Jared was right about her. Maybe she wasn't living up to her potential.

"The Lord God formed the man from the dust of the ground and breathed into his nostrils the breath of life, and the man became a living being." Marissa sat back on her heels. "God spoke the entire universe into being but He used His hands to make Adam. I've lost sleep over that one. Even in the beginning, He wanted that close relationship with us."

"Have you entered it in a show?" If the sculpture had tugged at me—the person who wanted to appreciate art but usually ended up admiring the jacket on the person standing next to her—there had to be something special about it.

"Come on. Our tea is getting cold."

I took that as a no. "Has Jared seen it?"

Marissa hooked her foot around a short wooden stool and pushed it toward me. "I haven't shown it to him."

"But if you can do something like *Genesis*…" I lifted the cup to my lips. Open mouth, insert tea. It was better than insert foot.

"Then why am I making dishes?" Marissa finished. "Because it's what I *want* to do. I want the pottery I make to be in people's homes. In their *lives*. I want there to be one of my tea sets in grandma's kitchen so her grand-daughter can use it to have a party with her dolls. Eating meals together is the way people stay connected. There's intimacy there. Something rich. Why do you think we have all those potluck suppers at church?" She laughed. "Someone is going to start their day pouring coffee into a mug I designed. Someone is going to grab a moment of solitude and see fireflies in the glaze. I never think of my work as making plates. Or cups. I think of it as…life."

"I'm sorry." I was apologizing for Jared. And for myself, because I was guilty of thinking the same thing he had. *Why was she wasting her gifts?*

"Don't apologize. My passion for my work takes over sometimes and I get a little vocal. You know how it is."

Marissa was giving me too much credit. I wanted to have a passion but I wasn't sure cutting hair was it. And I wasn't sure I wanted it to be. I loved it, but there had to be something buried in my soul that God hadn't mined out yet. A special gift that would create some-thing more lasting than a spiral perm.

"When did you know that this is what God wanted you to do?" I had to ask. "I know God has a plan for my life—He just hasn't unrolled the blueprint yet and let me in on it."

"He does have a plan, but sometimes I wonder if the most important thing to God isn't *what* we do, but what we allow Him to do *through* us."

Chapter Nineteen

No one told us womn have lists. (Text message
from Dex to Tony Gillespie)

What kind of lists? (Tony)

U wouldnt believe me. (Dex)

"Hey, stranger." Bree stopped in at the salon the next
day right at lunchtime. "Hi…Kaylie."

Kaylie flashed Bree a weak smile and fled into the
back room, muttering something about cleaning out the
fridge while she had a few extra minutes.

"Kaylie Darnell is working for you? You do believe
in living dangerously."

I winced. "Am I the only one who hasn't been grafted
onto the grapevine in this town? Someone should send
out a weekly newsletter."

"I think Mindy Lewis has that covered. I'll get you a subscription."

"Well, I'm keeping Kaylie. I don't know how Bernice did everything herself. I'm a mere mortal."

"Do you have plans tonight?" Bree went right for the suckers in the big plastic container next to the cash register.

"Jared and I have been playing phone tag since yesterday so I'm not sure. Do you want to go riding?"

"Is there anything else?"

"Let me think. Parasailing? Mountain climbing? White-water rafting?"

Bree wrinkled her nose. "Boring."

"True. You talked me into it."

"It's also bath night for the ponies so I told Riley we might stop over to help. His dad sets up a pony ring in the park during the Fourth of July celebration this weekend. You're going to be there, right?"

"I think so." My casual shrug didn't fool Bree for a second. I was still hoping that Jared would change his mind about the weekend. But maybe he was hoping I would change my mind. This was where things got complicated. I was beginning to realize that dreaming about a relationship was a lot easier than actually *being* in one.

"Let me guess. You're hoping to make plans with a certain someone before *you* make plans."

"I'm pathetic. I know. Stephen and Annie need help organizing games for the teenagers and I put them on hold, too."

"Because you don't think the Fourth of July Frolic is going to be exciting enough for Jared?"

"No." He'd made that clear enough. But I was waiting for him to change his mind now that he'd had some time to think about it. I wanted Jared to quit being the displaced artist and start being the appreciative art *student*. The one who acknowledged that Prichett had given him the opportunity to create a sculpture that would last…well, a long time. Even if it was a bronze cow displayed in the center of a town with a population of less than two thousand.

"But you like the guy." There was a question in her voice.

"Now you sound like Marissa."

"I do?"

"She seemed kind of surprised that Jared and I have been seeing each other." That still bothered me. "I'm not sure why."

Bree fished around in the container and pulled out another sucker. "This one's for Riley. Pineapple."

"You've got to love a man with exotic taste in Dum-Dums."

Bree grinned and waved it at me when she reached the door. "We'll talk later. I'll see you after work."

Kaylie emerged from the backroom after Bree left. I had a feeling her timing wasn't a coincidence. I had about ten minutes before my next appointment came in and for some reason, I was restless. Bree had deliberately cut off our conversation about Jared and it left me unsettled. Why was it such a surprise that I was attracted to him? I was going to have to come right out and ask Bree why she seemed so cautious about Jared all of a sudden.

Kaylie intercepted me mid-pace and handed me the sandwich I'd stashed in the fridge. And a bag of carrot sticks that hadn't come from my lunch box. "Wait a second. You didn't tell me that you were moonlighting as the Food Pyramid police."

"It was on my résumé."

I was finding out that even though Kaylie was shy, she had a great sense of humor. Which reminded me of the reason she was shy. Which reminded me that somewhere out there was a circle that had my picture in the center. With a line through it.

"Kay—please tell me your mom knows you're working here now."

The guilty look on her face gave her away. "I haven't had a chance to mention it yet. Two of my brothers both got poison ivy over the weekend so she's been busy marinating them in calamine lotion."

I took a deep breath and decided it was time to ask the question that had been nagging at me since Kaylie started working at the Cut and Curl. "Why is your mom so against you having the birthmark removed?"

"She's never told me why. Just that I should be happy with the way God made me. I've tried to ignore it, but I hate the way people stare—like it's all they see when they look at me. They can't get past it. Or else they try *not* to stare. Which is just as bad."

"Have you told your mom how you feel?"

"She won't understand. She thinks I should be a living, breathing example of a person who knows that it's what's inside a person that matters. But you know what, Heather? I'm *tired* of being that example. People get braces all the time so they have a prettier smile and that's not wrong, is it?"

I felt the need to tread lightly. I didn't want to come between Kaylie and her mom, but I didn't know if it was right to look at the birthmark as a test of Kaylie's faith, either. That seemed like an awful lot to put on a teenager who was already self-conscious and struggling to figure out who she was. Been there, done that. And not completely cured myself, to be totally honest.

"Tell your mom what you just told me. I had something going on that I was afraid to talk to my mom about and when I finally brought it up, she was more hurt that I hadn't come to her sooner than about what it was." I sent up a quick prayer that Mrs. Darnell would be the same way.

Kaylie looked uncertain. "Okay."

"And mention that you're working here. But maybe not in the *same* conversation. On second thought, you might want to leave a note."

Kaylie laughed. But I wasn't kidding.

She was quiet for the rest of the afternoon and I didn't bring up the subject again. I prayed Kaylie would work things out with her mom—and I didn't want to get caught in the middle.

After work, I skipped up the stairs and felt the railing quiver under my hand in response to the decibel level of Dex's radio. At least it was safe to assume he wasn't asleep on my couch. Even with the phone ringing nonstop and the constant stream of customers in the salon, it was always a peaceful oasis compared to the fun house waiting for me at the end of the day. My apartment.

I took a deep breath. *Here goes...*

The first thing I saw was something in the middle of my living room that looked like a scaled-down version of the ark. I went over to the radio and yanked the plug out of the wall.

"Hi, Noah."

"It's a bookshelf."

"Was that on Alex's list?"

"It's for the corner over there."

"I repeat—"

"It needed one."

I looked at the empty space near the window. He was right.

"Your dad called."

"You answered my phone?"

"It was ringing."

"What did you say? Did you explain who you were? Did you tell him why you're in my apartment?" If not, there was probably a SWAT team setting up a perimeter around the building as we spoke.

"He wants you to call him back. Something about a job being available when you get back to Minneapolis."

I sat down in the chair with a hard thump. "A job?"

"It's through one of the churches. Helping women make their transition back into the workforce. It's full-time, too."

"What about benefits?"

It was a good thing Dex was oblivious to sarcasm. It cut way down on the guilt factor.

"No, but there's some room for promotion down the road."

My palms got sweaty. Maybe this was *it*. God's answer to the question about my future. Right on schedule. Why do I pray for things but then I'm surprised when God answers? I hope that didn't mean my measure of faith could fit in a Dixie cup. I wanted it to be like Prichett's water tower.

"He's sending you the application. Priority."

"Anything else?" Again, sarcasm. Again, I couldn't help myself.

"Your mom says hi."

"You talked to my *mom*, too?" I was going to have to call them—soon—and do damage control.

"She thinks they might be able to come for a visit within the next few weeks. But don't worry about putting them up—they already talked to Alex and Bernice and they're planning to stay at the house outside of town." Dex flipped the bookcase onto its side. "She asked me if you were running the town yet."

"She did not." Even though she probably had. Mom liked to tease me about what she called my *managerial capabilities* and *leadership qualities*. I couldn't help it. Rearranging other people's lives was like organizing closets. Much more fun to tackle someone else's than your own.

"Some help here."

It was clear that Dex's daily quota of words had been

depleted by our conversation. I walked over and pushed my shoulder against one end of the board while he hammered on the other. That put us almost nose-to-nose. Close enough that I caught the faint scent of sandalwood and musk. *Expensive* sandalwood and musk. Interesting. I would have put Dex down as strictly a soap-on-a-rope kind of guy. My nose twitched in appreciation. I leaned a little closer.

The dull thwack of the hammer and Dex's yelp made me jump.

"Are you okay?"

Dex shoved his thumb in his mouth. Like that was going to help. "I'm fwine."

"Are you sure? Let me see it."

"I'm *fwine*."

"Okay. I got it. You're *fwine*." I tried not to smile. "This is probably a good time to quit for the day. I have to call my parents back and then drive out to Bree's…and you should put some ice on your thumb. Despite what you've heard, saliva doesn't have healing abilities. Unless you're a Dalmatian."

Dex pulled his thumb out of his mouth and stalked toward the door. Just like that. Leaving tools scattered everywhere and a coffin-size bookcase in the middle of my living room.

"Dex, get back here." No way was he leaving this mess for me to deal with. He was going to have to pick up his toys before he could go home.

He reached the door and glanced back at me. "I'm praying for you—about the job."

While I sputtered out a thank-you, he disappeared. Talk about sneaky.

"You're going to be a missionary. You shouldn't use prayer as an escape hatch." I had to shout through the door because he'd actually closed it this time.

The horses were saddled and ready to go when I got to the farm. Bree pushed Buckshot into a canter before we reached the edge of the field. Rose made an executive decision to keep up, which left me out of breath with my hands frozen on the saddle horn by the time we reached the pond.

"All right. What's bothering you?" I gasped.

Bree didn't answer right away, which told me I was right.

She leaned over and wrapped her arms around Buck's neck. "Riley said the M-word last night."

This was girl-speak and I knew exactly what she meant. "He asked you to *marry* him? And you waited this long to tell me!"

"He didn't ask me to marry him, he asked me if I ever *thought* about getting married."

"What did you say?"

"I told him I thought about it all the time."

I gaped at her even though I knew that was Bree. No games. No flirtatious smiles. No fluttering eyelashes. "And he said?"

"So did he."

"Wow." It was all I could come up with.

"Tell me about it." Bree sat up and spurred Buck into

a leisurely walk with her heels. Rose took her place at his side and they stepped out together like they were harnessed to a buggy. "I have three more years of college and now Riley's thinking about going to school to be a vet tech. I don't know if we should even be *thinking* about thinking about it right now."

"But if you were out of college, would you be thinking about thinking about it?"

"I think so."

We both giggled.

"All I keep hearing is a little voice inside my head that keeps telling me *there are a lot of fish in the sea.*"

The voice in *my* head was a squeaky rendition of a song that spun like a merry-go-round. *Someday my prince will come.* Which the logical part of me—the part that had absorbed every tip about dating from the books that Mom had strategically placed on the nightstand in my room—told me was unrealistic. And the guys in the YAC group had certainly *proved* it was unrealistic. So why was I still on the lookout for him? Somewhere along the way, I'd been brainwashed. And then there was The List…

Focus, Heather. This is about Bree.

"So you don't want to tie yourself down with Riley because you're worried there might be someone out there who's better for you."

"There might be someone out there who's better for *Riley,*" Bree corrected. "I've been away for a year and I'm ninety-nine-percent sure I'll never find anyone like him. It's hard to explain. We're so much alike but we're different enough to get into a good argument once in a while. One minute he looks at me like I'm from another planet and the next minute he understands exactly what I'm saying—even though I haven't said a word."

For some insane reason, an image of Dex flashed in my memory. The night he'd shown up at Annie and Stephen's when I was babysitting—not to gloat that I'd gotten myself into a messy situation (literally) but to help me.

Jared came over, too. And he brought cake.

He came over after the twins were in bed. When he could have you all to himself.

Where had *that* come from?

"You think I'm crazy, don't you?" Bree let out a gusty sigh.

"Crazy? No. Not at all." Not when I was the one with voices arguing back and forth in my head!

"My parents don't want me to rush into anything and I want to finish school…maybe it isn't fair to ask him to wait."

Bree was more concerned about Riley than she was about herself. The authors who wrote those dating books would have cheered if they'd heard her.

Don't look at what you can get out of a relationship; look at what you can give.

"Maybe he doesn't mind waiting. Maybe he's like Jacob, who'd wait seven years to marry you." Riley seemed like a patient guy. The kind of guy who didn't care if he made a place for himself in the world, as long as he had a place in Bree's heart.

"Maybe. I know I would. Neither one of us wants to

make a mistake—and we don't want to hurt each other, either. I don't think it would be so complicated if we'd met three or four years from now. But we didn't—so now we have to deal with things the way they are."

"I thought things were supposed to get *less* complicated when you met The One."

"I think that's only if you meet them under the right circumstances. Right age. Right personality. Right job. The right *whatever*."

I thought about that for a few seconds. "How often do you think that happens?"

"Not very often. Look at our parents. One thing I'm learning about God is that His plan isn't one-size-fits-all. That's why Riley and I are praying about it. It's too big for us to figure out on our own."

Prayer was something Bree and Riley understood. It was something *Dex* understood. Even if he did use it to make a quick getaway. But was it something that *Jared* understood? I was praying about our relationship, but was he? And did it really matter at this point? We were just getting to know each other. I wasn't planning to marry him. I wasn't even planning to fall in love with him. But did anyone *plan* to fall in love? And what if you did fall in love and it was with someone who didn't understand what it meant to love *God,* then what?

I sucked in a breath, realizing that's exactly what had happened with Bernice and Alex. Alex had been forced to look for God to figure out who He was and why He was getting in between him and Bernice. Three months later, he'd tracked me down during spring break while I was in Florida and told me how he'd become a believer. It was pretty incredible how it happened.

Bernice had told everyone at her bridal shower that God hadn't only been with her, He'd gone *ahead* of her. She and Alex had walked away from each other, not knowing they were taking a path that would eventually bring them back together.

But it didn't always happen that way.

That was the part I couldn't quite wrap my mind around. We didn't get to see the future, so how were we supposed to know if we were heading in the right direction? The only thing I knew for sure was that Bree was right—God wasn't a one-size-fits-all designer; His stuff was tailor-made. Unique. One of a kind. Like snowflakes. And couture.

"Why don't you like Jared?" I asked suddenly.

It took a few minutes for Bree to answer my question. "I don't *not* like him. I'm just not sure if I like him for *you*."

"You're going to have to explain that one."

"I don't know…I don't want to hurt your feelings."

"What are friends for?" I tried to make a joke out of it but Bree looked doubtful. "Look, I'm putting on my game face here. I can take it."

"Remember—you asked," Bree said, her expression so serious I was suddenly afraid of what she was going to say. "From the little time we've spent with him—it seems like he's all about himself. His art. His plans. I know one of the reasons you like him is because he sees a bigger world out there, but it's *his* world. And it doesn't seem like he lets other people in it unless they can do something for him. You aren't like that."

I wanted to argue with Bree but her words scraped away at my own doubts, exposing them. "People can change."

"I know, but promise me it won't be *you*."

Chapter Twenty

Need carriage, ball gown and prince ASAP.
(Heather)

The conversations I'd had with Bree and Marissa kept me up half the night. Which meant that I slept through my alarm the next morning. It was Snap who finally woke me up by strolling across my face. I hadn't done laundry for almost a week, so I was working my way through my B-list of clothes and couldn't find anything I liked. And then I couldn't find my Bible.

I always had my devotional time with God at the kitchen counter, where I nibbled on my breakfast with a side helping of guilt—thinking it would be more spiritual to have my prayer time in an uncomfortable chair while my empty stomach growled out a praise chorus. But when I took one of Marissa's plates out of the cupboard, I decided that for once I was going to let myself enjoy my morning conversation with God *and* the bagel He'd provided.

"Snap, did you take my Bible?" I could see her curled up inside Dex's bookshelf. Her ears twitched and her nose lifted toward the coffee table. There was my Bible. I sighed and went to retrieve it. Dex. He was going to be a missionary, for crying out loud. Didn't he have a Bible of his own? Which reminded me that I hadn't checked Haggai for messages in a while.

Sure enough. There was another note and a scripture reference scrawled on a ragged piece of brown paper bag, Dex's personal brand of stationery. He'd answered my question—are you talking about me?

Not you. Priorities.

It made me feel a little bit better that he wasn't singling me out. I glanced at the reference. Matthew 6:33. That sounded familiar. I flipped to it.

But seek first his kingdom and his righteousness, and all these things will be given to you as well.

Righteousness was a heart thing, right? Something that happened on the inside. If Dex hadn't written the message before I'd talked to Marissa, I would have accused him of eavesdropping on our conversation. Her words had stuck with me like a song that kept playing over and over in my head.

I tapped the pen against my teeth. It was weird that Dex was verbally challenged but managed to get his point across perfectly with one simple verse. I grudgingly decided he might be a good missionary.

Okay, God, I'm going to take a break from asking You to show me what You want me to do with my life. I'm just going to ask You what You want to do in my life today.

I thumbed through my Bible to find a piece of paper so I could write back to Dex and that's when I noticed something was missing. The List.

I paged frantically through the Song of Songs. Nothing. I even shook my Bible—gently—upside down and watched old church bulletins fall like confetti onto the carpet. No list.

"It has to be here somewhere," I muttered. The last time I'd seen it had been during the worship service on Sunday, when I'd been cruising through the Old Testament toward Isaiah. Maybe it had somehow fallen out and been disposed of by one of the ushers, who straightened up the sanctuary after church. I could accept that. My name wasn't on it, so even if someone had read it, they couldn't trace it back to me. It was certainly better than the alternative.

That Dex had taken it.

When I rushed down to the Cut and Curl, now officially seven minutes late, there was a box on the sidewalk outside the door of the salon. Kaylie walked up just as I was examining it.

"What's that?"

"I have no idea." I anchored it against my hip and unlocked the door. "Maybe it's the samples of the all-natural sunscreen I ordered last week."

It wasn't. It was a box of crepe paper.

"I wonder what this is for."

Kaylie peered over my shoulder. "I think it's for the float."

"What float?"

"For the Fourth of July parade on Saturday. I'm pretty sure the Cut and Curl always enters a float. Some city organization judges the parade and there are different categories. The most beautiful. The funniest. The most patriotic."

How about a category for *the one that's thrown together at the last minute?*

"Kaylie, it's *Thursday*. No one mentioned anything about a float." Not that I'd talked to Bernice recently, but I was pretty sure she would have warned me about a parade. Especially if I was supposed to enter a float.

"I'll help you."

"You will?" I'd been praying for an opportunity to spend more time with Kaylie, but why did it have to be *this* weekend? I still wasn't sure I was going to ditch Jared. I'd already let him down once and I was hesitant to do it again, just in case he didn't change his mind about spending Saturday in the park, watching the horseshoe tournament.

"Sure." She wouldn't look at me now. "It's not like I have anything else to do."

"Don't we need a truck or something?" I was grasping at excuses.

"It depends on the theme. We could pick something simple. Sometimes people just dress up in costumes and walk along the parade route."

I scraped up some enthusiasm because I didn't want to let her down. "Okay, we'll do it."

The rest of the day, Kaylie and I called out possible slogans to each other.

The Cut and Curl—when you're dyeing for a change.

Cut out bad hair days for good.

By closing time, we'd laughed our way through half a dozen ideas that might win first prize in the Lamest Slogan category.

"Nothing too crazy. Whatever we decide, we both have to be able to show our faces in church the next morning," I reminded her.

Kaylie didn't say anything for a few minutes and I figured she was brainstorming more ideas.

"I thought I could be the creative genius *behind* the float."

"No way. If I have to walk down Main Street dressed like a giant curling iron, so do you."

"Maybe we should just forget about it. You're right, we don't have a lot of time to come up with something."

As excited as Kaylie was about the float, she'd planned to sit on the sidelines. Again. I wanted to hug her. And shake her until her teeth rattled. "Why are you changing your mind? With our brilliant ideas, we could win first prize."

She looked down, something she hadn't been doing as often as she had when she'd first started working at the salon. "Then we better enter the *funniest* category instead of most beautiful. We'll never get that one if I'm in it."

Kaylie!

I took a deep breath and prayed for wisdom. And patience. The words that spilled out of me didn't sound wise or patient.

"You shouldn't have surgery, Kaylie. Not if that's the way you feel."

"What are you talking about?" She looked like I'd just slapped her. And maybe I had—unintentionally.

"If you get the birthmark removed, you think your life will automatically change, but it won't. You'll just find something else to focus on. Something else will make you insecure. You've let that birthmark control you for years—maybe people don't feel comfortable around you because you're not comfortable with yourself. You have to know that your value isn't based on what you look like on the outside."

She glared at me, bringing the tears in her eyes to a boiling point. "That's easy to say when you're *beautiful*."

"It's not easy to say *ever*. Every time I look in the mirror, I see a mouth that's too wide. A chin that's too pointed. The only thing I really like is my nose." I took a breath and forced myself to slow down. "And, Kaylie, you *are* beautiful. Whether you have the surgery or not, that's what you need to believe because that's what *God* says. If you don't believe Him for that now, the surgery won't make any difference."

I sank into the chair next to her. I hadn't meant to come on so strong—but once the words started, I couldn't stop them. Story of my life.

"I didn't mean to preach at you." This is why I had

a shampoo chair in my "office" instead of a couch. I was a rotten counselor.

She sniffled. "Yes, you did. But that's okay. You're kind of good at it."

"So…I'm *right?*"

"I didn't say that."

"Oh."

"I'm kidding." She actually smiled. And sniffled again. "You were on a roll there."

I groaned. "I'm sorry. Women come in here all day, hoping that a new hairstyle will make them a new person. I want them to make the most of what they have—not wish they had something else. I get a little crazy…" I stumbled over the word as another one flashed through my mind.

Passionate.

No, that described people like Marissa. And Annie. People with a calling. I could add Dex to the mix. Which was even more depressing.

"I want the surgery. I'm sick of being two people," Kaylie said, swiping tears away with the back of her hand. "I'm not even sure which one's me."

"I hate to break this to you, but you aren't the only one who feels that way. Let God work on your inside first and then you'll know what to do about the outside."

"I think the surgery might be easier."

She was right. But maybe because she'd acknowledged it, I knew when the time came, she'd make the right decision about whether to have the birthmark removed. "Kaylie, I didn't mean to hurt your feelings.

It's just…I consider you a friend. And I can't stand to see you hide yourself away from people."

I thought about Bree and how her honesty had stung. *Faithful are the wounds of a friend,* wasn't that what the verse in Proverbs said?

"I know. Believe me, I'm tired of it, too." Kaylie caught sight of her reflection in the mirror and slumped forward. "I can't go home yet. Mom is going to know something's wrong."

"I know what you need."

"Potato chips?"

"Nope. Better. Come on, Cinderella. Your fairy god-mother knows how to give an awesome manicure."

I grabbed Kaylie's hand and dragged her toward the little table by the dryers.

"I bite my nails."

"Not after I'm finished with them. You'd break a tooth."

I pushed Kaylie's fingers into a dish to soak while I looked for the perfect color of nail polish. "What do you think of this one? It's called April Showers and—"

"I have an idea for the float."

Suddenly, I knew what was coming and it was going to involve yards of taffeta. "We're going to walk down Main Street dressed like bottles of nail polish?"

"Cinderella—getting ready for the ball. We can come up with a cute slogan of some kind. But we're going to need a horse. And a carriage."

"No problem." I had Bree.

"And a prince."

Now it was getting complicated. Mmm. Riley. Getting him into hose would be tough, though. I'd have to have Bree put some pressure on him. Maybe flip her hair again. "Check. So which one do you want to be? Cinderella or her fairy godmother?"

"Cinderella wears a mask to the ball, right?"

"Not that I remember." I saw the expression on Kaylie's face. *One step at a time, right, Lord?* "But I don't see why she couldn't. Just this once."

My cell phone rang and Jared's name came up on the screen. I couldn't prevent doing a little tap dance around the kitchen.

"Hi."

"There's a farm wagon blocking the alley."

I winced. "I know. I parked it there."

"*You* did?"

"I found out yesterday that the Cut and Curl has to have a float in the parade, so Kaylie and I are going to be decorating it tonight. I promise it'll be gone by the time you wake up in the morning." I anchored the phone between my ear and my shoulder and shook a can of gourmet cat food onto Snap's dish.

It had been a challenge finding something to transform into Cinderella's carriage. Every tractor, truck and flatbed had already been commandeered for the parade. Even Bree's dad had lent out the buggy Elise had ridden in last summer for the parade given in her honor when she'd finaled in the Proverbs 31 Pageant. Riley had finally come through for us, but the wagon wedged in the alley looked more like something that had broken down on the Oregon Trail than Cinderella's coach.

"So this means you're staying in town for the Fourth?"

"It looks like it."

"I was hoping you'd change your mind."

I was hoping you'd change yours.

"We could use some help tonight. You're an artist—I'll bet you can make great crepe paper roses." I was nothing if not single-minded in my attempts to get Jared to discover the blessings of serving others.

"I have to work late tonight. The mayor informed me there's going to be an official unveiling of Junebug at the end of August. Nice of them to put me on a time schedule, wasn't it?" His sarcasm burned my ear. "I tried to tell her the foundry can't cast it until late November, but she said they're going to have it anyway *because no one's going to stand outside in the park and freeze their toes off in November to see a statue of Lester's cow when they can drive by his farm in their nice warm cars and see her in person.*"

I had guilt. "Ah…that was my idea. Denise wants new Christmas decorations for Main Street and I thought the PAC could raise money by hosting an event. The statue was the first thing that came to mind. People can't wait to see it." Maybe flattery would work.

"That's strange. Because everyone I talk to thinks the money should have been spent on a gazebo. Preferably one from a kit. After they go on sale, of course."

Or not.

"I'm sorry I forgot to mention it." I nibbled on the

end of my fingernail. I couldn't *believe* I'd forgotten to mention it.

"You've been busy."

He had a *tone*. Frustration sent me pacing up and down the narrow strip of vinyl flooring that bisected Bernice's kitchen. "The Cut and Curl is a Main Street business, which means I'm automatically drafted into the parade."

"Whatever." Jared sounded like he didn't believe me.

Dreaded silence. I felt like a Ping-Pong ball being bounced back and forth from Jared to My Responsibilities. My biggest fear was that Jared would think he was losing and walk away in the middle of the game.

"I miss hanging out with you."

I almost dropped the phone. A man who could express his feelings. From what I've heard, this was a rare breed. *Can I keep him, God?*

"I miss you, too. If you change your mind about helping out—you know where I live."

"Right back at you."

There was a knock on the door. Kaylie had promised she'd be back by seven.

"I should go. Kaylie's at the door."

"Heather—"

"I'll call you later." I snapped the phone shut, shouted for Kaylie to come in and started scrounging around in the cupboards for the iced tea mix I'd bought.

I could hear footsteps in the living room and when I popped up from behind the counter, a crowd of people was watching me. Kaylie. Annie. Stephen. Bree. Riley. Marissa.

"We heard you needed help with a float," Stephen said.

I charged past the counter and threw my arms around Annie. "I can't believe this." I looked at Riley. "And you're our prince, right?"

"Can't do it. I volunteered to drive the mayor's truck this year. But don't worry. I got you a stand-in. And it only cost me twenty bucks."

"The prince is *charging* you—"

"Call it a royalty fee." Dex wandered in, looking like he'd just rolled out of bed. There was a shadow of stubble on his chin and with his dark hair flopping across his forehead, he looked like a sleepy pirate.

"*You're* the prince? You don't like horses."

"Horses?" His face got pale under the stubble.

"What do you think pulls Cinderella's coach, man? A Chevy?" Riley slapped him on the back.

"I was hoping it would be a tractor."

Riley grinned. "You can ride beside the coach on Lily while Bree drives the carriage. Lily is what we call bomb-proof."

"And hopefully firecracker proof," I murmured, just to see him sweat. I could make a hobby out of teasing Dex because there was never a flicker of emotion in his eyes to prove he got it.

"All you have to do is smile and wave," Bree chimed in.

"I remembered I have something else to do tomorrow morning."

"Come on, Dex. Where are your *priorities?*"

He gave me a blank look. Like he hadn't been

guilty of secreting those notes into my Bible for the past month.

"Okay, people, we've only got a babysitter for an hour." Stephen clapped his hands and we all snapped to attention. "We've got white sheets, fake flowers and twenty rolls of crepe paper. Let's get moving."

"Cinderella?" Dex walked up to Kaylie and bowed, then offered his arm.

Come on, Kaylie. Remember what I said.

She stepped back shyly but she didn't duck her head or look away. Then she curtsied and took his arm. "My curfew is midnight."

We got giddy on root beer and worked on the float until the streetlight dimmed to a soft glow at ten o'clock. Did the people of Prichett know that Candy was saving money this way?

"What kind of costumes did you come up with?" Marissa asked, handing me a paper rose. The ones she made really did look like roses. Mine looked more like those little scratchy things used to scrub out pots and pans.

"Costumes?" The float had consumed my attention—I hadn't even thought about costumes. And it wasn't like I could call people this late at night to beg for some old formals.

Marissa patted my arm. "I've got some things that might work. I'll be back in a few minutes."

God, have I thanked You lately for friends? Because I'm doing it right now. Thank You!

A car pulled into the alley and parked by Jared's

garage. The next thing I knew, three people spilled out of it, laughing as they pounded on Jared's door. I was on top of the wagon, with an aerial view that allowed me to see one guy and two girls. Blonde One and Blonde Two.

A crack of light raced out of the garage and down the alley toward us when Jared opened the door. How long had he been home? And why hadn't he stopped over to help with the float? I scuttled over to the end of the wagon but couldn't hear what he was saying. Everyone disappeared inside and the door snapped shut. Now it was two guys and two girls. Two *pairs*.

I miss you.

So much that he'd found someone to take my place?

Chapter Twenty-One

I AM AFRAID… (Fill in the blank. Come on, you can do it!)

That someone is going to read this and think I'm a total idiot. Or a geek.
(Dex—written on page 22 of the book Real Men Write in Journals)

"Congratulations, Heather!"

Denise poked her head out of the door of the variety store on Monday afternoon and waved a mop at me as I swept the sidewalk in front of the salon. The city crew had made a halfhearted attempt to clean up the remnants of the Fourth of July Frolic but, borrowing one of Mom's phrases, they'd "missed a few spots." Like the piece of yellow taffy I'd just stepped on.

"Thanks," I shouted back, pausing to peel the keepsake off the bottom of my sandal.

"Tell Kaylie, too."

"I will."

When I got to work that morning, there was a message from Kaylie on the answering machine telling me she wasn't coming in. Her voice had sounded a little shaky, so I hoped she was feeling okay. I'd missed laughing with her.

After the parade on Saturday, Candy had tracked us down to tell us we'd won first place in the most beautiful category, which turned out to be a ten-dollar gift certificate at Bender's Hardware. Dex took the certificate and the adorable stuffed octopus I won at the karaoke contest in payment for performing his princely duty. I was fine passing along the gift certificate but disappointed he took the octopus. It was bright pink with little suction cups on the bottom of its feet and would have looked cute on my mirror.

I finished sweeping and went back inside to empty out the coffeepot so I could go home for the day. One thing about Amanda's book club and her free refills, the number of people stopping into the Cut and Curl for coffee was dwindling every day.

"Are you Heather?"

I hadn't even heard someone come in, so the sound of a voice startled me. A woman was standing a few feet away. She wasn't one of my regulars but she looked familiar.

"Yes, I'm Heather. I'm closing up for the day but I'd be happy to—"

"I'm Kaylie's mother."

Those three words sucked the air out of my lungs. "Mrs. Darnell. It's nice to—"

Her hand sliced the air like a karate chop and cut off the rest of my polite greeting. "Kaylie has been crying most of the day and she refuses to talk about whatever is bothering her. I can only imagine it has something to do with *you*. She's been a different person since she started working here—oh, I know all about you hiring her. And I should have known that a young woman like you would encourage her to have her birthmark removed."

A young woman like me?

"Mrs. Darnell, I didn't influence Kaylie one way or another. The truth is, I told her—"

"Annie Carpenter convinced me that Kaylie would be fine spending time with you. I shouldn't have taken her word for it. If you were really a Christian, you'd encourage someone like Kaylie to accept the way God made her."

The coffeepot I was rinsing out slipped from my hands and fell into the sink. Mrs. Kirkwood might have judged my skirt immodest, but no one had ever come right out and questioned my relationship with God before.

"I *did* tell Kaylie to accept the way God made her—"

"Kaylie is no longer working for you." Mrs. Darnell pivoted toward the door but hadn't quite run out of ammunition. She turned around and emptied the last round. "People stare at her enough—it wasn't necessary to put her on display in the Fourth of July parade."

"I didn't…" I gave up. The rest of the sentence was lost in the slam of the door as Mrs. Darnell charged away.

I stumbled up to the apartment. Tears blurred my

vision and when I thought I was in range, I launched myself onto the couch. I didn't land on cushions. I landed on a person.

"Hey!"

Arms and legs flailing, Dex and I scrambled apart.

"What are you *doing* here?" I hurled a pillow at him. I wasn't expecting there to be a witness to my meltdown.

"You're crying."

"I want…" I sucked in air. "To be alone."

Somewhere in the back of my mind, I was dimly aware that a woman's tears should send a guy like Dex running for cover. Instead, he tucked the pillow I'd just chucked at him behind his back and didn't budge. "What happened?"

I turned into a miserable puddle right in front of him. I squeezed my eyes shut to stop the flow, but it didn't help. Tears spilled over like a break in the Hoover Dam. "Go away."

The cushions shifted. Maybe he was going to leave. I felt his fingers touch my cheeks, framing my face. "Look at me."

"Dex—" I turned my face away. The ultimate humiliation. That someone would see me come unglued. No, that Mr. Unemotional would see me come unglued.

"Tell me."

I couldn't. Mrs. Darnell's angry words were still hammering away inside my head. "I messed up."

"Welcome to my world."

He made me want to smile. "I just need to be alone."

"Okay. I'll take you somewhere you can be alone."

Did I always have to be the one to point out the obvious? "If you leave, I'll be alone. If you take me somewhere to be alone, then you'll be with me and I won't be alone."

"You'll be as alone as you need to be. Come on."

Somehow he got me outside and into the Impala. It smelled like French fries. And old carpeting. He fished around in the back seat and then dropped a mashed box of tissue in my lap. The stuffed octopus I'd won was stuck to the dashboard and there was a blob of ketchup on the side of its head. If I could prove neglect, there was a chance I could regain custody.

I waited for Dex to start in on me, but he didn't say a word. Didn't turn on the radio. Didn't slide sympathetic glances my way every few minutes. He did lean across me and open the glove compartment with one hand, fumbling inside until he pulled out a melted candy bar. Which he ate right in front of me. For the first time, it occurred to me that *he* was upset. I just wasn't sure why.

"Is that Lester's place?" I wasn't too numb to recognize the farmhouse in the distance. It wasn't very far from the Cabotts'.

"I hang out there sometimes."

He drove onto the grass and followed a worn path past the barn to an old metal building. The doors were open and I could see a plane inside. The canary-yellow paint was faded but I could make out the words *Fancy Free* written in flowing script along the tail.

Crisis or not, I hadn't lost all of my ability to think straight. And I wasn't taking another step until Dex told me what he had in mind.

"Is that Lester's plane?"

"It's his brother's old crop duster. Lester has a hard time throwing things away. This is where I come to be alone."

My apartment, stocked with cold soda and unmelted chocolate, would have worked fine for me.

"You sit in Lester's plane?"

"You could say that."

"You don't…*fly*…Lester's plane?"

"Let's go."

"I'm not…you can fly a plane?" I squeaked. The world as I knew it was crashing down around me.

"I'm a licensed pilot."

Yes, but for *real* planes? Or the kind that shoots down alien spacecrafts?

"It doesn't look safe." I based that assumption on the rust spreading across the underbelly of the plane like a bad rash.

"Safety is highly overrated."

Who are you and what have you done with Dex?

It occurred to me, though, that if we crashed I wouldn't have to face Mrs. Darnell again. This thought alone sent me clambering into the tiny cockpit. When Dex got in on the other side, he reached over and buckled me in like I was a kid in a car seat.

"Ready?"

"No."

"Good. Let's go."

Five minutes later, the plane was bumping down Lester's pasture while Lester's cows crowded together at one end of the pasture to watch. If the plane did crash and we went up in flames, there'd be enough steak to feed the entire town. Mmm. If they charged admission, Denise would have enough money to buy the snowmen. I giggled. Dex glanced at me and frowned, clearly wondering if he should remove all sharp objects from the cockpit.

The plane shook and I forgot about PAC fund-raisers for the moment. I clung to the sides of the seat, which vibrated like one of those cheap massage chairs at the mall. "Let me see your license."

"You should have asked me that earlier. It's in the glove compartment of my car."

The next thing I knew we were airborne. And I was truly kidnapped.

"How long have you been flying planes?" I shouted over the hacking cough of the engine.

"A few weeks."

I almost threw up. Dex laughed. Except for that afternoon at Annie's, I couldn't remember ever hearing him laugh. *Now* he decided to reveal the sense of humor I'd known was lurking below the surface.

"Since I was nineteen. This is what I'm going to do. Fly medical supplies to missionaries in the field. Sometimes I'll fly sick people out for treatment." The plane rocked to one side suddenly and my head kissed the window. "Sorry. I was waving to those kids down there."

I peeked down and saw a group of people, as tiny as Polly Pocket dolls, swimming near the bridge on Marley Creek.

"Let me get this straight. You won't get on a horse but you'll fly a plane."

"Big difference. A plane has an engine, a horse has a mind of its own."

"But if you fall off a horse, you only fall a few feet."

The plane evened out and I gathered enough courage to peek out the window again. The sun was setting and if we kept going, we'd disappear into the whipped-cream clouds on the horizon. Maybe when we came through on the other side, I'd be a different person. Maybe I'd be back in Minnesota, far away from decisions about my future. And confusing guys. And Mrs. Darnell.

Dex must have read my mind. "You know what I love about flying? Everything that happens on the ground stays on the ground."

"That would be nice." If it were true. I could still hear Mrs. Darnell yelling at me.

"Did Ward do something?" Dex's voice was tight.

"Jared? No." *If only it were that simple.*

"You said you messed up."

I scowled at him. "Don't you know you're supposed to give people *space* when they're upset?"

"I thought we were supposed to help people carry their burdens. In order to do that, you have to be close enough to a person to *touch* them."

"You want to hear every miserable detail, don't you?"

"Yup."

I sighed. If I were going to die, it probably wouldn't hurt to have a clear conscious.

"Mrs. Darnell? Kaylie's mom? She came into the salon today and accused me of influencing Kaylie to have her birthmark removed. She said if I were really a

Christian, I'd encourage her to care more about what she looks like on the inside than the outside."

Every word she'd said was stuck in my head, playing over and over like a CD with a scratch on it.

Dex didn't say anything for a while. The plane banked to the left and skipped over a stand of trees, dragging my stomach along with it. "So this is about you?"

Hadn't he heard anything I'd said? My teeth snapped together. "It's about *Kaylie*."

"Is it?"

"Yes…no." I blinked and tears poured out of my eyes. I hated to cry. It messed up my mascara and now I probably looked like a raccoon. Which proved that Mrs. Darnell was right about me. I was the spiritual equivalent of marshmallow fluff. It wasn't fair that when Annie opened her mouth, wisdom poured out and when I opened mine, a person got a beauty tip.

"I thought you were shallow when I met you."

"Oh, thanks."

"You thought I was a geek."

I choked back a laugh.

"I get it. You *still* think I'm a geek." There was a smile on his face that didn't look geeky at all. I'd never seen that particular smile before and it woke up some butterflies in my stomach that must have been napping. Probably something to do with the turbulence. "Don't worry about it. Being a geek is flattering considering what I used to be. People aren't so simple, are they? Look at you. You're full of surprises."

I felt a flash of pleasure at his words. Grandma

Lowell said I was the kind of person who wore her heart on her sleeve, so it was nice to have someone hint that I was mysterious.

"So are you." I patted the door of the plane to prove the point. But he was right. People *weren't* simple. It was tempting to slap an invisible label on them. Dealing with layers took time. Sometimes it was worth it because you found things you didn't have a clue were there—and sometimes it left you disappointed because you expected to find things that weren't.

Doubts pelted me and I was vulnerable against the attack. Dex was right. It wasn't just about Kaylie. Mrs. Darnell's words had made a direct hit into the center of my insecurities.

"There are a hundred other things I'd rather be good at. Cutting hair doesn't really impact the world, does it?"

"No."

"Are you trying to cheer me up? Because you're really bad at it." I could feel tears bubbling up again so I stared out the grimy window. The cars on the road underneath us looked like toys. I should have been freaked out by this, but I wasn't. I was flying above the trees in an ancient airplane—with Dex—and I wasn't searching for a parachute.

"Kaylie's mom is wrong," Dex said matter-of-factly. "You didn't tell Kaylie not to have the surgery—you told her it wouldn't instantly change how she felt about herself. And you were right."

"How did you *know* that?"

"She told me. While you were working the parade

route, tapping little kids on the head with your wand, she was talking to me. I think she was afraid if she didn't distract me, I was going to faint."

If that was true, then why hadn't Kaylie come to work? Why had she been crying most of the day? It didn't make sense. But at the moment, nothing did. Maybe Dex wasn't the ideal person to pour my soul out to, but he was the one who'd kidnapped me so he had to deal with the fallout.

"I want to do something that counts. Something that *lasts*. Look at you—you're going to be flying medical supplies to missionaries. Why did God put you on that list? Why am I cutting people's hair and you get to do *that?*"

"Maybe because I took someone's place."

"Well, maybe someone can take *my* place, then, so Mrs. Darnell can yell at someone else." In the distance I could see the sapphire-blue shingles on the roof of Lester's barn. We'd flown in a large circle and were heading back to the farm. I wasn't ready to go back. Dex was right. Circumstances looked different when you were above them.

Both of us were silent as the plane thumped along the ground toward the pole building. It coasted to a stop just inside, the nose of the plane inches from the wall. Neither of us moved.

"Again?" I pleaded.

Dex leaned back, plucked his glasses off and rubbed his eyes. "No gas. We were flying on fumes the last ten minutes as it was."

And thank you for not mentioning that sooner.

"Dex…thanks." I wasn't sure what I was thanking him for. Maybe for listening. And for saying just enough.

His eyes narrowed. "You don't need a *hug,* do you?"

He sounded so uncomfortable that I laughed. "No."

"Because I can." From the tone of his voice, it sounded like he was offering to wear a wire and go into a room full of drug dealers.

"Really—I'm okay." Whether I wanted it or not, the real world was back and I had to face it. I opened the door but just as I was about to jump down, Dex was there. He grabbed my waist with both hands and swung me down. Automatically, I clung to his shoulders. Which ended up with both of us up to our ankles in sawdust, not as close to each other as we'd been when I'd landed on him back at the apartment, but almost.

"Heather?" His voice was low.

"What?" I forced the word out. The butterflies were awake again and I couldn't blame it on the turbulence this time. He hadn't put his glasses back on. I kept forgetting his eyes were that soft shade of blue, like the comfy footy pajamas Annie dressed Nathaniel in.

"Give me your phone."

I blinked.

"Your phone." He held out his hand.

I pulled my cell from my pocket and gave it to him. He flipped it open and started cruising through my address book.

"Don't call Kaylie…I can't talk to her right…Dex!" The phone was ringing and he pressed it into my hand.

I would have hung up except that I heard a familiar voice say hello.

"Mom?"

"Heather? I was just thinking about you."

He'd dialed *home*. I couldn't say anything past the lump in my throat.

"Honey? Is everything all right?"

Dex nodded at me. Prompted me to say something.

"Things could be…better." I gravitated toward a stack of tires in the corner and perched on top of them. When I looked up, Dex was gone.

Half an hour later, I found him leaning against a fence post, feeding dandelions to one of Lester's cows. I walked over and stood next to him but he didn't look at me.

"Are you sifting through the stuff in your head again?"

He and the cow both swung their heads around. Dex looked confused. Finally, an expression I was used to seeing on his face. The pilot Dex and the sensitive I-know-when-a-girl-needs-her-Mom Dex had totally thrown me off center.

"What does that mean?"

"Oh, nothing." I was embarrassed it had slipped out. "Annie just mentioned one day that you lived in your head a lot—sifting through stuff."

I think she'd used the word *junk*. Maybe not. What kind of junk would someone like Dex—Mr. Mission-ary Pilot—have cluttering up his head?

Dex looked down at the ground and scuffed the toe of his shoe against the sun-scorched patch of grass under our feet. He'd suddenly retreated into himself like a turtle. And I was the one who'd tapped on his shell. "Annie is something else."

I smiled. That was the truth. I bent down and picked a dandelion to feed to the cow, then noticed its ear.

"Is that *Junebug?*"

"Uh-huh."

I dropped the dandelion. "She's...vicious."

"She's a big baby." Dex scratched Junebug's crooked ear and she pushed closer. If she were a cat, she would have purred.

"That's not what I heard," I muttered, remembering the bite out of Jared's T-shirt.

Dex patted her nose and then brushed his hands off on his jeans. "I'll take you back to town."

I let him get a few steps ahead of me as we walked to the car.

It was inevitable that I had to go back to Prichett. I felt better after spilling my heart out to Mom, but the numbness hadn't completely worn away. Dex and I must have been at Lester's for several hours. The sun was settling comfortably on the horizon for the night, fluffing the clouds around it like feather pillows. My stomach realized this and growled a loud reminder that we'd passed the acceptable time frame for supper.

I would have been horrified if that had happened in front of Jared. But this was Dex. "Do you want to come over? I'll make us something to eat."

He didn't slow down. "No."

I wasn't sure if the disappointment I felt was because

he didn't want payment in the form of a grilled cheese or because he was back to using sentences that consisted of a noun and a verb. "Are you sure?"

"I have something to do."

An hour later, Mrs. Darnell and Kaylie showed up at my door.

Chapter Twenty-Two

I froze. Not even Kaylie's quick hug thawed me out.

"Can we come in?" Mrs. Darnell looked different when she wasn't on a crusade. Nicer. She wasn't fooling me. She'd come back for round two.

I stepped back and let them file past me. Mrs. Darnell glanced at Dex's bookcase, which was still in the center of the room, and found an empty spot on the couch next to Snap. Kaylie flopped down beside her.

The sudden silence in the room was very loud.

Kaylie leaned forward. "I'm sorry I didn't come to work today, Heather. Saturday was…hard. I didn't expect it to be so hard."

She had to be talking about the parade. Or maybe the karaoke contest. I'd convinced her to pair up with me in a duet for that. Or was it when I'd taken a bandanna and tied her—ankle to ankle—to the cutest guy in Stephen and Annie's youth group for the three-legged race? It didn't matter. I'd cheerfully bullied her into the limelight the entire day, forgetting she was more comfortable fading into the woodwork. Or maybe I'd just ignored it. I was convinced Kaylie had been squeezing her outgoing personality into a mold designed for an introvert and it was time for Heather's interpretation of freedom in Christ.

Scratch the gift of discernment.

"It's my fault. I shouldn't have pushed you." I cringed inside, expecting Mrs. Darnell to second the motion.

"You didn't push me. I pushed myself. And I had a blast. Max, the guy you entered me in the three-legged race with, told me he was leaving for college next month and he wished he had more time to get to know me. We've been in the same classes for four years and I was always afraid to talk to him. I wouldn't even *look* at him." Kaylie's voice cracked. "But yesterday—when the youth group led the songs during worship—that's when it hit me. All the things I didn't do. Not because of this birthmark but because I…hated myself. I thought the birthmark was all people could see but it was all *I* could see."

I'd been too nervous to sit down, but now my knees turned into pudding and I wobbled over to a chair. The pain on Kaylie's face jump-started my tears all over again. I'd put her through this.

"I told God how sick I was of living like this. Then I told Him I was sorry for letting a mark on my face get in the way of the person He wanted me to be—"

Wait a second. That sounded promising. *Maybe she wasn't blaming me…*

"And I thanked Him for you and Dex."

Me and *Dex?*

I must have asked the question out loud because Kaylie nodded.

"You both cared enough about me to tell me the truth. You said having the surgery wouldn't matter if I didn't accept that I was beautiful even without it—"

Was Mrs. Darnell hearing this? I let myself glance at her but not in an I-told-you-so way.

"What did Dex say?"

"Did you notice I wasn't wearing the mask during the parade?" Kaylie asked.

"Nooo." *Blushing.* I'd been too caught up in my role as fairy godmother, distributing pink plastic combs to all the miniature princesses that lined the parade route.

"I was about to put it on and Dex took it away from me. He said if I kept covering up my face, people wouldn't see Jesus in my eyes."

That sounded like a whole sentence to me. God had used Dex—and his blunt, unemotional way—to rewire Kaylie's thinking. Why was I surprised? He'd used a donkey to get through to Balaam.

"I'm sorry I jumped to conclusions." Mrs. Darnell's eyes caught mine and held them. "I thought you'd taken on Kaylie as your little project. That you wanted to give her one of those makeovers so you and the salon would look good."

Ouch. I guess Dex wasn't the only one who'd thought I was shallow. "Kaylie's already beautiful."

"That's what I've been trying to tell her for years, but it didn't come out the same way. She never believed me."

I looked at Kaylie. "Does this mean you're coming back to work tomorrow."

Kaylie's mouth dropped open and she twisted around to stare at her mom. "Did you tell Heather *I quit? Mother!*"

"You should have told me why you were so upset yesterday," Mrs. Darnell said, a bit defensively. "What was I supposed to think?"

Oops.

"Moms can't read our minds, they can only see us with the eyes that are in the back of their heads." I winked at Mrs. Darnell and she relaxed.

"That's true."

"I'm going to meet with Annie once a week for Bible study and prayer," Kaylie said. "Dex told me I should. He said she had some things happen that made it hard for her to see herself as beautiful, too."

There was a question in her voice that I couldn't respond to. Annie? She lived facing God. I couldn't imagine there being a time in her life when she'd been afraid to look at Him. But Dex was right. People were complicated. Maybe even missionary pilots who moonlighted as carpenters.

"We better go." Mrs. Darnell stood up, her arm wrapped around Kaylie's shoulders.

"I've got to work tomorrow morning and my boss can be a real slave driver." Kaylie bounced over and gave me another hug.

"I hope you can come for a cookout soon," Mrs. Darnell said. "We'd love to have you."

"I'd love to come." *Now that I know I won't be the main course on the grill.*

"Invite your friend Dex, too."

My friend Dex. Were Dex and I *friends?* When had that happened? Maybe somewhere between the kidnapping and the clouds.

"I can ask him, but Dex is kind of…antisocial."

Kaylie's eyes widened. "Antisocial?"

I rolled my eyes. Was I the only one who saw it?

A few seconds after they left, there was a tap on the door.

"This was on the step outside your door." Kaylie handed me a large white envelope. "You probably didn't notice it. See you tomorrow!"

I flipped it over and saw the gold foil label in the corner, printed with my home address.

"This might be it, Snap." I bulldozed her to the other side of the couch with a pillow and sat down. "My future. Delivered by God via FedEx."

I dumped the contents of the envelope onto my lap and started at the beginning—which was a detailed description of the job. It sounded perfect. Forty hours—most of them during the week but I'd also work some weekends…did I see the word *shopping?* There it was again. Shopping. Like in helping the clients shop for business attire if they needed it. Spending someone else's money on clothes. Was this my dream job or what?

I fanned myself with the application.

My cell phone rang, reviving me momentarily. The name that popped up on the screen would determine if I answered it or not.

"Hi."

"Mama B!" I squealed into the phone.

Bernice laughed. "I can have the worst day of my life and when I hear you say that, everything falls into place."

"The worst day? There are no worst days when you're on your honeymoon in Europe."

"True. I'm calling to apologize and I'll bet you know why."

"The parade."

Bernice groaned. "That was too quick. I'm surprised you're still speaking to me. I hope you had enough time to come up with a float. I know Candy wouldn't let you wiggle out of it just because you're the new kid on the block."

"Enough time?" I scratched the tip of my nose with the corner of the application. "I found a box of crepe paper by the front door on Thursday morning."

"I am so *sorry*. I'm going to have to do something really big to make it up to you, right?"

I laughed. "Right."

"Let me think. How about I turn over the Cut and Curl to you?"

My name was about to go down in Ripley's as the only person who'd ever sliced off the end of her nose with a piece of paper.

"Heather? Are you still there?"

"I think so." I pinched myself, just to be sure.

"I know I'll see you in a month, but Alex and I have been talking—and praying—about something since we left Prichett and I had to call and tell you about it. One of the charities Alex supports is a camp for at-risk teens. A *Christian* camp. He didn't even know that's what the emphasis was. *Definitely* a God-thing." She laughed and I joined in. Weakly. "The camp encourages artistic expression—painting, music, dance—and up until now, he's always mailed in a check, but the director of the camp contacted him last week and asked if he'd be interested in teaching a six-week drama course. The next one starts in the beginning of November and if Alex feels he should say yes, I'll go along for the ride. Maybe I can put my makeup techniques to good use again."

Trying to process everything Bernice was telling me was like riding a bicycle under water. "Ah…he'd be good at that."

"Which brings us back to you," Bernice said. "I have to confess that as much as I love the salon, what I really want to be is June Cleaver à la Mrs. Alexander Scott. I want to bake cookies and make pot roast—"

In the background, I could hear Alex shouting *No, no, no. Not pot roast.*

"—and I want to bring him his slippers at night—"
Hysterical laughter now.

"—and basically stick to him like a barnacle until he gets tired of me and scrapes me off." She lowered her voice. "Which doesn't look like it's going to happen anytime soon."

I couldn't resist smiling.

"Since you don't have a job lined up when you go back to the Cities, will you pray about managing the salon? Permanently. I can't think of anyone I'd rather pass the curling iron to and I know you'll let me come in and play with someone's hair if I go through withdrawal."

She was willing to give me the Cut and Curl. At twenty-one, I'd be running my own business. The application fluttered to the floor and drifted under the coffee table.

"Here, Alex wants to talk to you."

"Heather?"

It was still a surreal experience hearing Alex's voice. I'd been going to his movies for the past ten years and if I closed my eyes, I could see Devon Ross, undercover government agent.

"Hi, Alex."

"Don't think of this like we're doing you a favor," he said seriously. "You'd be doing us one. And you could hire as much help as you want or need."

Had I told Bernice about Kaylie? No, I don't think I had.

"I…ah, have a receptionist." Might as well put that out on the table right away.

"Great. I don't know how Bernice managed the customers and the telephone—"

"I ignored the phone!" I heard Bernice yell.

"I think your mom just sent a flock of pigeons to their death when she yelled," Alex murmured. "They fell right off the roof across the street. Do not pass Go, do not collect two hundred dollars."

Bernice needed Alex. She needed the laughter that he brought into her life. If I could find The List, I would have added *makes me laugh*. But it was still missing in action. "I miss you guys."

"We miss you, too," Alex said softly. "But whatever you decide—whether you stay in Prichett or go back to Minnesota—we're going to be like those barnacles Bernice mentioned. You're stuck with us, sweetie."

There was humor in Alex's voice but an undercurrent of warmth, too. And love. He didn't put any pressure on me to stay, but it was clear they wanted to keep me close. But I believed him when he said they'd trust my decision.

Bernice came back on the line. "I know this is a big decision. Talk to your mom and dad. Ask Annie and Elise to pray with you. Bree, too. And by the way, Alex is right…you're stuck with us."

"I like being stuck with you."

"Keep in touch. And don't hesitate to call me and complain if the PAC forces you to organize something. They're good at that."

"I will. And I won't." Best not to mention that I was heading up a committee for a PAC fund-raiser.

"Love you. We'll see you next month."

"Love you, too." I closed the phone. *Next* month. Half the summer was gone already. I reached down and picked up the application. Up until five minutes ago, I was sure it had been the answer to the question I'd kept asking God—*what do you want me to do with my life?*

Waiting for the answer had been challenging enough. I hadn't expected it to be multiple choice.

Chapter Twenty-Three

Has priorities in place.
(Addition to The List. If I could find it—Heather)

I convinced myself that Marissa was busy and I was being a Good Samaritan by dropping off the dresses that she'd loaned us for the parade. The fact that I would see Jared at the studio was unavoidable. I hoped. So was the fact that I hadn't heard from him since Blonde One and Blonde Two had parked their convertible on his doorstep Friday night.

"Hi, Heather. I was just thinking about you." Marissa was at the cash register, a pen tucked between her teeth. She had on a cute pair of cat-eye glasses studded with rhinestones. "We should have a meeting pretty soon about our August fund-raiser."

There was that word again. August. Hearing it had

never made me nauseous until now. "I brought back your dresses."

"There was no rush." Marissa came around the counter and I kept my eyes focused on her. Not on the doorway behind her. The doorway to the room Jared was working in. She took the two garment bags and draped them across her arms. "It's not like I'm going to be wearing them anytime soon. I was actually thinking about donating them to the high school. Maybe the drama club could use them in a play."

I couldn't believe Marissa would be willing to part with them. When she'd brought the dresses over and shown them to us, they were so gorgeous Kaylie and I were afraid to wear them. One was a creamy-white taffeta and the other dusty-blue, both tea-length and similar in style, with bell-shaped skirts over yards of stiff netting. I couldn't tell how old they were. The way fashion cycled, they could have been Marissa's or reached back another generation.

"Were they yours?"

"This one was." Marissa patted the white gown that Kaylie had worn as Cinderella. "It was my wedding dress. Do you have time for a cup of tea?"

The words *wedding dress* derailed my thoughts. For some reason, I'd assumed that Marissa had never been married. Maybe because she had that creative, inde-pendent soul—the kind that didn't go through life, glancing at The List. *Like some women.*

"Heather?"

What was the question? Something about tea.

"Oh, tea. Sure." Bree was going out to dinner with

Riley—an official date that didn't include horses, farm chores or a bonfire. She'd been so busy helping Sam with the farm they hadn't been able to see much of each other. I'd been invited to go along but I'd said no. Not because of the "third wheel" thing but because I was still trying to decide which circle to color in on my multiple-choice test. Now I knew what it meant to *pray without ceasing,* because that's what I'd been doing all day. And still no answer. Just when I thought God had been shining a spotlight down one path, He'd illuminated another and left me at the crossroads.

"Come on up." Marissa took the stairs two at a time but I lingered for a second, wondering if Jared had heard my voice and if he'd come out to say hello.

Marissa paused, glanced down at me from the railing and once again read my mind.

"I kicked Jared out of the studio today. He discovered that he has to have Junebug finished by next month and to say it put him in high gear is an understatement. He told me he didn't need a break but I told him that I did. From him."

"I confessed that I was the one who'd gotten him into that." I trudged up the stairs, disappointment making my feet heavy. Maybe he hadn't quite forgiven me.

My clothes melted against my skin the second my foot hit the top stair. The studio was like a sauna. A fan hummed in the corner, cheerfully churning the warm air around the room.

Marissa put the dresses over a chair. The gentle way

she arranged them didn't match up with the casual way she'd mentioned donating them to the high school. And the smile on her face when she looked down at them was…sad. How long had she been married? And what had happened?

"Would you like it iced or hot?" The sadness was gone now, swept away behind her usual serene expression.

"Iced. One to drink and one to dump on my head."

"I know it's hot up here. The air conditioner is on the fritz. I can't get anyone over here to fix it until Friday."

I didn't know how she could stand it. "What does Jim Briggs do?"

Marissa dropped an ice cube and it spun across the floor.

"Excavating. Why?"

"He just strikes me as the kind of guy who can fix anything. You should ask him to take a look at you…*it*."

"Oh, should I?" Marissa stared me down.

I'd watched some old Shirley Temple movies with Mom on satellite. I could do wide-eyed and innocent. "Just a suggestion."

"Uh-huh. Follow me." She pulled on a cord hanging above our heads and a piece of the ceiling dropped down. A rickety ladder that reminded me of the contraption Grandma Lowell used to dry her "unmentionables" was attached to it.

"Wow."

"I know. It's one of the reasons I bought this building."

Marissa scrambled up the ladder with the ease of a mountain climber and disappeared.

Up you go, Heather. This is a lot less dangerous than Lester's crop duster.

I tucked the glass of iced tea against my side and maneuvered up the rungs—which brought me onto the roof. And into a wonderland. Marissa was waiting for me in the middle of a garden. I wasn't an expert on artistic style but I could tell the sculptures scattered around us were Marissa's work. Pots overflowing with flowers and real live miniature palm trees crowded every inch of space around a circular stone patio in the center.

I couldn't believe this wasn't visible from the street.

Or maybe it was and I just hadn't noticed it. "This is incredible."

Marissa looked pleased and curled up in one of the umbrella-shaped chairs, drawing her bare feet under her. "This is my *being* place. When I'm up here, it clears out my head. The studio is my *doing* place. Even though I love my work, it's output. This is input."

Like Baby Bear, I wandered around the circle of mismatched chairs, poking cushions, until I chose a wicker rocker with a lumpy floral cushion. It reminded me of the furniture on Bree's sleeping porch at the farm. When I sat down, the scent of roses drifted up.

"I wish I had a being place." Even Dex had one—the musty cockpit of Lester's old crop duster.

Marissa smiled. "You'll find one. It takes time."

That was not comforting. I blew out a frustrated sigh. "What doesn't?"

"Let me think. Instant pudding. Hot dogs. Weeds."

She was right. And anything I said now would sound

like whining, even though whining would feel good. Really good. I crunched down on an ice cube to keep my mouth busy until I could come up with a safer topic than *waiting*.

"So, what are your plans at the end of the summer? Are you going back to Minneapolis?"

This was *not* a safer topic.

"I have a job opportunity with a ministry that helps single moms transition back into the workplace. It combines giving women advice about their lives and shopping. Two things that some people would say I excel at."

"Really?" Marissa murmured.

I searched for sarcasm. None there. I was free to move on. "It sounds like a perfect fit, doesn't it? And it's a *ministry*. I've been asking God to reveal His plan for my life this summer and I thought this was *it*. Until Bernice called last night—from Italy, I think—and offered to turn the salon over to me." I swirled the ice in my glass until it created a miniature whirlpool in the center.

"And you feel obligated to Bernice?"

"No! She and Alex told me they'd be fine with whatever I decided. I…" Was I brave enough to say it? "I love working in the salon. But that *can't* be the plan."

"Why not?"

She had to know the answer to that. Making a difference in women's lives verses trimming their split ends. This should be easy.

"Because it's…" I couldn't say the word *shallow*. Even though Mrs. Darnell had apologized, I still had some internal bruising. "Superficial. It's not important in the scheme of life. It's not a ministry." Even Dex had said so.

Marissa sat back in the chair and studied me. "You really believe that, don't you?"

I shrugged.

"Don't you think that God gave you the gifts He did for a reason?"

"That's just it. They aren't *gifts*. The things I'm good at aren't exactly mentioned in the Bible, but I have seen them in the class schedule for the cosmetology school I went to."

"That must be your answer, then. To apply for the job in Minneapolis…" Marissa's voice was as neutral as a referee's.

She was probably right. I could get excited about that one, too. When I'd read the job description, it sounded like it was designed specifically for me. So why did I still feel restless?

"…because people like Amanda Clark and Kaylie Darnell are customers. They aren't a *ministry*."

The iced tea took a detour into an airway it wasn't supposed to.

"They aren't just customers," I managed to squeak.

"No?"

My mouth dropped open. I saw where this was going. "You're good."

Now she laughed. "Food for thought."

And I was choking on it.

"Let me dust off my podium one more time." Marissa leaned forward. "Yes, God has a plan for your life, but

He usually doesn't play the entire thing all at once for us like a movie. Step by step. With Him. That's how it's going to unfold. You don't have to figure it all out right now. What God wants is *you*. He wants you to stay close. And if you do that, you'll hear His voice when He whispers in your ear—*this way.*"

That sounded too easy. And too hard.

Marissa must have sensed my confusion. "I have to get an order ready to ship tomorrow but go ahead and stay here for a while. I'm happy to share my being place with you."

"I thought I heard voices up here." Jared's head appeared in the trapdoor and then he hoisted himself onto the roof, smiling a guilt-free smile at me. "I stopped by your apartment a while ago."

"I was here." As if he hadn't figured that out for himself.

For some reason, my heart hadn't given that funny little kick I was used to feeling when I saw him.

"I wanted to take you for a ride. Maybe get something to eat." He glanced at his watch. "There's still time. It's only six-thirty."

The back of Jared's motorcycle was not a *being* place. And hanging out with him would be stirring another ingredient into my already muddled up head. Was this a good thing?

"So what did you end up doing over the weekend, Jared?" Marissa asked. "I didn't see you at the Fourth of July Frolic."

Was it my imagination, or did she emphasize the word *frolic?*

"I went to Madison on Saturday and Sunday morning

some friends of mine talked me into going swimming."
He glanced at me. "How did the float turn out?"

"We got first place in the Most Beautiful category. A
bunch of people came over to help." *But not you.*
"Marissa helped with the roses."

He must have heard something in my voice because
he reached out and took my hand. Right in front of
Marissa. "Every time I go somewhere in this town,
every Jethro Bodine and Daisy Duke stops me to ask me
how I'm doing on the statue. Then they give me a
detailed description of the clay dog they entered in the
fair when they were ten. I needed a chance to breathe
some air that wasn't tainted by cow manure. I knew
you'd understand. You're a temp, like me. I needed to
be in the real world. Get my center back."

"I'm not sure I'm a temp," I said slowly, testing each
word. They felt pretty good. "I might stay in Prichett."

He laughed. "Doing what?"

"Whatever God wants me to do." Saying that felt
pretty good, too.

Jared's eyebrow rose. It had been cute before, now it
looked…condescending. "If there is a God, He gave you
a brain for a reason. I think it's up to *you* to decide what
you want to do. All that God-stuff throws you off center."

If there is a God… Right then, I felt like an actress
in one of those natural disaster movies. The one where
the ground shakes and all of a sudden an earthquake
splits the ground between two people, leaving one of
them on one side and one on the other. With a crack as
deep as the Grand Canyon between them.

Jared was great. Gorgeous, funny, intelligent, creative. We had fun together. We had a lot in common. In the back of my mind I thought it would be really sweet of God to introduce me to my future husband while I was seeking His will about my future plans. Kind of like those two-for-one specials at the shoe store.

But something Kaylie had said that day at the salon came back to me. She was tired of being two people. If I got into a serious relationship with Jared, I'd end up trying to be two people, too. In small ways, it had already started to happen. And I knew myself well enough to know that eventually, just like Kaylie, it would tear me apart.

"Jared, I'm sorry I didn't tell you this before, but all that God-stuff? It *is* my center."

Chapter Twenty-Four

"Where do you want this, Heather?" Kaylie staggered into the salon, her arms wrapped around a suitcase-size cardboard box. I rushed over to help her.

Too heavy for crepe paper. "What's in it?"

"I have no idea. Denise said she found these in the basement and we could give them out as prizes." Kaylie turned her head and sneezed.

"I think Denise is unloading her entire inventory on us," I grumbled. The week before, she'd sent over a box of something she'd referred to as *decorations*. Definitely a stretch. When Kaylie and I had looked inside, it was overflowing with bunches of artificial purple grapes, attached to plastic leaves that were a sickly shade of yellow, as if the grapes had been attacked by a nasty blight. I would've rejected them even if our theme for Junebug's unveiling were An Afternoon in Tuscany instead of Art in the Park. It wasn't very catchy but it was better than Junebug Day, which Lester had been pushing for.

"Any guesses?" Kaylie put the box on the floor and grinned up at me.

"Giant pencils with tassels on the ends? Erasers shaped like monkeys?"

"I'll vote for the monkeys." Kaylie ripped off the packing tape and pulled back the flaps. "Ta-da!"

We both stared into the box, momentarily mesmerized by the gleam of gold.

"Ah, are those…elephants?"

"I think they're aardvarks."

"Aardvarks?" I pulled a plastic-wrapped figurine out of the box and studied it. It might have looked like solid gold, but it was so lightweight it had to be plastic. Whatever it was, it sat proudly on a matching gold base.

"It has to be an elephant. Look at its trunk."

"I guess so." Kaylie still didn't sound convinced.

I looked closer. Across the bottom of the stand, in block letters, were the words *THE BESS*. I pitched over onto my side and laughed like a hyena with a few uncontrollable snorts thrown in.

"What are you…" Kaylie started to say, and suddenly she was twitching on the floor next to me.

Thank goodness it was Annie who walked in and found us like that. Anyone else would have dialed 911. She made sure the contents of the box weren't something the feds needed to check out, and joined us on the floor.

I was the first one to recover. "Who do you suppose Bess is?"

"An aardvark?" Kaylie asked, which started the whole thing all over again.

"What are these *for?*" Annie gasped. "And can I have one?"

"Denise sent them over as prizes for Art in the Park day."

"I heard about that. Candy asked Stephen if the youth group could oversee the dunk tank that day."

I hated to contradict her. "We don't have a dunk tank."

Annie gave me a sympathetic pat on the knee. "Yes, you do."

I groaned. After two weeks of working with the PAC, I was beginning to see a pattern. The members of the committee worked, both individually and in pairs, to create chaos and my role, as chairman, was to chase along behind them and straighten things up.

The chaos had started with Amanda and Sally, who wanted the food served that day to be elegant. Now they were caught up in a feud with someone named Ed, who rolled out his portable hot dog stand for every town event. I, as chairman, was expected to be the mediator. Marissa had warned me when Ed, "the hot dog man," was going to come to the next PAC meeting. Whenever he'd shown up in the past, he'd dressed up like a giant ketchup bottle. I was already bracing myself for flashbacks.

Annie turned to Kaylie. "I ran into your mom at the grocery store and she mentioned you were working today. We're having a special speaker come in for our youth rally next week and I need someone to make sure things run smoothly that night. Interested?"

Kaylie hesitated. I knew she and Annie had been

meeting the past two weeks for prayer and I'd seen a real change in the way she interacted with people who came into the salon—but I had a feeling the Cut and Curl had become a safety net for her. Even when she wasn't working, she came in to straighten up the back room, check the inventory or restock the candy drawer.

"Think about it." Annie saw the expression on Kaylie's face and backed off. That's one thing I loved about Annie. Her ability to look into someone's eyes and read what was in their heart.

"Who's the speaker?" I asked, easing my way into the silence.

"Someone named Tony Gillespie," Annie said. "From what Stephen said, he's in high demand as a speaker, but he only accepts three speaking invitations a year."

"How did you and Stephen end up getting him to come to Prichett?" I loved Faith Community Church, but it was a small church—not exactly the kind that drew big-name speakers.

"Dex knows him. He's been helping Stephen get everything set up."

Maybe that explained why Dex had been a no-show at the apartment for the past two weeks. The day after he'd taken me up in Lester's plane, I'd come home and found the bookshelf upright and in the corner where it belonged. I'd checked Haggai but there were no new updates. It was weird, but I'd gotten used to having Dex around, messing up my life. Leaving notes in my Bible. Falling asleep on my couch.

Annie stood up and brushed off the knees of her

jeans. "It's been fun laughing hysterically with you girls, but I've got to get back to the nest."

Kaylie caught up to Annie at the door. "I'll help you."

I gave God an imaginary high five. *Yes.*

"Great. Next Wednesday. Be at church by five." Annie smiled at me over Kaylie's shoulder. "You can come, too, Heather. Technically this is for the youth, but bring a pan of brownies and I'll make you an official part of the kitchen crew."

"I'll try." Between working at the salon and organizing Art in the Park, I hadn't had much free time. But I was curious about Tony Gillespie, especially knowing that Dex had been instrumental in getting him to come to Prichett. Maybe Tony was a missionary with the organization that Dex would be working for. Flying planes. Who would have thunk it?

"She'll be there." Kaylie tossed a look at me. "She won't be able to help herself."

Brownies aside, she was right. My natural curiosity was going to get the best of me. Argh. Was I that transparent?

Annie's laughter followed her out the door.

I went back to the counter and put a line through one of my afternoon appointments, which had canceled because her daughter's monarch butterfly was about to hatch and they were videotaping it. "Are you ready for lunch yet?"

"It's Tuesday, isn't it?" Kaylie looked a little nervous and I didn't blame her. Thai Tuesday hadn't taken off, leaving Sally and Amanda poring over the world atlas to come up with another theme. The book club had gotten in on it, too, and come up with a creative alternative.

"'Talian Tuesday."

"Talia? Where's that? And what kind of food is it?"

"It's short for *I*talian, which means all-you-can-eat spaghetti and meatballs. And they have it to go."

"I'll be right back." Kaylie grabbed her purse and took off.

"Bread sticks!" I shouted just as the door shut.

I straightened the pile of magazines, checked the level of coffee in the coffeepot and wiped out the sinks. The phone wasn't ringing off the hook—maybe because the spies Candy had planted on the roofs of Main Street had seen Kaylie walking down the sidewalk to the café.

The door opened and I turned around.

"Do you have time for a walk-in?" Jared stood just inside the door.

I sucked in a breath and then let it out again. Slowly. "You want me to cut your hair?"

"The Buzz and Blade is closed. There's a note on the door saying something about a goat that let a bunch of cows out of the barn." I could tell by the gleam in his eyes he was hoping Junebug was one of them.

"That messed up my morning, too," I deadpanned. "And the monarch butterfly that's about to hatch. *National Geographic* is filming it."

Jared wandered in. He hadn't called me since the day we'd talked on Marissa's roof. Thirteen days ago. Maybe I wasn't the only one who'd seen that chasm open up between us.

"Kaylie went to get us some lunch, but she won't be back for a while because Amanda's drafted her into being their dessert taste-tester." *Rambling again, Heather.*

"Where do you want me?" Jared thrust his hands in the pockets of his jeans.

Sitting next to me in church on Sunday morning? Did I say that out loud? No, thank goodness.

"Over here." I patted the back of the chair.

He sat down and tilted his head to look up at me. "I miss you, Heather."

I knew what he meant. I didn't spend my spare time scoping out the alley for Jared-sightings (well, maybe a few times when I was emptying the recyclables) but he was good company. "Yeah. I kind of miss you, too. Have a seat. Because of the butterfly, I have time for you."

"I hope so."

Our eyes met in the mirror.

"I know I'm not high on your list right now…" Jared began.

Oh, you have no idea how high you are…

I squashed the thought mid-sigh. That was another thing unexpected alone time had accomplished. If I ever found The List, I was going to throw it away. Flush it. Incinerate it. Whatever. I'd come to the conclusion that if I could trust God with my future, I could trust Him to know exactly what I needed in a husband. I'd take that step by step, too, and listen for Him to whisper (or shout) the guy's name in my ear when the time was right.

"But I still want to hang out with you. We don't have

to pick out towels together or anything, maybe hang out together. Go for an occasional ride."

Do you think you, your ego and I will all fit on your motorcycle?

Mean, Heather. I scolded myself. It's not like I was perfect. "I'd like that."

Jared looked relieved. He stretched out his legs as I fumbled with the spray bottle. "By the way, I heard a rumor yesterday."

"Just one?" Must have been a slow day for the grapevine.

"Someone said you were related to Alex Scott, the actor. That you're, like, his daughter." There was laughter in his voice and he looked at me expectantly, waiting for me to deny it.

I exhaled, wincing at the sharp pain that rolled along with it. "That would be the truth."

Jared's eyes almost popped out of his head. "Seriously?"

Fleetingly, I wondered who'd told him. We'd been seen together enough that someone might have mentioned it, thinking Jared already knew. "It's true."

"I can't believe you're even thinking of staying in this one-horse town. You could be working on location somewhere. Traveling. Club hopping with the rich and famous."

I stared at him. Never in a million years had I considered asking Alex to find me a job. "I'd never use Alex like that."

"Don't think of it as using him. Besides, he must have walked out on you, right? He owes you something."

There was no way I was going to share my story with Jared. My hands were shaking and I knotted my fingers together. "I wouldn't feel right about doing that."

"This is where your religion clouds your thinking." Jared gave me a *poor deluded Heather* look. "When you see an opportunity, you should take it."

"How did you want me to cut your hair?"

He looked irritated that I'd changed the subject. "I don't know. Surprise me."

I picked up the scissors, lopped off his ponytail and handed it to him. Jared squawked and sprang out of the chair.

"What did you do that for?"

"I saw an opportunity and I took it."

Chapter Twenty-Five

"Heather—are you listening?"

I hadn't been but I couldn't admit it. Not when everyone around the table was staring at me. The regular PAC meeting was scheduled for next week, but I'd called an emergency session to finalize some details for Art in the Park.

"One more time?" I scribbled on the piece of paper in front of me, pretending I'd been taking notes. Note taking was more acceptable than daydreaming.

"What are you going to do about Ed?" Candy asked, as if Ed "the hot dog man" Bonnewicz wasn't standing in the corner as stiff as the Tin Man in the *Wizard of Oz,* listening to every word we said.

I smiled at him. "We're glad you could make it, Mr. Bonnewicz."

His left eye started to twitch when everyone's attention turned to him. Tall and gaunt, with wire-rimmed glasses and a handlebar mustache, he reminded me of someone in a Norman Rockwell painting. Minus the ketchup suit.

"This is a special event we're having in the park," Candy barked at him. "Special events call for special circumstances."

"My grandfather donated that park to the town, so I've got the right to sell my hot dogs at every goings-on there." Ed's foam cap jiggled with indignation.

"We're trying to make this event a little more…" Sally tried to find the right word.

"Upscale," Amanda said helpfully.

"And we're catering the luncheon from Sally's," Denise said.

I knew this meant Sally and Amanda were *carrying* the finger sandwiches and miniature cream puffs from the café to the park.

"But we *want* you to sell hot dogs, Mr. Bonnewicz," I interrupted.

"We do?"

"You do?"

Amanda, Sally and Ed's voices bumped together.

"Sure we do, but keeping our theme in mind—" I ignored Denise, who raised her eyebrows and mouthed the words *what theme* at Candy "—we were picturing you in, oh, a white vest and a snazzy red bow tie. Maybe even some *spats*."

Ed looked down at his feet, encased in gigantic red slippers. "Debonair. Mmm."

I gave Amanda a meaningful look and she stepped up to the plate.

"That's right." Amanda nodded vigorously. "The ketchup costume just doesn't make the most of your... physique."

Denise made a face and pushed the brownies away.

Ed looked thoughtful now, even with his cheeks stained as red as the suit he was wearing. "I suppose if that artist can get his hair cut and make himself look *respectable,* I can, too."

I started to choke but no one noticed.

"We need to vote on it." Denise crossed her arms and there was a chorus of agreement. *Now* they wanted to follow the rules.

"Fine. All those in favor of Ed in spats, say aye," Candy bellowed.

It was unanimous. Even Denise voted yes. When I raised my eyebrows at her, she smiled. "We have to keep things democratic here."

I was suddenly very tired.

"Everyone has their to-do list. We'll have another meeting next week. Adjourned." I started to gather up my notes and Marissa leaned closer.

"You didn't have anything to do with the artist's respectable haircut, did you?"

"Please don't ask me that."

Jim Briggs must have overheard our conversation, because he winked at me. "The apple doesn't fall far from the tree, does it?"

I had no idea what he meant by that. I'd have to remember to ask Bernice.

* * *

I was sure I'd turned the lights off in the apartment
when I left but as I got closer to the building, I could
see a glow behind the curtains in the living room. Maybe
Dex was back, working on an unscheduled project. Like
regrouting the bathroom tile. Or tearing out a wall.

I nudged open the door an inch. "Dex?"

"Where have you been?" The door flew open; I was
yanked inside and hugged to death.

"Mama B?" Smothered against her shoulder, I saw
Alex standing by the window, giving us some space for
our reunion. He was smiling at me while he waited for
his turn. "What are you guys doing back so soon?"

"When you've seen one ancient ruin, you've seen
them all," Bernice sniffled. "You look great. Doesn't she
look great, Alex?"

"I'm too far away to tell."

I held out my arm and Alex moved into the circle. His
hug wasn't as exuberant as Bernice's but I could feel the
strength in his arms as they went around me. And the
love. Tears spilled onto my cheeks.

"You should have warned me."

"I know, I would have killed someone if they'd done
this to me." Bernice laughed. "But you surprised me that
time, if you remember. I owe you one."

"How could I forget?"

Arms wound together, we stumbled over to the couch
like we were competing in the three-legged race at the
Fourth of July Frolic. Snap immediately leaped into

Bernice's lap and began padding up and down her leg, purring madly.

"I was at a PAC meeting," I told them. "If I'd known you were coming, I would have scheduled it for another night."

"*You* scheduled it?"

"It was an emergency meeting because of the hot dog man. I'm in charge of Art in the Park—Junebug's big unveiling ceremony." I held my breath, hoping she wouldn't mention Jared. I wasn't ready to talk about him yet. "Overall, things are pretty much the way they were when you left."

"I love that." Bernice sighed deeply and looked around. "How did the carpenter work out? It looks like he's been busy around here."

"The carpenter? Oh, you mean *Dex*. First of all, he's a missionary, *not* a carpenter. But he did pretty well." *If I didn't count the poisonous vapors from the floor varnish, Snap's mysterious disappearance and my missing faucet.*

There was a tap on the door and when I opened it, Candy was there. "I saw the car parked outside. Figured it had to be *his*."

She peered over my shoulder.

"They're back. Come on in." I stepped to the side and heard Bernice's squeal of delight.

Within the next half hour, Elise, Sam and Bree showed up. Then Sally, with two banana cream pies, and Denise, followed by Marissa a few minutes later, wearing a flowered robe that looked like a kimono. When

Stephen and Annie came in with the twins, though, it was like Christmas morning. I perched on the arm of the chair, watching Bernice cuddle Nathaniel as everyone talked over each other. Alex, Sam and Stephen found an empty corner and held up the wall while they talked.

"So how's the town been?" Bernice asked. "It's hard to tell when it's sleeping."

"There've been a few changes." Candy's eyes met mine. I sucked in a breath and waited. "For the better, I'd say."

Sally nodded. "You'll have to try my coffee, Bernie. People say it's better than yours."

Bernice and Alex stopped in to see me at the salon the next morning, but eventually Alex was squeezed out by the continuous stream of women who'd heard through the grapevine that Bernice was back.

"I'm going to try Sally's coffee. I'll be back." He tried to escape but Mrs. Kirkwood walked in and blocked his path. She pulled a dainty handkerchief out of her purse, rubbed the lenses on her bifocals and balanced them on the end of her nose.

"You look younger on television."

"Ah…thank you." Someone opened the door and Alex made a break for it.

Mrs. Kirkwood presented Bernice with a foil pan. "It's about time you stopped skipping around the world and came home. You're too old for that kind of nonsense. Here. I made you some cloverleaf rolls."

"That's so sweet, Mrs. Kirkwood—"

"Don't eat too many. On your type of figure, they go straight to the hips."

I heard Kaylie gasp. She probably wondered if she was next in line for the firing squad. She'd already had her stress quota filled for the day when Bernice and Alex had walked in just after we opened. I inched in front of Kaylie, offering myself as a sacrifice, just in case. My pitiful attempt to shield Kaylie backfired. Mrs. Kirkwood marched up to me.

"Mrs. Kirkwood, would you like a cup of coffee?" Bernice tried to distract her, too, but the elderly woman waved her away like she was a pesky fly.

"You know I get heart palpitations just sitting next to that coffeepot." She took a step to the side and so did I, blocking her view of Kaylie.

Kaylie's confidence had been growing the past few weeks but one word from Mrs. Kirkwood could inflict enough damage to send her to the back room for the next five years.

Kaylie eased out from behind me before I could stop her. "Hi, Mrs. Kirkwood."

"The proper way to greet someone in a business establishment is with a *good morning* or a *good afternoon*." Mrs. Kirkwood glowered at Kaylie but she responded with a grin.

"I'll remember that, Mrs. Kirkwood."

"Be sure that you do." She swung around and Bernice and I both ducked. "Next Thursday, eight o'clock."

After she left, Kaylie disappeared into the back room, just like I was afraid she would. When I followed her, she was standing by the candy drawer, her eyes wide. "She was mean to me."

I was about to apologize but I noticed Kaylie was still grinning. Maybe it was Kirkwood-induced post-traumatic stress syndrome. "Don't pay any attention to her. She's mean to everyone."

"I know." She still looked like the Cheshire cat.

I was missing something here. Kaylie must have seen my confusion. "She treated me like she does everyone else."

"Kaylie, I'm not sure that's a reason to smile."

"Oh, yes it is. It means she doesn't feel sorry for me." Kaylie handed me a piece of chocolate. "Eat this, Heather. You look a little pale."

Chapter Twenty-Six

Tony Gillespie wasn't at all what I expected. He looked like a surfer, with sun-bleached hair, vivid green eyes and a brush of golden freckles across his nose. For some reason I'd expected someone older but Tony was close to my age. And he was in a wheelchair.

I took a seat in the back of the church while the teenagers squirmed in the pews, whispering. I looked around but there was no sign of Dex anywhere.

Stephen introduced Tony, who wheeled himself as close as he could to the audience. When he said hello, I understood why. Even with a microphone, his voice was low-pitched and husky. Then he leaned forward. "You should see the other guy."

There was a faint, nervous ripple of laughter but in that moment, everyone in the room fell in love with Tony Gillespie. Including me.

"Churches ask me to come and give my testimony," Tony said. "I never quite get that. My testimony is the same as it was five years ago, when the car I was driving rolled over and hit a tree. I got to know Jesus in Sunday school when I was eight. When I was thirteen, I decided He was telling the truth about who He was. When I was sixteen, I went to a youth rally and committed myself to God—and to full-time ministry. That's my testimony." Tony let a silence fill the room. We knew there was more. And so did he. "My love for God didn't change, even though my plans for the future did."

"My senior year, I started a Bible study that met after school on Fridays. The study happened to end the same time as detention, so every Friday a guy walked out the door with me and gave me a hard time about God. It was a big school but I'd heard about him. That he was a troublemaker. Was on his way to a serious alcohol problem. We started to talk. I'd tell him about God and he'd make fun of me. One Friday night, close to graduation, I was on my way home from the video store when an oncoming car crossed the centerline. I didn't have time to react. It hit me pretty much head-on." Tony paused and I could hear the silence stretching across the room. "Now I don't have to worry about wearing out my shoes."

Silence.

"Come on now. Even if a joke's bad, if a preacher's telling it, you have to laugh."

The laughter was soft. Hesitant.

"People ask me why God would allow something like this to happen. I'd committed myself to Him. To full-time ministry. Now I can't walk. But I want you to hear something. I *am* in full-time ministry. It doesn't look the way I thought it would, but there was a reason God allowed the accident to happen. Maybe it was because the first person I saw when I opened my eyes was my friend from detention. He was the first person I saw because he was the one who hit me." Tony broke off suddenly and smiled. "The best part of my story isn't what happened before the accident, it was what happened *after* it. My friend—the one who said he'd never seen evidence of God—is going into full-time ministry. God can take the worst day of our life and make it better. He loves to multiply things. Instead of one missionary, He got two. And those two are going to multiply again. To fifty. Or a hundred. Or a thousand."

I noticed Dex standing in the shadows in the back of the church. I motioned to the empty seat beside me, but he moved away in the opposite direction. Typical.

The youth group surrounded Tony after his message, so I went into the kitchen to get the snacks out. Stephen had ordered pizzas and I put them all out on a long table, skipping the silverware because these were teenagers, so what was the point? They swarmed into the kitchen like one of Pharaoh's plagues and ate everything in their path. Since it was smart not to be too close when that occurred, I loaded up the cardboard boxes and took them outside to the Dumpster.

Dex was leaning against the wall, staring up at the sky. I had the feeling he was wishing he were in his plane.

"Hey. There's pizza inside."

He didn't look at me. Strike one. I claimed the spot on the wall beside him.

"Tony has a powerful message, doesn't he?"

"Yeah."

"Annie said he's a good friend of yours."

Dex didn't answer. A tear suddenly rolled down his cheek. What shocked me the most wasn't that he was crying but that he didn't bother to try to hide it. Mr. Unemotional? *Crying?* Without thinking, I reached out and grabbed his hand, giving it a little shake to get his attention. "I'm sorry, Dex. Did you know him before the accident?"

Dex looked down at me. "Yes. I knew him *before* the accident."

There was something in his voice now that didn't belong there. I tried to sort through it. Not just pain. It was deeper than that. The instant I realized what it was, Dex nodded.

"Yeah. I was the guy who hit him."

He eased his hand out of mine and walked away.

I didn't see Dex the rest of the evening but Tony waved me over, as I was about to leave.

"You're Heather, aren't you?" He had an infectious smile that made you want to smile back. So I did.

"Yes, I am."

"So…did you decide to stay in Prichett?"

That surprised me. Annie must have said something to him.

"I'm not sure yet. Still praying about it."

"God has a way of turning things upside down. But later on, we find out they're really right side up. The way they were meant to be. It was *us* who had them upside down."

"You're going to have to write that down for me."

Tony laughed. "He said I'd like you."

I bent down and gave him an impulsive, holy kiss on the cheek. "Who's been talking about me? Stephen?"

He tilted his head and looked at me, his eyes clear and lively. "Dex."

"Why would Dex talk about me?"

Tony laughed again and shook his head. "Why wouldn't he?"

The kitchen crew finished cleaning up just before eleven and I turned down several offers for a ride home. I needed time to process so I wandered down the middle of Main Street, guided by the streetlights.

I tried to imagine how Dex felt every time he relived his past in Tony's testimony. A troublemaker. Skeptical about God. Turning to alcohol to cope. Then I added the few things Dex had told me about himself. That he'd been raising his siblings. That he was going into the mission field to take someone's place. *Tony*'s place. Did that mean even though Tony accepted the way his life had changed, Dex still felt guilty because he'd been the one who'd forced Tony's life down another road? And those tears…the accident had happened five years ago, but the pain in Dex's eyes told me that he relived it every day.

I tried to put the Ian Dexter I knew back into the little box I'd created for him when we'd met, but he didn't fit anymore.

God, whatever Dex is going through right now, show him that You're there.

That's when I remembered something Dex had said in the plane. About bearing each other's burdens and having to be close enough to touch them in order to do that. I knew where Pastor Charles lived so I changed directions and sprinted down a few side streets until I found the house. The lights were still on but I didn't question my impulsive decision until I was standing at the front door. And *after* I rang the bell.

Dex answered the door. Too easy. I pulled him outside. "Come on."

I'd taken him by surprise, but now he dug his stubborn heels in the dirt and wouldn't budge. "I'm going to bed."

"No, you aren't. If you were wearing your *Star Wars* pajamas, I'd believe you. Let's go." One more tug and he was moving. Except now that I had him, I wasn't sure what to do with him.

"You can let go of me."

I let go of his hand but kept a close eye on him. Those television magicians couldn't compare to Dex when he decided to pull one of his disappearing acts.

"Where are we going?"

"I have no idea." I hated to admit that. I should have had a destination in mind. "Just work with me, all right? I'm making this up as I go along."

"Why?"

The question hovered in the air between us. I didn't know the answer to that one, either, but I could tell he was waiting for an answer. "Maybe I thought you'd want to be alone. Like you thought I wanted to be alone that day Mrs. Darnell came into the salon."

'We turned the corner at Main Street. Now that we were out of the shadows, I tried to read his expression. There was a faint smile on his face. "You aren't going to take me up in Lester's plane, are you?"

"Don't dare me or I'll have to try. I hate to admit it, but I'm that kind of person." I suddenly knew where I was going to take him. I snagged his elbow and steered him across the street toward the park. When we reached the swings, I pushed one toward him and sat down in the one next to it.

"I suppose you want to hear every miserable detail?" Dex asked.

"Yup." I knew he'd manage to condense the story in ten words or less.

Dex was silent and I thought he'd done the turtle-thing again. He pushed back with his heels, setting the swing in motion.

"It was like Tony said. My mom—who happens to be Pastor Charles's half sister—was an alcoholic. She worked nights for a cleaning service and slept all day. She drank to forget that Dad left her for his secretary. That left me taking care of things at home. Grocery shopping. Feeding my brothers and sisters. Making sure they got their homework done. I got sick of it—and decided if alcohol helped Mom forget her troubles, maybe it would work for me, too. And it did, for a while. I got in trouble and ended up with three months of after-school detention. That's how I met Tony. I couldn't stand him. The guy was seriously deranged. I mean, he was happy *all the time*."

I heard the warmth in Dex's voice and waited.

"I hadn't been drinking when I hit his car. I fell asleep at the wheel for about five seconds. *Five seconds.* One of my sisters was sick and I was up with her all night. I walked away without a scratch, but Tony…Tony was driving one of those little matchbox cars. It spun around and hit the ditch. I thought he was dead and I was so ticked off at him. If anyone should have been dead, it should have been *me*. I started yelling at him, telling him that. He opened his eyes and told me that *I* wasn't ready to die and to shut up because I was giving him a headache." Dex smiled at the memory.

"When I finally scraped up the courage to visit him in the hospital, he took advantage of my guilty conscience. Every day it was, *Dex, can you read John chapter one to me? Dex, can you read Romans 8:28? Can you look in the notes in the back of my Bible and remind me what it means to be saved by grace?* The day I became a Christian was the day he told me that my soul was worth more than his legs. Hatred, anger, resentment—those were things I'd seen all my life. Forgiveness and second chances were all new to me."

I looked down, hoping he wouldn't notice I was about to cry like a baby. Tony's testimony had been powerful but, for some reason, Dex's affected me even more. "Why don't you and Tony travel together? Give *your* testimony?"

Dex shook his head. "Because of my background, I need a lot of space around me. God's still working on that part of my life. Tony's always been outgoing. He's like you. He connects with people. I fly planes."

"You connect with people better than you think you do. Kaylie. The residents at the Golden Oaks. You just proved you can talk when you want to." I was teasing him but Dex didn't look at me. He tilted his head back and stared up at the sky.

"It's hard to talk when the person you're with takes your breath away."

It took a few seconds for his words to register and when they did, I was the one who couldn't breathe.

He stood up. "I'll walk you back."

Just like that.

"I think I'll stay here a little longer. I need to think." *About what you just said. And what it meant.*

Dex was already walking away, blending into the shadows of the trees. Suddenly he turned around and started walking backward. I could see the moonlight flash across his face. "I think you should stay here."

"I *am* staying here."

"Not in the park. In Prichett."

"You were the one who said cutting hair wasn't going to impact the world!"

"It won't. But *you* can." I heard the laughter in his voice. "If you've got a pair of scissors in your hand at the time, it'll just be more fun for you."

I stayed in the park for another hour, thinking about Tony. Praying for Dex. And for myself. Remembering the conversations I'd had with Marissa. And Jared. All the thoughts racing through my head should have muddled things up even more, but it was just the opposite.

I'm not sure that God isn't more interested in what we let Him do in us than in what we do.

Cutting hair won't impact the world…but you can.

I thought that Prichett would be a quiet place to listen to God reveal His plan for my life. Was it possible that Prichett *was* the plan?

When my cell phone rang, I'd just finished winding the swing up like a top, giddy with the knowledge that Tony was right about God turning things upside down.

"Hello?" I managed to flip it open and gasp the word into it as I spun myself dizzy.

"Go home."

"How do you know I'm not home?"

"Because I've been sitting on your stairs for the last hour, waiting for you to show up."

"Dex? You're right. I'm going to stay. In Prichett. At least until Bernice and Alex come back in December. It makes sense right now." One step at a time, that's what Marissa had said. I wanted to say more, but I couldn't. Something had changed between us and I wasn't sure what it was. Whatever it was, it felt so fragile I didn't want to damage it with hasty words.

Dex mumbled something.

"What?"

"Tony asked me to go back with him. I've got ninety percent of my support raised and Faith Community is going to supply the rest."

"You're *leaving?*" I planted my feet and the swing

lurched to a stop. He was going to disappear again but this time, it was for good. My stomach wobbled—and it wasn't because I'd spun myself dizzy on the swing.

"Tomorrow afternoon."

"Oh. Tomorrow. I'll be praying for you." Ugh. Everyone said that. It was the Christian equivalent of the "have a nice day" the rest of the world handed out. But I *meant* it.

"What are you going to pray?" Dex read between the lines of Christianese, pushing me. He was more like Tony than he thought. His faith made me want to be more faithful.

I closed my eyes and recited the blessing that Annie had said for Greta. And I didn't feel weird doing it, either, because this was Dex. And Dex—for all his quirks—understood. "God bless you and keep you. The Lord make His face shine upon you and be gracious to you. The Lord turn His face toward you and give you peace."

There was a soft click. He'd hung up on me. Again. But this time, I thought I heard him say goodbye. I ran all the way home but when I got there, Dex was already gone.

Chapter Twenty-Seven

Best part of today
(From the book *Real Men Write in Journals*)

Looking forward to tomorrow. (Dex)

"I can't believe you pulled this off." Bernice linked her arm through mine as we stood in the shade of the Cut and Curl's awning and watched the park fill up with people.

"There is quite a turnout." I smiled, inwardly twirling and shouting out a *praise you, God*. The things I could control—like Ed wearing a red silk bow tie and removing the plastic Roman columns Denise had positioned around the statue of Junebug—had turned out fine. The things I couldn't control, I refused to obsess over. And it looked like I didn't have to.

Art in the Park wasn't officially scheduled to start until noon but Main Street was already packed with cars and people. The August day was sunny and warm, with puffs of white clouds in the sky and enough of a breeze to keep everyone comfortable. As close to perfect as a day could get.

"I'm not talking about the turnout. People are so starved for something to do around here they would've shown up if the PAC announced they were holding an apple-bobbing contest. I'm talking about the way you got the committee to do something *different*. I've been trying for ten years to push them out of their rut."

"We did things pretty much the same but added a few twists."

"Twists are your specialty." Mom smiled at Bernice over my head and the two of them shared The Look. I grabbed Mom's hand and gave it a squeeze. This should have felt weird—like we'd been sucked into a movie on the Hallmark Channel—but it didn't. Mom and Bernice weren't anything alike but they liked each other. And they both loved me. Mom had said that that was the only common ground they needed.

Mom and Dad had come to Prichett the night before and stayed at Charity O'Malley's bed-and-breakfast, affectionately called The Lightning Strike Inn by the locals. After they'd settled in, I gave them the official behind-the-scenes tour of Prichett. They both fell in love with it, which surprised me, because Dad was raised in the city and Mom knows the employees at Bloomingdale's by name.

Over pie and coffee at the café, I'd told them I'd decided to turn down the job in Minneapolis and stay in Prichett longer. That kind of news I had to tell them in person. I was worried they'd be upset, but the parental radar must have indicated I'd been leaning this way even before I knew it myself.

"Interested in checking out the dunk tank?" Bernice whispered.

I tried not to smile. Prichett had its own unique way of making sure people stayed humble. Jared's statue may have been the reason the town was celebrating, but Jared had been given the seat of honor in the tank.

"I think I inflicted enough damage on Jared," I said, still feeling a twinge of guilt about my imitation of a Samurai warrior. "I already gave him a new hairstyle. I probably shouldn't dunk him, too."

"You don't have to dunk him." Mom smiled innocently. "You can just watch."

"You two are terrible."

"Uh-huh." Bernice grinned. "Let's go."

"All right, all right." I rolled my eyes and let them tug me across the street.

Annie saw us and waved both arms to get our attention. She and the twins were sprawled on a colorful blanket spread out under a tree. Elise and Esther Crandall were sitting with her.

"Where's Bree?" I looked around.

"I think she and Riley mentioned something about the dunk tank," Elise said.

I gulped. "I'll be right back."

"Go ahead, honey. We'll catch up with you in a few minutes." Mom was already cooing at Joanna and Bernice was reaching for Nathaniel.

I wormed my way through the crowd and suddenly came face-to-face with Junebug. The *real* one. As coordinator for the event, I knew she wasn't on the guest list. But at least she was on a lead rope—which Lester was holding.

"Lester? What is Junebug doing here?" *And did the town's insurance policy cover cow attacks?*

He looked confused at the question. "She's the honorary guest."

Jared might disagree with that, but okay. "Lester, Junebug has a reputation for being…" *How to put this in a nice way?* "Unpredictable."

He shrugged off my concern. "She's in a good mood today. Look at her. Pleased as punch to be here."

I wasn't going to argue with the good mood part of his statement. I took a wary step closer. She did look kind of cute. Lester had tied a big blue bow around her neck and given her a pedicure—there was black shoe polish on her hooves. I glanced at Lester, looking for signs of a struggle. He was wearing new overalls, the fold lines still fresh, and the handkerchief around his neck matched Junebug's bow. And he looked pleased as punch, too.

"I suppose she can stay." I wasn't going to be the one who pointed a finger at the No Pets Allowed sign at the entrance of the park and banished them to the farm.

"Heather! Over here." Bree's voice was almost drowned out by the sudden cheer from the wall of people I was trying to push through. She flagged me down by waving her cowboy hat over their heads.

"What's going on?" I called.

"See for yourself." Several people stepped to the

side, giving me a courtside view of the dunk tank. Jared was sitting on the platform, wet and seething. I skirted around a deluxe stroller that looked like a day care on wheels to see who was responsible.

Dex.

I blinked, just to make sure he didn't disappear. No. He was still there, standing at the line, tossing the baseball up in the air and catching it with one hand. *But he'd left town.* The sudden warmth that spread through me had nothing to do with the sunshine.

"Did Dex dunk him?" I whispered.

"Six times so far. The guy should go pro."

"Six times…" He really was full of surprises. It could take *years* to figure out someone like Dex.

Splash. Cheer.

"Seven."

Jared crawled back up the ladder, shaking water like a Labrador retriever during duck season.

"Hand me another one, Candy." Dex deftly caught the baseball she tossed at him.

I sidled up to him. "Let someone else have a turn, Mr. Ruth."

Riley winked at me. "I'll take over."

Candy dug around in a box and handed Dex a gold elephant that proclaimed he was *THE BESS*. "I believe this is yours."

"What are you *doing* here?" Was I grinning like an idiot? Because it felt like I was.

"I came back for the weekend. I couldn't miss the chance to support Junebug's career."

He'd come back for a cow.

What did you expect, Heather?

There was no defining my relationship with Dex. And did we even have a relationship to define?

My attention snagged on the subtle differences I saw in him. He looked more relaxed, as if there was a smile lurking just below the surface of his serious expression. I gave him a subtle head-to-toe scan. The faded khakis and white T-shirt he wore weren't exactly cutting edge but, when added to those nerdy absentminded-professor glasses, he looked *good*. For the first time I noticed the eagle tattooed on his forearm. *Whoa*. I couldn't take any more surprises.

We stared at each other until Bree coughed. "Riley and I are going to get a hot dog from Ed's stand. We'll catch up with you guys later."

"Did she just say something?" I frowned.

Dex pushed his hand through his hair. "I'm not sure. Walk with me?"

"Okay."

As if someone had choreographed it, we went straight for the swings on the other side of the park. I sat down but Dex didn't. He put one hand on the chain of my swing and looked up at the sky.

"Dex—"

He shushed me. "Wait your turn."

I pressed my lips together and pretended I was turning a key. Dex put out his hand and I dropped the "key" into it. His fingers closed around it.

"The first time I met you—and I swear I didn't notice

you were wearing a bathrobe—this is what I saw. A girl who wore shoes that matched her earrings—" He must have seen the sparkle in my eyes because he rolled his. "Yes, I noticed. I noticed the expensive clothes and the pink lipstick, too."

"I know…you thought I was shallow."

He shook the invisible key in front of my face and I pressed my lips together again.

"Maybe for the first five minutes. After that, I thought you were like the best Christmas present under the tree—the one that didn't have my name on it."

My throat closed. I wanted to hold those words and study them but Dex kept talking, so I had to keep up.

"All summer long I tried to stay away from you and I think God laughed every time He put you in my path. There was no getting away from you."

There was no getting away from you. And here I'd been thinking I couldn't get away from *him*. But I'd also thought he couldn't talk and was disconnected from his emotions, which proved when it came to Dex, I knew nothing at all. But I wanted to know more. That amazing thought hit me, knocking every coherent thought out of my head. Even if Dex had given me back the key, I wouldn't have been able to say a word.

"There are things in my past I haven't worked through yet. I don't deserve the life I have now, so I wouldn't have the guts to ask God for more. Especially someone to share it with. But I had to see you and tell you that your friendship is…important. I didn't want to leave without you knowing that."

Forget the key. Fortunately, when something rendered me speechless it was a temporary condition.

"So that's what we are? Friends?" I tested the word.

"If that's okay with you." Dex's eyes met mine.

"So I'm supposed to write to you while you fly planes somewhere in South America?"

"You could call the headquarters once in a while. They'd track me down."

"You could call me, too."

"I could." The smile was in his eyes now, warming them.

"You'll be gone two years."

He pushed his hand through his hair, leaving a row of tousled strands. "I know. It's a long time."

Step by step, walking with Him. Listening to His voice. For a girl who liked to jump ahead, it didn't seem so scary anymore. "A lot can happen in two years."

Dex's smile came out in full force.

"I'm counting on it."

Epilogue

Loves surprises
(The List. Number 23)

A gust of wind grabbed my scarf and wound it around my neck several times, like it was playing tetherball. The keys to the salon bunched in my mitten and I fumbled for the right one before I reached the door. The snow that had fallen in the night sifted into the tops of my shoes, promising a white Christmas. Above my head on the streetlight, Denise's snowman cheerfully waved his plastic arm at me.

A brown package, dusted with snow, blocked the door. I scooped it up with one hand, unlocking the door with the other. No one had warned me about a Christmas parade, but if there were red and green rolls of crepe paper in the box, I'd know what they were for. And I'd put Kaylie in charge.

I nudged the lights on and set the package down, noticing one side of it was crushed. And it was plastered with strange-looking stamps. *Yes!* I shook off my mittens and let them plop on the floor. It was better than crepe paper. It was from Dex. I twirled around, creating my own miniature blizzard in the salon as the snow blew off my coat.

How he'd managed to time it to arrive three days before Christmas—which also happened to be my birthday—was beyond my comprehension. It hadn't taken us long to discover that mail delivery between Prichett and a certain missionary station was—and I'm putting this nicely—unreliable. We'd given up on snail mail and relied strictly on e-mails, but I hadn't heard from him in over a week and I was trying not to worry.

I ripped open the box, fished around in the packing peanuts and pulled out something soft. My octopus. The one he'd taken from me at the Fourth of July Frolic. I collapsed in the chair, giggling. Its tentacles were wrapped around a piece of paper. I plucked it out and smoothed it open on my lap. And almost slid to the floor.

It was The List. *My* list. My list that had gone MIA over the summer. He'd taken it! All this time when we'd been writing back and forth, he'd never said a word. My humiliation was complete. But why was he sending it back now? For blackmail purposes?

My eyes flew over the paper, noticing there were

large black checkmarks everywhere. And an occasional comment.

Adventurous *(Pilot!)*

Outgoing *(is this negotiable? Can I substitute likes cats instead?)*

Creative *(just fixed an engine with a butter knife and a coat hanger. I'm counting it)*

Smiles a lot *(working on this one—should have it mastered sometime next year)*

Romantic *(no clue what this means)*

The words got blurry. As the meaning behind the comments began to sink in, I decided to forgive him for stealing The List. The truth was, I'd forgotten all about it. It had never even occurred to me to compare Dex to it. I was still amazed by the things I was finding out about him through our long-distance friendship. We were nothing alike, but we had everything in common that mattered.

At the very bottom of the paper, there was another message.

P.S. My list is shorter. Loves God. Loves Me. Green eyes with gold flecks that look like fireflies.

I smiled, pulled a pen out of my purse and put a checkmark by *Romantic*.

The door opened, letting a rush of cold air in.

"Ready to go?" Alex stomped the snow off his boots and went straight for the suitcases lined up by the counter. Bernice wrapped her arms around me. The envelope crinkled and she looked down. "Is this something you want me to mail?"

"No." I laughed. "It would take weeks to get there. I'll just deliver it…in person."

Bernice gave me a knowing smile. "He's going to be surprised when you show up for a visit, isn't he?"

"I'm counting on it."

* * * * *

QUESTIONS FOR DISCUSSION

1. Do you remember a time in your life that you felt like you were waiting for God to reveal His plan? When was it? What were you feeling? What was the outcome?

2. Heather's lack of confidence that she was in God's will was the sign of a deeper heart issue. What was it? Can you relate at all? Discuss.

3. What do you think are the greatest challenges Christian women face these days when it comes to dating and relationships?

4. If you created a "Top Five" in the list of character-istics you'd like your (future) husband to have, what would they be? Be honest!

5. What drew Heather to Jared in the beginning? Discuss the differences you saw in her relationship with Jared and the relationship she had with Dex.

6. Read *1 Peter 4:10*. What were the gifts Heather had that she didn't recognize as gifts? Why didn't she value them? Do you ever downplay the gifts and abilities you *do* have and wish God had gifted you in another area? Discuss.

7. What are some of the things we, as women, do to make ourselves feel more confident? More beautiful?

8. Do you believe that "God's timing may not match ours but it's always perfect"? How has that statement been true in your life?

9. Do you agree or disagree with Marissa's statement that "what we do isn't as important as what we allow God to do *through* us." Share your thoughts.

10. Grandma Lowell had a favorite saying: "Make it an opportunity for grace." Share a circumstance from your own life when you've done that.

11. What was your favorite scene in the book? Why?

12. What was Heather's turning point over the course of the summer? If she had made a different decision about Jared, where might it have taken her? Do you think she made the right decision to stay in Prichett? Why or why not?

13. Do you have a "being place"? Where is it?

14. *Proverbs 27:6* says, "Wounds from a friend can be trusted…" What do you think this means? Has there ever been a time when a friend told you something that you didn't want to hear? What was the outcome?

15. If you had a chance to "write an ending" for any of
    the following people, what would it look like?
    Heather and Dex
    Bree and Riley
    Kaylie
    Jared

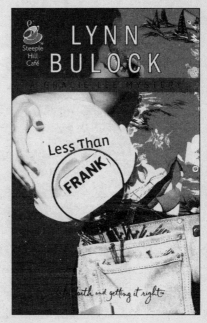